Praise for Carla Swafford

This is the first book in the series and I will be looking out for the next book.

— Reviewer on Amazon for Jake

This savage contemporary is filled with action, deception, and emotional and sexual tension that leaves readers panting right up until the highly anticipated climax.

— Publishers Weekly, starred review for Hidden Heat

Exciting and breathtaking. Carla Swafford is an up-and-coming author not to be missed!

— Sherrilyn Kenyon, New York Times bestselling author

Jake

A Southern Crime Family Novel

Carla Swafford

Ebook ISBN: 9781386021292

Paperback ISBN: 9781956518054

Hardcover ISBN: 9781956518139

Chapter One

"I hope you rot in hell, old man."

Jake Whitfield leaned over the grave and spit as his father's casket slowly disappeared into the blackness. When a violent shudder brought the crank to an abrupt stop, he shot a sideways glare at the cemetery worker.

The man wiped a sweaty forehead on the upper sleeve of his faded gray uniform and kicked the contraption. "Stupid old thing," he muttered as he avoided Jake's gaze.

With a painful screech, the device started up again, rattling and jumping, and finally a solid thuc came from the hole as it reached the bottom. If he believed in ghosts, he'd swear the hateful bastard wanted out to kill him.

Jake's attention fell on the mourners surrounding the gravesite.

Their jackets flapped in the hot wind like vultures settling around a carcass as most of the men stared at the ground beneath their feet. No one looked into his face. Though the minister shook his head at Jake's disrespect, he and the others didn't say a word. They understood his hatred. Everyone who attended would love to do the same, if they had the backbone. All were business associates and most came not so much to grieve for the man's death, but to receive assurance that his dad had died.

Many of the people in Sand County owed Dick Whitfield their livelihood and endured his heavy-handed manipulations, but none suffered as much as the Whitfield brothers. The old man had reveled in tormenting his bastard sons more than he did his associates. Besides their last name, the old man refused to give the boys anything without a deal or concession involved. Then again, maybe an agreement had been made when they were born, a bargain with the devil for their souls.

Releasing a snarl, Jake turned and nodded at his brothers. Townsend—or Sen, as he was known—and Ethan fell in step beside him as they headed toward the old man's white limo idling next to the curb. No one said a word.

Another gust of wind tugged at their jackets. A bouquet of dead flowers blew across their path to become stuck between an urn and headstone.

Behind dark sunglasses, Jake scanned the area. Tension from the funeral and a gut feeling warned that danger lurked. Nothing appeared strange or out of place. But life with the old man had taught him to be extremely cautious whenever emotions ran high. With new leadership at Whitfield Industries taking over, many of the smaller players wanted a part of the business and conspired to oust the brothers. He knew without a doubt, no one would take one brick or dollar without a fight. After years of being under the old man's rule, they deserved every piece of his ill-gotten money and property. They each had worked hard and often for pennies compared to others who worked for the old man and did far less.

He glanced around again without being obvious. The old cemetery covered acres of well-tended plots that held numerous large memorials and oak trees. Several people headed toward their cars while others remained near the burial site, talking and gesturing toward the grave being filled. In the distance, he heard traffic swooshing by, but strangely, the birds stopped chirping in the swaying limbs.

Steps away from the limo with the chauffeur waiting inside, Jake passed a life-size marble statue. The head exploded, spraying chunks of the white stuff. The confirming snap of gunfire sent everyone running for cover. Screams and shouts of concern punctuated by more shots echoed around him as he scrambled for the other side of the limo, its bulletproof body offering better protection than a tree or headstone. He motioned for his brothers to follow. In no time they hunkered down with guns in hands.

"Damn! Who do you think it is? Some asshole out to get Jake for sleeping with his girlfriend?" Ethan sat on the ground with his back near the car's engine, watching for anyone coming from behind.

In his usual calm manner, Sen checked his Beretta and then edged closer to the taillights. "Probably the girlfriend."

His brothers loved to rag him about how his last girl-friend had another guy on the side. When he kicked her out of his home, she must have told the other boyfriend a tall tale as the dumbass came at him with a gun. It almost became messy. When the boyfriend realized whose door he had knocked on, the poor dude drove out of town so fast he left rubber on the road for a half mile.

Jake shook his head and white dust fell around him. His forehead stung. A light touch came back with blood. He'd been nicked. "Most likely someone who's wanting to take over the old man's businesses," he said as he ignored his brothers' comments. "Or possibly the person who set the fire." Leaning over, he ruffled his hair, showering the ground with powder and bits of stone.

He sneered. They'd already received warnings that someone outside the county planned to make a move soon. He hadn't expected it to be at the cemetery. The old man was barely cold in the ground.

Several more shots zipped by and dug into the asphalt a few feet away. Followed shortly by a couple more over their heads.

Damn! They needed to concentrate on stopping the sniper. Normal people ran and kept moving when fired upon, but no, not the Whitfield boys. Maybe he and his brothers were as insane as the bastard they buried.

Sen nodded to where the road looped into the cemetery near the interstate fence. "I think the shots are coming from that direction. See the old rusted-out black van?"

"Yeah." Ethan peeked over the limo's hood.

"The sliding door is cracked opened. You think he's still in there? The smart thing for a shooter to do is leave with the crowd." Jake referred to the mourners cranking automobiles and screeching tires on their way out.

"I'll go around and come up on the opposite side." Without wasting time, Sen stooped low and ran alongside the cars parked by the curb.

Jake shook his head. He always wondered if his middle brother had a death wish. "Tick!"

The rotund driver inside the limo rolled down the window, showing only the top of his pale bald head and large blood-shot eyes. "Yeah, boss?"

"Scoot over. I'm coming in."

"Sure, boss."

"You get in the back." Jake nodded at Ethan. With a jab, he returned his gun to its holster beneath his jacket.

"Sure, boss," his brother said, mimicking Tick.

In seconds, they eased the limo down the lane toward the van. Jake caught a glimpse of Sen dashing behind a tree a few yards away. Then the side door on the van slammed shut, and a figure dressed in black jumped into the driver's seat. No way would he let the asshole escape. He flatfooted the gas pedal and the old limo T-boned the van.

The crunch of metal and broken glass rang in Jake's ears as he pushed hard on the door and sprinted to the other side. Two fellows ran for the trees. He tackled the nearest one as Sen sprinted after the faster, smaller one.

"You son of a bitch!" Jake flipped him over. Fist pulled back to slug the sniper, he stopped. "Sally? Sally Tally?"

Light green eyes in the middle of dark liner and eye shadow glared up at him. Chin length ebony hair tipped blood red stuck to a sweaty pale face. A grimace stretched her crimson lips lined in black as she waited for the downward swing.

He lowered his arm and examined her clothes. No wonder he'd mistaken her for a guy from the back. She wore an ankle-length leather coat with thick-soled biker boots buckled to her knees, the tight black pants tucked in. The only feminine clothing was the stiff red corset holding up plump, creamy white breasts, heaving with each intake of breath.

"No one calls me Sally anymore. Call me Angel."

The last time he'd heard that husky voice, they had been teenagers, and she'd stolen his wallet. He'd retaliated by turning her over his knee, lifting her short skirt, and giving her nearly bare bottom a good sound spanking. During the chastisement, an unexpected dilemma had emerged. He remembered how much he enjoyed it. Way too much.

His body hardened with the memory. Squeezing his eyes shut for a few seconds, he tried to regain control by erasing the mental picture of a pink lace thong. Damn, he'd gotten expelled for physical abuse after that. Despite how furious the old man had been at the time—as angry at the school as he'd been at Jake—he'd forced the school board to repeal the sentence.

After Jake had returned to school, the rumors flew around with varying degrees of outlandish speculation. Some claimed they watched him beat her to a pulp. While others said he'd dragged her off and raped her. The outcome everyone had agreed on was that his old man had paid off the officials. The only part that had been true.

In turn, rumors said Sally Tally had transferred to a girls' school. Between being teased about her unfortunate name and a father who was in prison more than he was out, she had it rough, even after her wealthy grandfather stepped in to help. Jake never knew what happened to her, but he did know his old man had enjoyed making Jake pay back every dime spent on lawyers. Because of her, his last two years in high school had been hell.

"Get off of me, you freak!" She shoved at his chest.

When his eyes focused on the mature version of Sally, all gothic angel, wiggling between his thighs, he returned to the problem at hand. "Who was with you? Why was he shooting at us?"

She sighed and rolled her eyes, looking away as she remained silent.

The wind picked up again, blowing her strangely dyed hair across her neck. He clasped her wrists. Her full lower lip trembled, yet no tears simmered. Unable to resist, his gaze returned to her full breasts. Sally-Angel had filled out quite nicely.

"My eyes are up here, dickhead."

He dragged his gaze back to hers. "You've grown up."

"Get off me now." Her words sounded tough but the worry in her eyes told a different story.

Before he moved, he heard Sen shout, "Hey, Jake, look at what I got!"

With a firm grip on a slender arm, Jake stood, hauling her up with the aid of her backpack. Then he forced her to the van. Sen held onto a lanky teenager with one hand and a Remington rifle with another as they walked out of the tree line. The boy wore black leather pants and a matching tee shirt with the words "Suck This" above two streams of red.

Jake returned his attention to Sally-Angel. "Kind of young for a boyfriend."

"You're sick. He's my brother. Leave him alone." She pulled on her arm but he squeezed tighter. "You're hurting me," she said between clenched teeth.

For some reason, he didn't believe her—beneath the leather he felt solid lean muscles—but he eased his grip.

"I thought your granddaddy taught you better than that. Didn't he ever tell you Whitfields were mean sons of bitches?"

"Oh, I already knew that."

She jerked at his hold again.

He grasped both arms and pulled her to him, leaving not a fraction of an inch between their bodies. Her breasts rubbed below his chest, and his cock jerked. Damn. What was it about her that revved his engine?

Leaning down to her ear, he said in a low tone, "Be still and I won't hurt you." He'd never physically hurt a woman in his life, but she didn't need to know that. "Anyone else in the van?"

The softness of her hair and the smell of leather and woman caused him to lengthen more. Like he needed this. She had trouble written all over her hot little body. He shoved her back enough to regain control, while keeping his grip and glancing over to the van.

Ethan leaned into the open door. He then looked over his shoulder to Jake and shook his head. No one else was inside.

He returned his attention to Sally-Angel. "You better tell me, why did your brother try to kill us?" His tone modulated as he wanted her frightened but not to the point of being speechless.

"Maybe you deserved it for killing my granddaddy." Her dislike oozed out with each word. She nodded her head toward the teenager. "Anyway, who says *he* shot at you? It could easily be me."

He didn't have time to play her games. With all of the gunfire, the police would be coming soon.

"There's a possibility I deserve to be shot for many things, but I had nothing to do with your grandfather dying in that fire. Did you forget my old man died in it, too? That has to tell you we weren't involved," he said, hoping it sounded convincing.

"He's lying! What did I tell you?" The teenager reached for the rifle, but Sen quickly twisted his skinny arm up behind his back. He squealed, bowing his body to escape the painful pressure.

"Quit hurting him!" She wrestled with Jake's hold, trying to reach her brother. With a smooth step to the side, he avoided her kick. Then he grabbed the back of her neck and squeezed until she quit fighting.

"Look at me." He shook her until her gaze met his. "You and your brother are in enough trouble. I don't have time to turn you over my knee again." Memory of a hot red handprint on her rear jarred him.

"Another reason you should be dead," she said, her eyes narrowed.

He could tell she meant it. Interesting. Few men had the guts to say that to a Whitfield, no less a female.

"Kill him, Angel. One less Whitfield we have to put up with. You know how." The teenager wheezed when Sen's elbow met his stomach.

"You two have lost your minds," Jake said with disgust. At that moment, the sound of sirens drifted across the cemetery, coming closer by the second.

He shouted over his shoulder, "Tick!"

The chauffeur straightened from checking the damage to the limo's front end. "Yeah, boss?"

"Is the limo drivable?" he asked.

"Yes, sir. Mr. Whitfield had it made special to take a beating." Tick reached for the driver's door.

"Then let's get the hell out of here." Jake dragged Sally-Angel over to the back door.

Her body brushed his. Before he could figure out her game, the heel of her palm slammed beneath his chin, jarring his whole skull. Stars floated in front of his eyes long enough for her to regain her freedom. She stepped toward her brother.

Jaw throbbing and his eyes blurred, he blindly reached out and wrapped a hand in her hair and hauled her back. This time, he clasped a wrist and lifted it high behind her back. When she kicked out, trying to bring him to his knees, he pulled her arm higher until she bit off a groan.

He brought his mouth to her ear. "Try that again, and

I'll make sure you feel the same kind of pain before I break your arm and then I'll start on your brother's limbs," he said as he waited for his vision to clear.

Hell, the woman had a punch. His threat was no more than hot air. He had boundaries, and intentionally hurting women or children crossed the line. Her whimper alerted him that he might have reached that line with her. He released his hold. With her he hoped the Whitfield reputation for cruelty, actually the old man's rep, ensured her cooperation. Usually it worked, but her attitude so far proved nothing frightened her.

Worry sharpened the glare she gave him, but she quickly pulled herself together when she spotted Sen loading the teenager into the other side of the limo. They scooted into the bench seat facing the back. Her shoulders slumped. Maybe she understood he threatened her more as a means to encourage her cooperation. Though he refused to wage war against the weak, the teenager was big enough for him to keep an eye on. Relieved she didn't plan to fight any more, Jake pulled the backpack off her shoulders and threw it to Ethan.

"Check this and make sure there aren't any weapons," he ordered.

Then he shoved her inside. Once Ethan jumped into the front with Tick, the limo shot down the lane.

No less than a minute passed and Ethan held up a gun. How much more dangerous could the woman get? His brother tucked the gun into the console and shook his head.

Jake jabbed the seatbelt into the latch and leaned over to do the same for Sally-Angel with her trying to slap his hands away. He ignored her as it clicked in place. Then he barked at the others to do the same. The way Tick drove, an accident loomed in the near future.

As sirens faded behind them, he caught her wrist and held it on his thigh, her heartbeat popping furiously against his fingers. The way she eyed the door handle, he refused to let her have an opportunity to do anything else foolish.

They left the cemetery by way of the dirt service road exit behind Quinn Funeral Home. When they hit the interstate, Jake loosened his hold, took a deep breath, and leaned back. He grinned when she jerked away and shook her wrist.

A few more miles down the road, he mentally sighed with relief. No police followed. If needed, he would deal with the authorities later. At the moment, he had an important meeting to get to, and along the way, he wanted some answers from these two.

His gaze passed from her to her brother. The teenager glowered from the seat facing them. He wanted Jake's blood pooling on the floor for touching his sister. No one said a word but Jake had a lot of practice reading people's body language.

Old man Whitfield's temper had swung from one end of the spectrum to the other in a split second. By paying attention to the downward sweep of his mood, it made a difference between walking out of a room and being thrown. These two were amateurs in hiding their concerns. They had a good reason to tremble. The boy twitched and squirmed until Sen snapped, "Be still."

The woman next to Jake stiffened. So she didn't like anyone raising their voice at her brother. Dangerous to let others know what could be used as leverage.

"So tell me, what made you believe I had something to do with your grandfather's death?" He folded his arms and glanced at the woman next to him.

"We don't have to tell you shit, you lying motherfucker!" Her brother moved toward Jake, but Sen slapped an arm across his chest and rammed him back into the seat.

"Damien," she said, her tone cautionary as she shook her head. "Shh!"

"Watch your mouth and shut up," Jake said at the same time, pointing a finger at the teenager. He remembered being that age and full of resentment at anyone telling him what to do. "Show some respect in how you talk in front of your sister."

The teenager opened his mouth, looked at Sally-Angel, and then shut it. For the next minute or so only the sound of the radio filled the automobile as everyone tensely waited for what might happen next.

Jake turned in his seat to study her. He'd hoped the breather would give her time to mull over her decisions so far. She stared out the passenger window with her shoulders stiff and straight.

"Sally."

When she continued to watch the passing scenery he gritted his teeth and tried for the other name. "Angel."

She slowly faced him, hostility tightening her lips.

Not a bit amused by her insolence, Jake narrowed his eyes.

"I don't have a lot of time to waste on this. I can turn this limo around and take you and your brother to the police." She actually snorted? Damn, he kind of liked her spunk, but for the moment, he needed answers. "Tell me everything. Don't make me do anything you'll regret. There are messy ways for me to find out the truth." When she made a move to look out the window again, he caught her jaw, felt it flexing beneath his fingers as he forced her to look at him. Oh, yeah, he took pleasure in seeing those light-colored eyes spitting fire with the need to tell him off.

But he didn't have time for this. "Throw him out of the limo," he said to Sen as he kept his gaze on Angel.

His brother opened the door and grabbed the back of the teenager's shirt.

"Let me go, you slant-eyed bastard!"

"Damien!" She faced Sen with a look of unmitigated horror. "Oh, I'm so sorry. He's upset or he'd never say that. Please close the door. Don't hurt him." She unbuckled her seatbelt and tried to dive over Jake's lap. He held her back by the waist. "Damien, you apologize to him right now," she shouted at her brother.

Lips stretched tight, Sen, whose mom had been Vietnamese, shoved the teenager's head out the door. "That's no way to talk to your elders, especially one holding your life in his hands," he said.

The teenager's arms waved in the air as he scrambled for a hold on the side of the door. His screams became partially lost in the stream of air sliding by the fast-moving car. Fighting Sen was hopeless for the teenager. The exotic looking man was the family's collector and worked out daily. Collector was a nice word for the person who made sure others paid what was owed. It often involved broken bones and bruises, and the occasional disposal of a body.

"I'm sorry, sorry! I swear," the teenager shouted. "I don't know why that came out of my mouth. I never even wanted to say that before." Tears glistened on his cheeks and snot ran from his nose like a two-year-old.

"Okay! Okay! He apologized. I'll talk Please don't." Angel held out her hands as if she could reach her brother and pull him back in.

Jake was a little disappointed she'd cracked so fast. Twice, she'd shown by controlling her brother, he controlled her. He understood how protecting a sibling was important, but self-preservation ensured they came back and fought harder.

When he and his brothers were kids, they often found their punishments worse whenever they defended each other against the old man. They realized to survive they needed to stand on their own two feet. Take what was coming and then plan vengeance as a team.

Not everyone learned that lesson growing up. Maybe that was a good thing. Otherwise, he would not have the upper hand like now. Besides, Sen would never throw out the boy, but after being shot at, they needed answers quickly. Fear was a great motivator to get someone to talk.

Angel turned to him, tears in her eyes.

Jesus H. Christ. That was the last thing he needed. He hated it when women cried. It turned his insides into mush as he did anything to make them stop. His mom only had to tear up for him to start looking around to make it better. He took in Angel's smeared mascara and streaked face.

Was it real? She could be playing with his sympathy.

"Leave him alone," she begged. "I'll tell you whatever you want. I don't understand why you're pretending not to know, unless it's all to prove you're just as big of an asshole as your dad."

He nodded toward his brother. With an effortless move, Sen tossed the teenager onto the seat and closed the door. The kid's hands shook as he locked his seatbelt.

At the same time, Jake braced his arm over her collarbone and pressed Angel back into her seat.

"I don't play games. If you think calling me and my brothers names will piss us off, then you're mistaken. The old man was one of the biggest assholes in the Southeast, and I took all of my lessons from him. I'll show you how big of one I can be if you don't hurry up and talk." His interested gaze drifted down to her chest. She inhaled as if attempting to make her breasts smaller.

To ensure that she understood, he leaned in and placed an arm around her shoulders. She needed to be aware of how helpless she was in the situation. For whatever reason, he'd never been so desperate to prove to a woman how much of a bastard, figuratively, he was too.

"I remember how pretty and red your skin looked, but I didn't remember how soft," he said in a low voice the others couldn't hear. Using one finger, he followed the edge of her corset to the little satin bow in the center. The tip of a blunt finger slipped beneath the material and caressed her warm skin. Her breath became shaky, glittering eyes drifted halfway closed. Just as quickly her eyes popped open, glaring at him.

Interesting. He liked how responsive she was even as she fought it.

"Get your hands off my sister!" Though the teenager's voice shook from his near fatal exit, Jake couldn't help but respect the kid's determination to protect his sister.

"Stay out of it," Angel demanded, without taking her gaze from Jake's.

"Start talking and make it quick," he whispered. He inhaled and breathed in the light clean scent from her hair.

She swallowed and then closed her eyes taking a deep breath. Her lovely breasts buoyed up and almost stopped his heart. He forced his gaze to her face. She lifted her chin and opened her eyes.

"We have to get married."

Chapter Two

Angel slumped into the seat while she waited for the big guy to quit laughing. She hated how he acted so amused by the horrible fact. It wasn't the first time the male species laughed at her. Growing up, people made fun of her all the time. They laughed about her hand-me-down clothes or her rhyming name. But the last few years, when she started working for her grandfather, they realized how much of a mistake it was to treat her so. Often it had been too late. That was, after she knocked them to their knees, bleeding.

So far, the only reasons why she'd been so patient with Jake—as patient as she knew how—and not tried drastic measures to escape were because they had her brother and she needed Jake's cooperation. They were to marry. Even she knew better than to start off a relationship by giving the groom a black eye.

Hell, she needed to tell him the truth about who shot at him. Why did she care that he thought she was lying? Maybe she wanted him a little worried about what she would do next.

When they'd pulled up to the cemetery checking on the flowers at Granddaddy Mac's grave, there were the Whitfields in all their glory. The oldest, who constantly landed on his feet no matter the circumstances, stood over the grave glaring at all of the mourners, while she struggled to hold together the family's businesses and take care of the only family she had left. Desire to kill Jake had crossed her mind, and just as quickly dissipated. Rather ironic that someone else wished to put a bullet into his cold heart. For certain, if she had given into that weak moment, his brothers would be coming after her, and no one lived long after that. Instead of shooting Jake, she found herself saving his life. He'd never believe it. One moment she was watching the Whitfield funeral, and the next, she spotted the sniper in the trees. Before she knew what she was doing, the rifle, normally resting in the rack inside the van, was in her hands as she eyed the sniper through the scope's crosshairs.

Sure, she'd been angry about the requirements of Mac's will and planned to confront Jake, but not until later in the afternoon before they read his daddy's will.

She watched him laugh. Thin lines fanned from the corners of his eyes; the type a person received from being out in the sun too much or from laughing. He had a wonderful laugh. Full and sexy. The sound helped her relax as his gaze heated more from amusement than lust.

"Hon, I haven't seen you since high school. You'll have to find you another baby daddy." He finally released her and sat back.

"No, no. I didn't say anything about a baby. You don't understand—"

"Hey, how old are you?" The youngest Whitfield—Ethan?—leaned over from the front, arms and hands hanging down the back of the seat, interrupting her explanation, and waited for her brother to answer.

"He's too tall. So he has to be too old." Sen tilted his head.

"They grow 'em big nowadays," Ethan bit back.

"True. Look at us." Sen nodded.

"Fourteen." Her brother's eyes widened.

"Thirteen," she said at the same time as her brother. "He won't be fourteen until October. But that has nothing—"

The other Whitfield, holding her brother in place, nodded, and butted in. "The timing is about right."

"No way." Jake shook his head.

She looked at Jake and then her brother.

Shaking her head, she held out her hands as she tried to stop their speculation.

"Hell, no! Damien is my brother, remember?" Her mind refused to wrap around their logic. "Just because I said we had to marry, you jump to the conclusion I'm preggers or he's our kid?"

Everyone started talking at once. Her head ached from trying to keep up with the insults and accusations. As she was about to release a frustrated scream, a piercing whistle shut everyone down. They turned toward Jake.

"None of that matters," he said to her. "What the jackasses don't know is we never had sex." He looked at his brothers. "So the kid isn't mine," he confirmed in a firm tone.

"You bet he's not. That's just scary." She wrinkled her nose and crossed her arms beneath her breasts.

What a disaster this was becoming. He refused to listen. She was shutting her mouth. He could just find out the truth the hard way about why they had to be married.

"They're just yanking my chain." He shifted in his seat and pulled out a crushed pack of cigarettes. After lowering the window a little, he lit one and inhaled, closing his eyes for a few seconds. Then he looked at her from beneath heavy eyelids as he blew smoke from the corner of his mouth toward the opening. "What's so scary about being with me?"

How could anyone look so sexy while smoking a cigarette? She sighed and resisted the urge to roll her eyes. Bad boys never grew up. When his gaze dipped down, she dropped her arms. No need to draw his attention in that direction again.

"Scary?" Then she remembered what she'd said. "Well, it's scary because I would've been a kid at the time I had him." Sarcasm dripped from every word.

"The rumor was going around that you left to have a baby." Masculine lips puckered to take another draw. The tip flared bright.

Oh my, he oozed sex and heat. Her attention refused to move away from how his lips parted to release the smoke. He looked even more dangerous doing something so bad for him.

"Mom was sick after having Damien, and she needed me at home to help out. I know when the rumors started. It was after some of the kids from school saw me holding him at the grocery store, assuming he belonged to me. You know, trailer trash equals baby." Sure Granddaddy Mac had money, but he'd owned his first nickel and refused to help anyone including family. He firmly believed everyone had to work for it. What money he paid her dad to do odd jobs had been spent on drugs and alcohol, and when good old dad didn't work or was in jail, they lived on welfare. Funny how little had changed. Even though she had money the last couple of years, guys still thought she slept around because she was a Tally. Idiots.

"I heard about your mom. That's rough," said Sen.

Angel glanced his way. His sincere expression helped ease the tension in her shoulders a little. Then she remembered hearing about his mom's death a year before hers.

"She'd been sick a long time. I was sorry to hear about your mom, too."

He lifted his chin in acknowledgement of her shared sympathy. Then he looked away.

She'd never heard how his mom had died. For her own, what could she say? That her mom had never been there for her, and her suicide only finished the job. She forced her gaze to the window.

"Where are you taking us?" she asked.

"We still have a lot to talk about. What with all the shooting and marrying involved. . ." The laughter in his tone warned he believed she was trying to pull a fast one on him. He pinched the fire on his cigarette and flicked both out the window. "So tell me the truth."

"Maybe it's simply I don't want to be married to you," she said, concentrating on keeping her face emotionless. How could he pretend he didn't know about the two major parts of the codicil to Mac's will? Marriage was nothing compared to the other requirement.

He leaned over, and she pressed her shoulders into the seat. If it was his attempt at intimidating her, it worked.

"Quit talking about marriage. That has nothing to do with you wanting to kill me. Should we open the car door again and see what answers we get from your brother?" He tugged at her hair, she jumped, and he sat back. His infuriating grin spread across his handsome face. His grin told her he liked unsettling her.

"I told him if you were dead, I wouldn't have to marry you. Nothing more and *that* simple." It was a lie, but Jake didn't need to know. He'd eventually find out the truth. She didn't plan on making it easy.

She dared not look at her brother. When he lost his temper, he blurted out things best kept quiet, or never voiced, or thought about for that matter. He'd already proven that. Besides, he hadn't seen the sniper. She really needed to tell everyone the truth. Then again it would serve the Whitfields right to stew for a while. The push-pull she felt when dealing with Jake always drove her nuts. The thought of her doing anything that helped a Whitfield was almost abhorrent to her. Maybe holding back was part of her stubborn nature.

His blue eyes turned icy as he stared into hers. Then with a flicker, as if he thought of something new to torment her with, they warmed again.

He nodded. "We're home. I don't have time to argue now. Later, I'll certainly get straight answers. Yeah, later." His gaze brushed over my lips. "You're lying about this nonsense, but I don't know why. You and I are going to have a long talk. For now, my brothers and I have a meeting to attend first. So don't even try to leave."

"Sure. Whatever." Her mind wasn't on what he'd said or how he looked at her but on the house at the end of the long drive. Built forty years earlier in the Victorian-style with numerous turrets, large windows and wraparound porch, even the roof was covered with slate instead of asphalt shingles. She'd loved the house from the first and only time she'd seen it.

Not long after the incident at the school, she'd gone with Mac to meet with Dick Whitfield. Instead of listening to the old men yammering about what they should do about their two *young'uns*, she'd sat quietly hoping for a glimpse of Jake. He wasn't her type—he was a Whitfield—but as any normal girl, she enjoyed looking at him. Back then he wore his hair long. Sun-kissed brown hair, tall, with an athletic build, he played several sports, but was often kicked out because he didn't follow instructions well. All the good girls wanted him and bad girls had him for a night or two. Maybe deep inside she'd wanted his attention. She'd been neither a good nor bad girl, just a Tally. Hated for her blood. That didn't stop her from having a little crush on him. She did know something had changed in her after he'd taken her over his knee.

Her legs quivered as she remembered those strong arms holding her, the feel of his bare hand on her near naked backside. The memory brought a tingling between her legs.

Nothing like that was going to happen and certainly not with Jake Whitfield, no matter how attracted she was to him. Even living in the same small town, she'd seldom caught sight of him over the years, and on the rare occasion their gazes met, he never spoke to her. Maybe the families' long standing habit of mistrusting each other remained ingrained in his subconscious, despite that they both had felt a connection on that fateful day. She liked to think he had though he hadn't exhibit such a sentiment in all this time. Then again, their families' lack of communication had a lot to do with their unspoken mutual desire to keep down hostilities while money continued to flow into their businesses.

Exhaling in frustration, she decided at that moment she'd rather tell him to take a flying leap off the town's water tower.

Her gaze followed the long driveway with various trucks, SUVs, and luxury cars lined up on one side. When the limo passed a large black SUV, a huge man exited the driver side and watched as they drove to one end of the house. She doubted if Big Judd Richards could see through the tinted black windows. So she didn't bother waving, and instead stared in amazement at the six-car garage.

Who in their right mind needed that many vehicles? She couldn't imagine paying their insurance and maintenance bills.

She twisted in her seat hoping to see the cars parked behind each closed bay, but the driver stopped several yards away next to a side door leading into the house. A tall, thin woman stepped out onto the small porch and watched them exit the limo. Their housekeeper had been with them for years and everyone in Marystown knew her. Probably the only woman over fifty not rumored to have slept with old man Whitfield.

"Tick, show them to the den downstairs and make sure they don't leave. Tell Jimmie Sue to give them something to drink and snack on until supper." Jake's gaze swept over Angel, and a teasing glimmer returned to his eyes. She almost melted from the look. "Behave yourself. All of our guns are locked up, so I expect you to be there when I'm finished with my meeting, understand?"

She hid her surprise. He didn't really believe she was dangerous, no matter how much he accused her of shooting at him. She found his attitude to be a curious contradiction.

"Do I have an option?" She wanted to go home and forget how he found it so easy to push her around. And for some unknown reason, she let him. Truthfully, she needed to be as angry at herself as she was with him. But what good would it do?

He laughed and turned away, walking with his brothers toward the front of the house. Satisfied that he didn't know everything, she grinned. He was going to be plenty angry when he found out the truth.

Seeing Judd there reminded her he hadn't called with the time and place to complete the requirements of her granddaddy's will. She couldn't wait to hear one certain asshole's reaction to it.

Her attention drawn by Jake's broad shoulders slid over his jacket stretched tight to the point she wondered if the seams would split like the Hulk's. The image of his shirt and pants tattered, slipping off with each step, revealing taut pecs and biceps glistening in the waning light caused her face to warm.

Tick cleared his throat behind her. Uncomfortable being caught dreaming about Jake's clothes falling off his naked form, she forced her gaze to the big man called Tick and glared. His knowing grin irritated her.

"Come this way, and I'll get you settled." He tossed her the backpack, and she smoothly caught it. It felt lightweight. Her small Beretta was probably still missing inside. Tick continued to talk. "Wait until you see the room. It has an eighty-six-inch TV and stadium seating and a sound system that will blow you away. There's also a popcorn machine. Jimmie Sue keeps two jars of cookies on the bar." Tick put an arm around Damien's shoulders and waited for her to walk ahead.

Her brother stared at the house with amazement. She knew he'd never been in the mansion. Even though their granddaddy had money and property—still nothing like the Whitfields—old man Mac Tally lived in a mid-size home. The man was frugal to the point he could make a penny scream. She and Damien lived in the double-wide they grew up in. It wasn't until their mom died last year that Mac asked them to move into his house. She and Damien refused. Being under his thumb while she worked for him would be a bit too much.

She blinked a few times to get rid of the extra moisture. Despite her grandaddy being a hard-ass, she missed him.

The sun reflecting off the sparkly clean windows emphasized the difference in how they grew up. For that matter, Angel had a hard time not looking around. She guessed she would always have a feeling of awe. Only it was more about the man who lived in it than it was the house.

And what a shame Jake was similar to all the men she knew who never listened to what women said. When would he find out his bachelor days were over?

Chapter Three

The old man's cousins, Teddy Bear and Rat Boy, stood in the foyer, waiting for Jake when he walked into the house. Nicknames in the South made it easier for all the Michaels, Brians, and Matthews. When it came the two men standing in front of him, he no longer remembered the stories behind their nicknames, and Jake didn't care, just as he refused to refer to them as his cousins. Too many memories of their jeers when he was a kid. They enjoyed abusing him including throwing rocks and calling him a bastard.

At the time, he'd wanted badly to be a part of a real family. With a mother more child than parent and a father who'd rather curse and slap him across the room, he never had a family that resembled the ones he seen with other classmates. When he discovered blood didn't mean family, he treated the cousins with caution and avoided their presence as much as possible. But as the years went by, he had learned how to deal with their asinine ways, even while working with them through the family business.

For the last few years, they'd wiggled their way into the

organization by providing transportation for the untaxed liquor Whitfield Industries brought in and distributed. No matter how he warned his old man, the cousins took over the family businesses' freight logistics, especially the products requiring movement under the local authorities' radar.

"Jake boy, we need to talk."

"This isn't a good time, Teddy." Eventually he would need to deal with them, but the reading of the will took precedence. He sidestepped Teddy and headed toward the study with Ethan and Sen following.

"I believe it'll be in your best interest to listen to me, boy." Teddy's tone warned of trouble if ignored.

Boy? The redneck had no common sense at all.

Jake stopped, nodded to his brothers to go on, and then turned to face the man. At five-eight, Teddy was nearly a half foot shorter, and with his rusty color hair and freckles, he looked like what people imagined as an older Tom Sawyer. Rat Boy looked nothing like his brother with greasy black hair and beady dark eyes.

"Me and Rat Boy have a proposition for you. I think you'll want in." He smirked and crossed his arms.

Tempted to knock him on his ass, Jake gritted his teeth and pointed to the dining room. If they wish to feed him some bullshit, he might as well be seated properly.

"Okay. What do you have to offer?" He leaned back in the chair and folded his hands above his belt.

On the opposite side of the table, the cousins sat next to each other.

"Cousin Dick was a real dick." Teddy chuckled at his own lame joke and glanced over to Rat Boy who shook his head and indicated that he should move on. "We figure you hated him as much as everyone else. He did love baiting you and your brothers. I remember that one year he refused to let Jimmie Sue wash or buy you boys any clothes, not that he was ever generous. I hadn't seen such filthy kids in my life. Whew-wee! Ya'll stunk to high heaven before Social Services came after him. Or how about that time—"

"You don't know shit about me and the old man. If that's all you got, people are waiting." Jake shook his head. He stood, preparing to tell them to go to hell, when Rat Boy stood up and blocked his way. Rat Boy was only a couple of inches taller than his brother, but he didn't scare Jake one bit as he towered over them both. He would love a reason to beat the shit out of him. With the old man dead, there would be no one stopping him.

"Give us a minute more. You know how Teddy is. Let him finish. He'll get to the point now." He shoved his brother's shoulder.

"Yeah. Right. See, me and Rat Boy have a plan. We're guessing that you don't really want anything to do with the old man's businesses, what with him treating you and your brothers like shit all the time."

Jake just stared at him. Teddy was as crazy as he acted. He remembered being beaten by those two often, until he was big enough to fight back, about the same time the old man quit slapping him around. Besides, what would they know about what he did or didn't want?

"Seeing that we're older and know a lot more about the business overall than you and your brothers. The old man held his dealings tight to the chest, but we know a lot. So me and Rat Boy can run Whitfield Industries for ya, and we'll make you honorary vice president. That's right. Honorary has a nice ring to it, doesn't it? All you have to do is draw your paycheck and not do a thing. You can buy a nice modern place—better than this old dump—kick back and not lift a finger. Leave all of the hard work to us, and we can make you even richer."

Were they out of their minds? Had they believed the old man when he called him lazy and stupid? From their eager looks, they obviously did.

"I tell you what. I'll think on it and talk to my brothers and let you know our decision in a couple days." That would give him enough time to set his plans in motion.

"I understand. You want to give your bast—half brothers a chance to express their opinion." At Teddy's intentional slip, Jake narrowed his eyes. "But don't wait too long. Then again, the old man always said you were a smart ass." Teddy laughed at his sorry joke again. A really bad habit he'd regret one day.

Jake turned toward the hallway, catching Rat Boy's expression. Yeah. Teddy did all the talking, but Jake knew who to watch. It would be best not to underestimate Rat, as his cousins underestimated him.

Judd Richards waved to the numerous chair provided for the meeting.

"Gentlemen, if you would all have a seat, I'll read the section of Dick Whitfield's Last Will and Testament you've been waiting for in just a few minutes. For now, I've hit a snag. We're missing one more person."

Big Judd had been Dick Whitfield's lawyer for as long as Jake could remember, but he didn't trust the son of a bitch. Years ago, the old man had helped get Richards's youngest son out of trouble. Mike "Tick" Richards wasn't the smartest man alive, but he'd been loyal to the old man ever since, and now father and son's loyalty belonged to Jake. When it came to Tick, he trusted as much as he could anyone who weren't his brothers. He could only hope he was wrong and the elder Richards was as trustworthy.

Richards adjusted his glasses and squinted at his cell phone. "It appears I've just located the last person named in the will, and she's in the last place I would've expected. She should be here any second." He turned to Jake with eyebrows raised.

She? Had the old man forgotten to mention another woman? Jake knew of two women in town the old man had visited on occasion, but they understood the arrangement. They provided a service and a little company, and they received the old man's attention and a nice allowance. The other possible scenario was a dead end, too, for the old man had told him he'd gotten himself fixed after Ethan's mom turned up pregnant. So there was no chance of another sibling.

Jake glanced around the room to see who could be missing or if anyone had a clue to the mystery woman. Sen and Ethan shrugged their shoulders. His mom flashed a grin at him while the old man's cousins sniggered from where they sprawled out in the chairs arranged at the edge of the room.

Rat Boy burst out laughing after Teddy mumbled something.

Then it hit him. Angel. Maybe he should have listened to what she had to say after all.

The door opened and with a swirl of black leather, she walked in and flopped into the chair Richards pulled out for her near the old man's desk. She appeared upset but hard to tell beneath that white makeup. He did know that he liked seeing her pale breasts rise and fall with agitation above the red lace trim of her corset.

Jake tore his gaze from Angel and looked at Tick

standing in the hallway, giving him a thumbs-up. He better mean the teenager remained in the den guarded by one of the other men. Keeping Damien in his control meant he controlled the sister, and he felt it would be very important before this was over.

The woman sat rigid, ignoring the whispers that circulated the room. Then Teddy spoke up. "Hey, what's a Tally doing here?" The way he emphasized *Tally* sounded the same as something found beneath their feet.

Richards shuffled some papers and shot the men a look. "Shut the fuck up. The ball game starts in two hours and I plan to be sitting in front of my TV with a large bowl of salsa cheese dip, chips, and a cold one."

A few nervous chuckles scattered across the small group until Richards cleared his throat.

Impatient, Jake shifted his chair. "Don't even bother with all the legal gook, get to the meat of the will."

"That's my plan." Lowering his reading glasses toward the tip of his nose, he cleared his throat again. "A week before Tally and Whitfield were blown up, uh, died at the Juicy Goose, and we still don't know how it happened—"

"Get to the point." Jake crossed his arms.

Everyone knew the old man had been trying to negotiate a peace treaty with Mac Tally. While Whitfields owned all of the clubs in the tri-county area along with controlling several bookies, the Tallys ran the high-stakes poker games in the back of their restaurants, convenience stores, and bait shops. The night club, the Juicy Goose, was the old man's pride and joy, and he spent most of his evenings there. Instead of coming home at the usual time of midnight, he'd stayed drinking with Tally, supposedly celebrating a truce and the place blew up around three that morning, burning to the ground before the volunteer fire department arrived. They'd found two bodies burned beyond recognition, and the dental records matched.

Someone somehow stopped the two old men from leaving. It had to be murder.

Whenever Jake found the killer, the authorities wouldn't find a tooth to match to their records. He'd do that not out of love. The old man never invoked love from anyone but his mom. No matter how evil he'd been, he hadn't deserved death by explosion or fire. People needed to know how dangerous it was to mess with a Whitfield. Now more than ever, Jake and his brothers had to show how strong the Whitfields were together. Letting anyone get away with murdering the old man would be a sign of weakness.

"The point is thirty-thousand each goes to the cousins here," he nodded toward Teddy and Rat Boy and their other two siblings, "and twenty-thousand each to Mike Richards and Jimmie Sue." Jake had known Tick and the housekeeper were included in the will, and the gifts were no surprise though he never really expected the old man to give anyone a cent. "For Lydia Morgan, she'll receive a hundred thousand and his newest Caddy and her allowance to continue for life."

His mom had never harassed the old man about not marrying her after having Jake. So she actually was one of the few the old man put up with after he got what he wanted. He refused to live with her anymore, but he did adore her in his own way.

"Jake Whitfield receives Swhitfield Liquor Distribution and the warehouses, Townsend the pawnshops and novelty shops, and Ethan the bars and night clubs. But they will share equal ownership of Whitfield Industries." Richards swiped his forehead with a handkerchief. What was he so nervous about? Those were the same businesses they'd managed for the old man the last eight years between a few interruptions. Once again, not a surprise.

"This house and the one in Gulf Shores belong to..." Richards shifted a sheet of paper to stare a little harder at the words. "Sally Angela Tally, on the contingency of her marriage to Jake Whitfield, and two million will be transferred to her account once the marriage is consummated."

"What the hell?" Jake shouted as he stood. Angel turned wide eyes his way when he leaned over her. "Did you have something to do with this? How much did you pay Big Judd?" he asked in an accusing tone.

"I didn't—" Before she had a chance to say more, Richards slammed his hand on the desk.

"Enough! Jake, sit your ass down." Richards held the edge of the desk. "I'll ignore that you insulted me." The big man blinked as if he realized he pushed a dangerous man. He was smart to know Jake's control had worn thin.

Jake shifted his jaw in frustration. Then decided some one-on-one time would be necessary to straighten everything out.

"This reading is over. Everyone out! You two stay and you, too." Jake motioned to his brothers and Angel to remain seated. "Where the hell are you going?" He pointed at Richards to return behind his desk.

Richards actually paled.

His mom stopped in front of him. "Jake, darling, there had to be a reason for your dad to want you to marry...uh...a Tally." She looked at Angel as if she couldn't figure out the joke.

"It'll be okay, Mom. Go with Jimmie Sue She'll fix you a glass of sweet tea. If I can, I'll check on you before you leave."

Behind his mom, the cousins smirked as they walked out, eyeing Angel and laughing.

"If you're sure." His mom gave him a sweet smile.

Why Lydia Morgan moved in with Dick Whitfield when she was only eighteen and the old man a little over fifty, Jake never understood. Sure, she claimed she loved the old man, but he knew she wasn't loved in return. Hell, the old man often laughed about how before the first year ended, he'd figured out Lydia's daddy had hit her in the head one too many times. Maybe that was the reason she survived all the craziness the old man put her through.

When Jake was a kid, he heard Lydia's one and only temper tantrum had come about when she was pregnant and discovered two other women expected the old man's babies, too. A week after he was born, she'd found her stuff moved out into a nice condo in a new section of town. Ever since then, she'd been drifting from one hobby to another, trying to fill in the hole the old man had filled when she was younger.

He chucked his mom beneath her chin. "I'm sure. Go on." He waited until the door closed, then he pointed a finger at Angel.

"You! You have a lot to explain."

Chapter Four

Angel wanted to be anywhere but in a room filled with too much testosterone, especially the Whitfield type. Everyone stared as if they waited for her to hiss and bare fangs. Seeing herself reflected in a picture frame, she smirked. Maybe they had a reason to feel that way.

"Well, Sally?" Jake pressed.

"Angel," she said between gritted teeth. Why was it so hard for him to remember? He probably did it to irritate. "Big Judd should've already told you. That's why my brother and I can't believe you didn't already know. He's our lawyer, too."

A wash of relief lifted the pressure from her shoulders when Jake's cold stare turned toward the big man.

Judd lifted his hands, palms out. "Client-attorney confidentiality. No matter what you think of me, I know when to keep my mouth shut." He shifted his eyes from Angel to Jake and back. "Unless you want me to—" When she glared at him, he snapped his jaw shut.

"Yes. Might as well now. He should've been there when Mac's will was read," she said.

From the dark expression on Jake's face, he didn't care for the accusatory tone.

And it really wasn't Big Judd's fault. But then again, she was tired of being surrounded by men who let their gonads think for them instead of using common sense.

"Of course." Big Judd lifted his briefcase and pulled out a sheet of paper. "You will find the details here, but the overall gist of Mr. Tally's will is that Angel must marry you if she wants to maintain control over her brother's estate. Her brother inherits everything of Mac's. She has a small trust set aside that will help her pay some bills, she won't go hungry, but nothing else unless she marries you."

When Big Judd stopped, Angel motioned for him to continue. "That's not all. Tell him the last bit."

"About Buddy?"

She glanced over to Jake. So far he'd been quiet though his piercing blue eyes cut into her. No way could she look at the other two men in the room. The brothers were as scary as their older brother. "He's talking about Damien. Like me, he prefers to go by his middle name." Returning her attention to Big Judd, she nodded. "Tell him about Damien."

"Yeah. That. I was getting to it. Per Mac's Last Will and Testament, you've been named Damien's guardian."

"And why in hell didn't someone come and get me, so I could attend the reading?" Jake leaned over the desk, hands flat on top.

"We did. But we were told you were too busy to be bothered. You were celebrating your good fortune." She spit out the last word. The day after his dad died, he and his brothers had gotten drunk at another establishment owned by the Whitfields. Mary's Place was more of a neighborhood bar than anything fancy. She really didn't have a word to describe how she felt about their behavior. To think of it, disgust worked perfectly.

He turned his head. Hatred caused his eyes to nearly glow. Were they only going to replay what had been going on for the last three generations in Sand County?

Mutual hatred was common between the Tallys and Whitfields. Her granddaddy had never gone into the details of how the feud started but she'd heard the rumors. Dick Whitfield had loved her grandmama even after she tied the knot with Mac. They said it was why Dick never married any of the women he impregnated. Everyone had thought the feud would end when Mary Tally died from cancer at the age of forty-nine. When the grudge continued, they'd hoped it would end a couple years later with the birth of Jake, followed shortly by Sen's and Ethan's arrivals. But instead, Dick opened a new bar and called it Mary's Place and then declared the crossroads where the bar was built as Marystown. Mac wasn't amused to see his dead wife's name everywhere by another man's decree, and being a stubborn man, he refused to move.

But things changed after the incident at school. She couldn't say her granddaddy's hatred of the Whitfields had waned, but the last few years, the two old men acted as if they had repented of their past and wanted to bring the feud to an end, but weren't sure how. That was what she thought until the will had been read. Obviously, they thought they had the ideal solution. A peace offering of a sort. Only, she was their sacrificial lamb.

She refused to be anyone's sheep.

"Someone told you a lie." His square jaw shifted.

Her focus returned to the present. "Why would Tick lie?" That got his attention.

He narrowed his eyes and looked over to the big man behind the desk.

"Don't look at me. Tick probably misunderstood some order you gave." Big Judd held his hands up and took a step back. Though he likely outweighed Jake by fifty pounds, he would never win a fight against the Whitfield brother. Jake wasn't known for fighting fair.

"Then tell me about this guardianship. What do I get out of it besides watching after a snot-nose know-it-all teenager who hates my guts? And what happens if I refuse to marry her?"

She just raised her eyebrows when he shot a look her way. Did he think she intended to protest the truth?

"In Mac's will, you've been given a large stipend to see to his needs along with a controlling interest in the Tally businesses while you're his guardian." After another swipe of his handkerchief across his forehead, Big Judd added, "And Angel cannot get within twenty feet of the boy or place a foot on any Tally or Whitfield property unless she marries you."

Her heart tightened. She was homeless as of that moment. Well, if Jake didn't marry her. The guardianship was a separate entity. He could still be Damien's guardian and control businesses that were Tallys before. How would her people react to the change? They probably all would be murdered in their beds before it was over.

"Sounds like I come out on top if I marry her or not."

Judd shuffled and cleared his throat. "That was Mac's will. In Dick's, all of the Whitfield assets will be sold off and funds placed into a trust for her and her brother. She can't touch the trust until she's forty and Damien at twenty-five."

"How is any of this legal?" Ethan spoke up.

"It isn't, but considering how much trouble it will be to

go to court and have the wills thrown out, do you really want to go through that at this juncture? Not counting how it would bring to light some less than savory businesses all of you own. Let's say Teddy and Rat Boy wouldn't be happy with their measly thirty-thousand dollars by the time it was settled." Big Judd was a plain spoken man.

Of the four men staring at her, Jake's distrustful stare bothered her the most. Old crush or not, she knew better than to think they'd have anything but business between them. That was okay with her. She didn't need a man's attention to feel good about herself.

But it would be nice to feel like a person, instead of a weapon to be used like Mac had treated her. Yeah, it would be wonderful to be desired and wanted as a woman. Ha! Who wanted a freak like her?

They continued to stare her way. She shook her head and caved in. "What?"

"Don't you have anything to say about this?" Jake crossed his arms.

She had to hand it to him, he surprised her by asking. After dealing with Mac on a daily basis for over ten years—he believed kids, even grown up ones, should do what they were told without any lip—and living with a self-absorbed teenager, she found it refreshing to be asked her opinion. That same teenager was the only immediate family she had left and no way would she allow someone to teach him how to be a criminal. She wanted him to graduate high school and go to college. Become a better man than their dad and granddaddy and certainly better than the Whitfields. For that matter, better than her.

Of course, she hadn't explained what she'd been doing in the van. It was her fault that Damien also believed she'd fired on the asshole staring darts at her. How was it her fault that Jake and his brothers angered the wrong person? A person who wanted them dead at their father's funeral.

Pure stubbornness had stopped her from telling the truth before. Maybe her granddaddy had rubbed off on her more than she thought. Thank goodness, she managed to keep Damien away from the old grouch's machinations.

She should set a good example and tell the truth, but after protecting her brother all his life from the lower elements in Marystown and Sand County, she'd come to the conclusion there wasn't hope for her. The choices she made had been tough, and she regretted a few. Yet she'd make them again if it meant Damien became a good, honest man, and lived a normal life. Similar to those people living in the beautifully landscaped neighborhoods she occasionally drove by in Birmingham.

"That's what I like, a woman who knows how to keep her mouth shut." Jake turned to face his brothers. They busted out laughing. The condescending assholes.

How dare he turn his back on her as if she didn't mean anything. He meant something to her. A new life. A life taking care of her brother like she should.

Fed up with everything that happened that day, she pulled a knife from her coat sleeve.

"Jake! Look out!" Sen kicked out just as her fingers released the knife. His foot hit her in the sternum, sending her body flying through the air and landing backwards into the chairs.

The knife zipped by Jake's ear and crashed through a glass pane behind the desk. Her toss had been faster than Sen. His interference hadn't directed the knife into Jake's back, pitching him face first across the desk. She wasn't stupid. She'd purposely missed. Just a warning. Anything different, and knowing what she heard of the Whitfields, she would have been dead seconds after.

"What the fucking hell?" Jake went to the window and looked at it in disbelief. Before she shoved a chair away and regained her feet, he marched across the room and pulled her up by the coat's lapels. Her nose almost touched his, toe tips brushing the floor. "In my house? You attack me here?"

"As if where really matters," she scoffed. Her temper and mouth ran away from her.

Swallowing deeply, she forced her lips to sneer. He thought because he was a Whitfield, people should be afraid of him. True, the fury shining from his eyes did cause her insides to quake and not in a good way, but she was determined to show how he couldn't push her around.

She lifted her chin. "Maybe killing you would solve all of my problems. Then I wouldn't have to marry your ass."

Big Judd cleared his throat. "Angel, you misunderstood, and I take partial ownership of that error. When I said Jake was the guardian, it was because the will indicates the eldest of Dick Whitfield's living sons. Should anyone"—he looked over his glasses at her—"kill or interfere with his ability to perform the requirement of the wills and his marital duties, the next oldest son becomes the guardian and receives the inheritance."

Jake still had hold of her coat so her movement was limited, but her gaze cut over to Sen. Though exotic and sinfully good-looking, the salacious grin he gave sent chills down her spine. She'd heard of how dangerous he could be with or without a weapon. There was good reason Dick Whitfield used him as the family's collector. Few people dared to be late with payments or cheat the different Whitfield businesses when they knew he'd visit. Despite the skills she'd honed over the years, when it came to hand-to-hand combat, he was a hundred times deadlier.

She looked at Jake and kicked. For such a tall, solid man, he moved fast. He held her away from his body as he turned to the side, her foot missing his knee. His other hand clutched the front of her corset. His fingertips scraped the skin between her breasts.

"Dammit!" He shook her until her stomach roiled. "You're lucky that I refuse to hit a woman."

"If you don't quit, I'll throw up on you." She gagged, and he tossed her to his feet.

Palms down, she stopped herself from landing face first on the rug. She was tired of them shoving her to the floor. In a well-practiced move she pushed off, twisting in mid-jump to a ready stance, hands out, and holding another knife, blade slicing up. Though she'd done it as a threat, the long cut across his ribcage had gone a little deeper than planned. She normally had better self-control, but she kept letting him stoke her temper. He needed to quit treating her like a bag of trash. He thrust her away, and she landed on her butt once more. Bastard.

Her elbow, knee, and rear end hurt from the mistreatment. Fury heated her face as she gritted her teeth. She slammed a fist to the floor. Damn, he made her so mad.

He pressed an arm over the bleeding wound. "That does it. I've put up with your brother shooting—"

"You chauvinistic asshole! It was me shooting, not my brother! And if I had wanted to hit you, you'd be dead."

Before she added that she'd been aiming at a sniper, she caught his brothers' expressions. She knew they didn't believe a word she said, and they intended not to listen to any more explanations. They stepped forward with murder in their eyes. Big Judd mumbled something about needing to make a call outside and left.

"Sen. Ethan. Guard the door and make sure I'm not interrupted. I believe *Angel* and I need to settle a few things." Jake glued his gaze to hers.

Now he got her name right.

"You don't need to—" Ethan stopped when Jake lifted a hand. Sen stood next to his younger brother, his hands in a tight clench.

"I'm fine. Go," Jake ordered. They glared at her and then turned away.

Jake waited until the door closed before he stalked toward her. She eased to her feet.

Wary of his intentions, she stepped back. A wildness flushed his face, stretching lips tight as his eyes narrowed. He wore a blood-soaked shirt and looked ready to hunt down his prey. Surely a scratch wouldn't bleed that much.

"You have to understand." Unable to stop, she backed up another step. "I'm desperate to keep my brother away from Whitfields...uh...that is, I want him to grow up to be a good...you keep jumping to conclusions. Quit looking at me like that!"

Her face turned ice cold. All her life, she'd fought for respect from those who should willingly protect her. So why should she expect the man in front of her to care? She'd learned quickly, she could only depend on herself.

She raised the knife.

Jake stopped only a foot away from her, ignoring the steel point aimed at his chest. He grabbed her wrist and leaned down until they were almost nose-to-nose. "You and I are going to come to an understanding right here, right now. We're not going to leave this room until we do. I can't worry that you're going to maim or kill me in my sleep or while I'm walking down the hall to the kitchen for a snack. I prefer feeling safe in my home, and it appears that you'll be living here for the next few months. At the least, until we can get this fucked up predicament straightened out. How you come to terms with whatever my crazy-as-a-bat old man dreamed up with your screw-loose grandfather is up to you. But you better do it quick."

The knife's tip surely dug into his flesh through his shirt even as she tried to pull away from his hold.

He glanced down at the knife. She released it. It tumbled until the blade stuck point-first into the wood flooring between his shoes. That was close. Her temper quickly cooled.

"I don't have time to fight you, the will, and whoever is killing our people. With the death of my dad and your grandfather, we have to be vigilant. Other organizations will want to take over. They'll think we're weak and disorganized. We can't have it. Too much internal fighting will make us an easy target. Make us appear weak. You and I are going to settle our situation now."

She looked up into his mesmerizing eyes. The sexual intensity in the room ratcheted up a hundred degrees. Intensity radiated from his body in waves, and when he clasped her shoulders, tingles of excitement raced down hers. Only once before had she felt so alive, so turned on. Only one other time had he focused his attention on her to the nth degree. That was years ago when she'd stolen his wallet in high school. His reaction had been electrifying, and she'd used those short moments to fuel many a lonely heated night.

Her chest rose and fell with each breath. She felt her heart pounding, wanting out.

Obviously, he felt the intensity, too, as his gaze heated and then dropped to her breasts and traveled up to her lips.

She'd never been a tease, but she unconsciously licked her bottom lip, showing a little tongue. A new glimmer flared in his eyes. His broad hand eased its way to her neck as his thumb traced the edge of her jaw. His head dipped to hers.

"Or what?" Her voice cracked. Frustrated with how nervous he made her, she needed Jake to back off. No matter how he tempted her, he represented a means to an end and nothing more.

He stopped to stare into her eyes. The sigh he released feathered across her lips and warned that her words had brought finality to his indecisiveness. She knew it wasn't in the way she intended as he pulled her body closer.

"I believe you're due for another spanking," he whispered in her ear.

Warmth flowed over her face and other parts of her body. The feeling excited her to the point she wished she could experience it again and again. But why did her skin burn in the same spot where he'd touched her on that fateful day?

The quietness in the room closed in on her. She needed to regain control of herself.

She roughly shrugged her shoulders, knocking his hands off, and stepped away, keeping her arms loose at her sides. Self-control remained the key to surviving the travesty being played with her and Damien's lives, and so far, she hadn't shown a whole lot of it.

"You have a sick fascination with what happened years ago." Good, she sounded firm and unaffected by his threat, not counting his nearness. Her self-defense lessons with her grandfather, Mac, had taught her not to show any emotion if at all possible. Just as a dog would attack a person when sensing their fear, a man's need to dominate intensified around a weak woman. They respected strength. "I already know you're bigger and stronger. I thought you said you don't hit women."

"I can promise you, honey, spanking isn't hitting." The sultry tone in his voice sent shivers down her body.

Taking a deep breath to regain her senses, she met his gaze.

"Let's talk about what we should do about the wills and my brother," she said.

His eyebrows rose. He hadn't expected her to change the subject.

"We?" he asked. Cynical amusement flitted over his face. What was so funny? "I don't think you have a clue yet. There is no *we*. There's only me. You better learn that I don't run a democracy in this house. In my house. I'm the ruler, master, and lord."

She'd thought about saying it would be her house after they married, but thought better of it. That would be close to a death wish without the chance of dying. At the moment, she preferred living. And really, for some reason she wasn't afraid of him. His gruff voice and words actually excited her. Besides, despite all of the threats he made, he hadn't hurt her intentionally.

"What are your brothers? Peons?" She did wonder if he loved his brothers as she did hers.

"They have their own homes, their own jobs. They understand their positions in the organization." He crossed his arms and looked down his nose at her. "Do you under-stand yours?" Before she could answer, he placed his hands on the wall behind her, framing her in. "Now tell me. Why did you shoot at me?"

Yes. He put her in her place. His forceful and dominant stance quickened the pace of her heartbeat. Even as a teenager, he had that aura of leadership. She admired that. It freaking melted her panties.

She eyed the bulging veins on his arms, beautifully sculpted by hard work or lifting weights. Her money was still on gym-made muscles. Having all the riches he'd grown up with, his work probably required no more than lifting a pen and his wallet.

"You're the boss." She tried to keep the sarcasm out of her tone. "I'll walk one step behind you. But I have to talk to you about my brother." She could place her pride to the side as little mattered to her beyond taking care of Damien. If she had to sleep with the devil to protect him, she'd do it. And when the devil looked like Jake Whitfield, who said she was sacrificing anything.

Once again, he surprised her. He lifted her by the shoulders and flattened her with his body against the wall before she could move. He gazed into her eyes as her toes barely scraped the floor.

"No. That bullshit can be left for last. Why were you shooting at me?"

She struggled, working at his hands as his hips pressed against hers. "Let go of me before I hurt you." Turning her head away, she tried to keep her mind off how much she loved feeling his firm body against hers and the strength of his hands.

"Why, sugar, you couldn't hurt me if you tried."

"Your bloody shirt says differently."

His evil chuckle didn't reassure her when he let go, allowing her to stand on her own. Yet he remained in her personal space.

"Yeah. That was an anomaly, and you do owe me

another shirt. This was my favorite one. The blue matched my eyes," he said with a teasing tone.

She had cut him, and he only worried about his shirt? Maybe he was as crazy as his father. After another peek, she had to admit the color did look good on him. His wearing nothing would look even better. She mentally groaned.

With her feet flat on solid support, wearing two-inch-thick-soled boots, she was eye-level to his mouth. For such cruel-looking thin lips, they appeared soft. The type she'd probably enjoy biting. She shut her eyes and released a shaky breath.

Had she really thought that? What was it about this man that made her feel weak, feminine, and horny? The kind of thoughts flitting through her mind she'd learned to ignore years ago, except when alone. Mac had said there were only two reasons to have sex: to produce children and to control someone. She'd never understood who controlled whom. One thing she learned was if Mac caught her flirting with a boy, he would lock her in her room for days. The isolation had kept her out of trouble, but her imagination had done so much more.

Even with her eyes closed, she sensed a shadow crossing her face before she felt his warm breath on her cheek. Then male lips gently pressed to hers. She gasped, her heart racing as his tongue stroked and dipped into her mouth. Unable to resist the temptation, she opened wide and joined in, tasting and rubbing her tongue along his. She clutched his forearms and dug her nails into hard muscles, wanting to beg for more.

He tasted like what she expected: a mixture of smoke and something indefinably masculine. Each time her tongue met his, the passion of the touch built until she forgot to breathe for a couple of heartbeats. Seconds passed before she realized he'd broken their kiss, and she'd been following his mouth with hers. The room swirled as she gulped in air.

"I've got to see and feel them," he muttered.

His large hands grabbed her corset and then shoved down the edge beneath her breasts. Her stiff nipples landed in rough, warm palms as he cupped and massaged. His touch felt good. Her heart thumped so hard she had difficultly catching her breath. She'd always suspected she would love it rough.

"Damn, I've been aching to do that," he said in a raspy voice. His gaze devoured the view as he lifted them.

She probably should protest, but his touch and hungry look enthralled her to the point that forming words felt impossible. How long had she dreamed of having him touch her? The way he rubbed his thumbs over the sensitive nubs brought a whimper to her lips as she arched her back. With each caress, she ached for more.

"You like that, huh?" He chuckled and lightly tugged at them. "Then let's see how you'll like this." His hands clasped her ribcage and lifted until her breasts were even with his mouth. Her hands clutched his shoulders. He rested a knee against the wall. His thigh supported the vee of her legs, providing enough support for his hands to roam.

He sucked in one tight nipple and tongued the tip. Every inch of her body zinged as nerves she'd never knew existed came alive. Whenever she'd been alone in her bedroom and tugged at them, it hadn't felt as delicious as what he did with his mouth. She clasped his head and looked at the ceiling with unseeing eyes. Surely they'd rolled to the back of her head. Her heart pumped so fast, she expected it to burst. She clenched her teeth with the tiny amount of restraint she possessed to hold back the scream. The last thing she needed was to alert his brothers on what he was doing—correct that—in what *they* were doing. She didn't want him to stop. No one had ever made her feel this way. Self-gratification would never do the trick again.

He moved his mouth from one breast to the other and back, while his hands slid down her torso. With ease, he unhooked, unzipped her pants and then his fingers slipped beneath the waistband of her pants to cup and massage her buttocks.

When had her ass become an erogenous zone?

He lifted her enough to open her pants all the way until cool air touched the moisture pooling between her legs. Pressing her shoulders back against the wall, he tilted her hips as his knee returned to support her.

His mouth continued to suckle, and his teeth tugged. Her fingers threaded through his thick hair just as calloused fingers rubbed between her slick folds. Dizzy from lack of oxygen, she was thankful for the support of his strong body and the wall behind her. She widened her legs and thrust her hips, enjoying how he knew exactly where and how to touch her.

Losing herself in his expertise, she jumped when someone banged on the door.

"Hey! We got a problem!" The male voice sounded pissed. Sen's?

Jake released her breast with a smack and then gave it a lick. His thumb continued to massage the small knot, bringing moisture with each rotation. She should say something, protest, hit him. She only knew she didn't want him to stop and didn't care that someone stood a few feet away with a mere interior door between them, probably listening to her every moan.

Her gaze searched his, worried about what he planned next.

"Shh, sugar. Don't worry. Sen won't open the door. If it'd been Ethan, I couldn't swear to it. He loves to watch," he said in a soft tone. Then he raised his voice "What is it?"

He kept his gaze on hers. Unable to even blink, her gaze transfixed to his blue, blue eyes. A flush warmed her cheeks, her eyelids drifted half closed. Without hesitating, his fingers pulled at the sensitive bundle of nerves between her legs, and she shuddered. His fleeting grin attested to how much he enjoyed having her at his mercy.

Her head spun from trying to understand the man. He had too many layers, from caring one moment to devilishly provoking to tantalizing and on and on.

"You better quit what you're doing and get out here." Sen's voice remained on the other side of the door.

"If it isn't life or death, it can wait a little longer." Jake's voice was edged with dark impatience.

Terrified that Sen would open the door, she pushed at Jake's hands. She needed to straighten her clothes, pull her shredded dignity around her. His hands finally slipped from out of her heat and pants.

"Let's finish this quick. I'm nothing but considerate," he whispered,

And before she realized what he planned to do, with one arm around her ribs and another behind her knees, he scooped her up and placed her on the edge of the desk. He swiped away the papers, lamp, and odds and ends and then spread her on top. He unfastened a couple of buckles and jerked off her boots and pants. Knowing his brother and who knew how many others were outside the door, she fought at his hands without saying a word. One Whitfield was bad enough, but if she shouted, others would come. No way could she handle them all.

She reached out to snatch her clothes back, but they flew across the room to land next to a large vase in the corner. When his hands seized her knees and lifted, she landed on her back, the breath knocked out of her. She scrambled to hang onto the cool top. Unable to regain her senses and tell him he was a son of a bitch, his mouth covered her folds. His tongue speared into her, finding the tender knot, and he sucked hard, finishing what his fingers had started. Her body arched as she threw back her head.

Sticking the side of her hand into her mouth, she bit down to silence the scream. Her heels dug into his shoulders. Then the best orgasm in her life washed over her wave by wave. That felt so gooood.

The man knew his way around a woman's body, even if he went about it demandingly and rudely. Who was she kidding? She loved it.

"Sugar, you okay?"

The buzzing in her ears subsided. Limp and brain dead, she looked at him in surprise. How could any man know how to do that? He knew her body better than she did. Who had taught him that?

He wrapped an arm around her waist and hauled her up against his chest. Grabbing her hand, he flipped it over. That was when she noticed the blood. She'd bitten into the meaty portion near the thumb.

With his long reach, he pulled a tissue from a box sitting upside-down on a nearby chair and swiped at the red beads. "Damn. Like I said before, you're beautifully responsive. That's hot. Molten lava hot." With unexpected tenderness, he brought her hand to his lips, kissing the wound, while his other hand slid up and down her bare thigh as if to soothe her.

She fought the urge to part her legs again. Her fingers itched to cup his crotch, to see how hard he was from his attentions. Oh, God, she hoped he was hard It would be so disturbing to think he could do that to her and not feel anything.

As if he knew what she was thinking, he reached down and adjusted himself.

"I'm so fucking hard, I'm surprised I didn't come in my pants." He grinned and looked her over. Her breath shortened. "You and me. Later. When we have more time."

A flash of devilment appeared in his eyes as he lifted her hand again and sucked in her middle finger. Zap! Hot pleasure shot straight to between her thighs.

"I'm going to send Ethan in, if you don't hurry," Sen said with exasperation in each word.

Jake pulled out her finger and licked a path down her palm. Did the man know every erogenous zone on a woman's body?

"Your brother's waiting for you," she managed to say in a breathy voice. She really needed him to quit touching her. Maybe then she could reclaim her common sense and salvage some control over her own body.

"Yeah. You're right. But I'm glad I got to taste you. You're real sweet." He ran his thumb across his lips and licked the pad as if he anticipated another meal on her behalf.

Unable to look at him any longer without begging him to take her, she glanced at the door.

He clutched her hair and slowly pulled her head back. "Look at me. I'm the one you need to worry about, the one you need to make happy," he said roughly, possessively. Her heartbeat raced. When his gaze dropped to her lips, she knew. He was angry with himself for losing control and going down on her, for wanting more just as much as she did. She shuddered from the deep hunger boiling beneath the surface, brought on by his rough treatment. "You fascinate me. With your black, red-tipped hair." He slid a knuckle down her face. "Even your pale makeup. Wild and unpredictable. So I've decided to meet the old man's requirements for now. I saw the lust in your eyes when I yanked down your top. Even now, you like how I'm holding you, controlling you with your wild, beautiful hair. Let's say I want to find out more about you and how you'll react to all of my particular tastes," he said in his deep, husky voice.

His fingers tightened until her scalp stung. Part of her wanted to fight back, but she never felt so alive, so freaking turned on. Her nipples tightened until they ached, and she wanted his mouth on her again. Then he turned the hand with the smeared makeup on the knuckle and lapped at each finger that had been in her seconds earlier, his gaze staying on hers. She whimpered again, wanting those glistening digits inside her, working their magic.

The pleasure crossing his face captivated her. Whatever he saw on hers satisfied him enough to let her go.

"I need my clothes," she said barely above a whisper. Her dry throat hurt from panting so hard.

Remaining on the desk, passive and attentive to his every move as he gathered her black jeans and boots, she raised one eyebrow when he stuffed her black panties into his pocket, silently daring her to protest. Then he helped her dress and straightened her corset. He rearranged and buttoned and zipped his clothing without her help. She merely watched, but when he wrapped his fingers around his cock and moved it to one side of his pants, her breath quickened. Nothing sexier than watching a man situating his package.

"Sugar, you still haven't answered me about why you shot at me, though I have a feeling it's all tied into your anger management issues. So for now, go to the kitchen and tell my mom and Jimmie Sue I'll be with them shortly. Introduce yourself to your future mother-in-law." He grabbed her chin. "And be nice. If you hurt those ladies or make them uncomfortable, I'll tear up your butt twice as bad as I did when we were in high school."

When he turned and reached for the doorknob, she did it before she even thought it through. A thud echoed in the room. Near his ear, a letter opener was stuck into the wood paneling, the mother of pearl handle quivering.

Did he believe he could talk to her like that?

His cold gaze stared at it for a few seconds and then he glanced over his shoulder at her. Blue eyes darkened, giving her a warning. She knew without a doubt the line was drawn, and he expected payment for that show of disobedience. Excitement zinged through her veins.

He opened the door and strode out, greeting his brother without another look her way.

There was no doubt he would make her pay for that final defiance. She caught her breath at the thought. Sure, she needed to learn to control her temper, but she wanted his unspoken promise. His threat had spiked the desire to revisit her so-called *just desserts* for being bad. She'd wondered for years if the sting of his hand was as sweet as she remembered.

Chapter Five

"Whatcha find out, Luc?" Jake slipped into the front of the hearse parked at the end of his drive and faced the man behind the wheel, waiting for an answer.

"You were right. Mac and the old man had been shot. From what they found, the shots were from a distance, probably across the dance floor, hitting each through the heart. Whoever did it was an ace shooter. He then partially covered the bodies with an accelerant to burn as much evidence as possible." Luc offered Jake a cigarette and then shook one out.

Lucius Quinn owned and operated the one and only funeral home in Marystown. Like many of the long-time citizens, he'd owed Dick Whitfield, and in turn, owed the brothers. His payment came about by sewing up knife and bullet wounds without the necessary reporting to the authorities, and providing insider information through his friendship with the small county's M.E. The report on the old man hadn't been released to the family; mainly because the local deputies hated the Whitfields and did everything they could to make their life a misery.

Jake understood the cops feared more people would die if it was known that the old man had been murdered. From the beginning, he'd suspected homicide, especially after what Angel had blurted out in the limo, and the way the kid hated him. Somehow, she had found out the truth before Luc had.

The oily smell of lighter fluid drifted in the air-conditioned space as Luc offered the flame to Jake. Taking a long draw, Luc pressed two buttons on the door, lowering the windows slightly, and exhaled a stream of smoke. The wisps disappeared with the help of the air conditioning blasting full force.

Jake settled into the leather seat and watched the red tip of his cigarette glow brighter. Smoking always calmed his nerves. Since he was hornier than a dog chained in a barn full of bitches in heat, he needed the smoke badly. Leaving Angel had taken every bit of his willpower. Next time, he wasn't sure if he could walk away without fucking her bowlegged.

"Whoever did this, the old man must've known him. No way would a stranger get that close to him before he shot back." Jake blew a thin stream of smoke out the cracked window. "Any bullet wounds show up recently?" Jake knew Luc helped a few others outside the Whitfield organization.

"Nope. I checked with the clinic. None there either. There's a chance he waited until he reached the suburbs of Birmingham to get stitched up." Luc shifted in his seat and pulled out a handkerchief from his back pocket and swiped at the sweat beading along his receding hairline. "Damn, it's hot. First week in June and the temps are almost hitting three digits. The air conditioner can't fight back hard enough."

Jake took another long pull before he stepped out of the hearse, dropped the butt on the cement, and rubbed it out with his boot. He spotted a UTV coming from the tree-line and waved.

Turning back to Luc, he leaned down to the opened door. "If you hear anything more, call me."

"You know it." Luc nodded as Jake closed the door.

He watched the hearse drive away. Something wasn't right.

The old man had never been sloppy with security and the same for Tally. Their guards saw no one enter the building or heard a thing before smoke billowed from under the door. How did someone move past armed men and walk into a locked building, killing two grown men who were more deadly than most?

"What you suspected was right?" Ethan stopped next to him in one of several UTVs they used to do work around the compound. With so much land to maintain and some in flood zones, the two-seater vehicles came in handy, not counting the long drive to the mailbox outside the gate.

He hopped in and held on as Ethan hit the gas, causing the front wheels to jump off the ground.

"Yeah. But it appears to be a professional hit. Only someone efficient with firearms could've shot within seconds two armed men through the heart. That doesn't include getting away with no one seeing a thing after setting the place on fire." He eyed the trees lining the drive, noting some needed trimming after the spat of tornadoes they'd had that spring. The old man taught them to always take care of the land as the land would take care of them. If only the old man cared about his sons the same way.

He grimaced at the *pity me* thought. What was done was done.

"Sen probably knows better than anyone who we need to talk to," Ethan said.

Of the three of them, Sen had it the roughest. The old man thought nothing of slapping them around when they were kids and treating them like less than dogs, but Sen received the brunt of it. By looking different in a vanilla town, he was an easy target for people to point their finger at whenever something went wrong. As he grew older, he'd learned how to keep a low profile, and over time, despite their fear of his position in the organization, most of the townspeople grew to trust him, something about his calm manner earned their confidence.

Ethan brought the UTV to a sliding stop. "Looks as if he's waiting for us."

Sen stood at one end of the porch in the shade, probably less to do with the heat than to keep out of sight. He claimed to learn more by being quiet and listening than by pounding information out of people, though he was willing to do both.

Before his middle brother even said a word, Jake knew something was wrong. The more stoney his face became, the worse the situation.

"What happened?" Jake asked.

"You know a couple years ago we heard that the Tallys had a new collector."

"Yeah. Since he didn't mess with our people, I haven't heard much about the guy." Jake glanced over to Ethan. His brother shrugged.

"I felt the same way, but today I decided to introduce myself." Sen's subtle grin brought Jake's eyebrows up. His brother rarely smiled, and when he remained quiet, Jake knew he wouldn't want to hear the answer.

"Are you going to tell me or not?" Jake lifted his chin.

"It's Angel."

"You're shitting me!" Ethan laughed.

That explained a lot about the guns and knives. Yet, he never expected old Mac Tally to be so open-minded about having his granddaughter as a collector.

"Okay. She's a good shot and crazy about knives, but there's no way she could intimidate anyone into paying their bills," Jake said.

"Strength isn't always needed to put fear in a person's heart." Sen leaned a shoulder on one of the large white columns.

"What's that? Some wise ancient Chinese saying?" He loved picking on his brother.

"How the fuck would I know?" Sen shrugged.

"That woman is—what's that riddle thing you always say?" Jake asked.

Sen shook his head. "It was Churchill. He said, 'A riddle wrapped in a mystery inside an enigma.'"

"Yeah. That's her." Jake rubbed his chin. The woman was different. So different he thought about her every five minutes. When was the last time a woman occupied his thoughts so often?

Ethan opened the front door. "You boys can stay out here, but I'm getting out of the heat."

As they stepped into the foyer, Jake's eyes narrowed. He spotted Tick taking two steps at a time down the large sweeping staircase, glancing at his feet and over to them with each step.

"Boss, boss, I'm sorry but I searched everywhere. They're gone."

Jake didn't need to guess who he meant by *they*.

"Then why the hell were you upstairs?" Did he think they escaped to the attic? Jake took a deep breath. Yelling at Tick only caused the big guy to choke. Then he would never get the information out of him. 'Tell me what happened," he said in a calm voice.

"I just turned my back for a second to get a beer." Their family room had a well-stocked bar in the corner. The old man had loved his liquor.

No need to point out to Tick that while he was on guard duty alcohol was off limits. He never listened. Jake raked hair out of his eyes, smoothing it back until his hand stopped on the back of his neck, looking at Tick from beneath his eyebrows.

"Where's Matt?" he asked.

Whenever Tick was running errands, Matt kept an eye on the place. Most likely, he had guarded the kid when Tick brought Angel to the study for the reading.

"He went to check the garage while I searched the house. Damien had talked about how an old house like this would probably have ghosts, and I thought maybe he'd wandered upstairs." Tick shifted his feet as if he was anxious to leave.

"Ethan, see if you can find Matt and meet us in the study." Jake didn't want Tick disappearing. He'd wander off in a heartbeat, thinking the problem not his. Jake dipped his head, silently indicating Tick and Sen to go with him down the hall to the office.

Someone had placed a sheet of plywood over the busted window and cleaned the broken furniture and blood.

He sat behind the desk and ran a hand down his shirt, feeling the bandages beneath. Earlier as he headed toward the door to meet Quinn, Jimmie Sue had ordered him to stop long enough for her to doctor the cut and place a few butterfly bandages over deeper parts, and then efficiently handed him a shirt from the laundry room. He rolled his shoulders, ignoring the ache across his ribs. Some women knew how to cut deep with their tongue; obviously, he knew one who could do it with a knife, too. With a little effort, he swallowed a chuckle.

Angel had some spunk.

Sen rested one hip on the edge of the desk.

"You know they're long gone by now," Sen remarked.

Jake leaned back. "Yeah."

He closed his eyes as he made plans of how to bring them back and make her stay. Of course, the brother was the key. But he wanted her to stay for more, for him. Funny, he never thought he would want a woman as much as he did Angel.

Chapter Six

ngel ran her hand across the soft beige leather. A weakness she'd never been able to indulge in was the ownership of an expensive vehicle. She'd always wanted to own a Corvette, and the black Stingray was a fine piece of machinery with zero to sixty in less than four-seconds. *Wowza!* Not that her Mustang was anything to be ashamed of, but it wasn't new and shiny like this one.

Her granddaddy's businesses were never as successful as the Whitfields, and the man rarely parted with a coin without expecting equal compensation. So until the day he died, he drove a 1998 white F150 Ford pickup and often shook his head at others' needless spending to buy the newest model.

Her brother had wanted her to steal the Hummer from the Whitfields' garage, but she pointed out it was so huge they wouldn't get far without being spotted. Though she had to admit the Corvette wasn't that low profile either. But, what little money she had on her would be gone in seconds as the thing surely guzzled gas as a drunk downing water after a three-day binge.

So they'd found the black Corvette's keys in a metal box hanging on the wall near the door. She'd only taken a few minutes to disable the GPS. Amazingly easy if a person knew where to look, and she did. All she had to do was disconnect the special battery, and it was dead to the world.

And when Damien checked the center console, he found the Whitfield brothers believed in having a weapon nearby at all times. A Beretta Px4 Storm fitted perfectly in the space. Without hesitation she held out her palm. He handed over the weapon, and she stuck it in her coat pocket. Only right she held on to it. The Whitfields still had her much older gun. A Beretta, too. Not as nice or pretty as this one.

They'd been traveling for about thirty minutes when she looked over at her brother. Relief lifted her spirits upon seeing the huge grin on his face.

"What are you smiling about?" she asked.

"Did you decide where we're going?" Damien pulled out a cigarette and lit it after cracking the window.

"Where did you get that?"

Aghast at his daring to smoke in front of her, knowing how she hated it, she shook her head. Her brother constantly tested his boundaries, but he had never tried to smoke before. It was easy to guess who he imitated.

So far, she avoided thinking about Jake and what he'd done to her in his study. So what if he had a way with his tongue and fingers? She shifted in her seat. Her breath caught when the tenderness between her legs brought memories of his beard-rough face sliding along her thighs. Her cheeks flushed and the air in the sports car vanished.

Stop thinking about it!

The most important person in her life was sitting next

to her and he needed her full attention. He couldn't help looking up to the wrong man. What other kind had come around? None who deserved his admiration. It was sad but she found herself chuckling as thoughts came to mind of other lessons he'd learned the hard way. Like the time he tried chewing tobacco, and he threw up for hours. She was thankful that Mac had given up the disgusting habit soon after, though it had nothing to do with Damien, and had more to do with being diagnosed with oral cancer.

"While you left me in the basement of that old creepy house, I found some inside a cabinet. I also tried out their bourbon, tequila, and gin. The gin tastes like rubbing alcohol. How do people drink that shit?" He inhaled on the cigarette; the tip glowed bright enough to set off sparks, and he started coughing.

She leaned across the console and snatched the cigarette, tossing it out the window before he could protest.

"So that's why you're acting goofy. I thought it was because I woke you from a nap. But no, it's because you passed out. See. Drinking made you think you could smoke without me saying anything." Tears welled in her eyes. She worked so hard to keep him on the straight and narrow. Some days her brain felt as if it would split in two. Working for Mac and looking after her brother were two full-time jobs. She'd tried so hard to keep them separated. Damien only recently found out what she did for a living, and as predictable as many teenagers, he thought it cool. No matter how many times she stated how he was wrong.

When Mac had decided a granddaughter followed orders better than his drug-addicted son, he'd taken advantage of her expulsion and put her to work in the family business. Being former Special Forces, he used the skills he'd honed in the service to teach her how to be the family's collector.

During those years, she'd worked hard and did whatever her granddaddy told her. Two years ago, he explained it was time for her to fill the job he'd trained her for. He explained if she didn't, he would begin training Damien. She wasn't about to let that happen. So she dove in head first, insuring Mac wasn't disappointed in his decision.

Only she knew the guilt that weighed her down, and how she resented Mac for the things he forced her to do all in the name of protecting the family.

"What can I say?" His lopsided grin tugged at her heart.

No, she needed to stand firm.

"You can start with saying I'm sorry, and I'll never do it again." Her voice remained even and firm. "Do you want to end up like Dad?"

He crossed his arms and pushed out his bottom lip. "You forget you're my sister, not my mother. You need to chill and get off my back. Just because I had a few sips, doesn't mean I'll go off the deep end and start smoking crack. I'm not Dad." Slumping in his seat, he stared out the passenger window.

Guilt floated to the top of her conscious. Not that it was her fault they had gotten stuck with lousy parents. But she wondered if she could've done more, been there for him more? She might be his sister, but she loved him as if he were her child, totally and unconditionally. From the moment he was born, he had been cared for by her. She'd changed, fed, and watched him as much as possible.

"Let me just say this. Because of our family history, we're prone to addictions, and you're smart enough to know it often starts with alcohol." Really, she hated preaching, but he needed to think about the consequences. Easily part of the reason she avoided alcohol and cigarettes.

She fought other types of compulsions over the years. Yes. How many black leather pants, skirts, coats, and boots did she own? How many colors had her hair been? She had many others, but all were harmless compulsions. She fought the whole shebang. Only she lost on occasion. She looked in the small rearview mirror at her black hair with red ends.

What could she say? She liked how it looked.

Before she could say more, cartoon-style snoring came from his side of the car. So phony. She chuckled and shook her head. At least he wasn't irritating her with complaints or questions on where they were going. She had no idea at the moment.

When they passed the large blue Welcome to Mississippi sign, the weight on her shoulders felt so much lighter. Despite her panic in leaving and heading west, Mac's right-hand man could handle things until she figured out how to avoid marrying a Whitfield. A little over two hours later, the car zoomed past the Louisiana sign. She smiled big. Hopefully, the Whitfields would never expect her to keep driving, and the more distance between them, the better. Wherever they stopped, it would be much better than Marystown.

Sure, she thought she'd come to terms with marrying that man, but after their time together in the study, she had decided he was one obsession she needed to stop cold turkey. Obsession? Yes. She'd kept tabs on him through contacts, the Internet, and the local paper. And of course, it bothered her a little...no, make that a lot that he hadn't thought of her once since high school. Was she running away because he'd forgotten her and hadn't been obsessed with her as she'd been with him? There was *that* word again. Obsessed. Obsession. She was a sick puppy. Maybe Jake Whitfield was her drug of choice.

Stupid, stupid, stupid.

She needed to do what Southern women were good at doing: she'd think about it tomorrow. For the moment, she needed to be as far from him as possible.

By the time they passed a Shreveport sign, her eyes tried to drift closed. She snapped them back open. Luckily, she remained on the road. Time to stop and get some rest.

Spotting a small motel off I-20, she drove up the exit. A few hours of sleep and she would be right as rain before they continued west. From the looks of the area, the expensive Corvette would be out of place. Maybe everyone would assume it belonged to a drug dealer or someone had been lucky in the local casino. And considering what she'd found out about the gas mileage, they were welcome to the car. Goodness, it was not much better than the Hummer after all. She guessed if a person was rich enough to afford it, they could afford the gas.

The attendant halfway listened to her request for a room on the ground floor. When she paid with cash, he raised his eyebrows and grinned. She wondered if his employers would even see the money. Thankfully, the room worked out better than she expected. A back door opened into a short hallway that led to a fenced-in pool area. Perfect for a quick getaway.

From the smell of old cigarette smoke and dust overlaid with a cheap floral deodorizer, she hoped the sheets and towels were clean. She seriously wanted a shower.

After herding Damien out of the car and into the room, she locked the door. Nudging open the curtains a tad, she looked out into the parking lot. Nothing unusual. At the few stops they'd made, she'd checked for any vehicles she'd seen before. None jogged her memory. If not for Damien, she would've kept going and taken a chance of falling asleep behind the wheel, but she would never risk his life. That was, no more than she had already.

How had Jake taken the news of their escape? She felt bad for leaving her people in a lurch. They weren't exactly thrilled to have her as a leader, but she needed time to think over all of the craziness. One day, everything would be her brother's. Until then she had to devise a plan to keep it out of Jake's hands and convert all of the front businesses into the real deals, profitable real deals.

She turned her attention to where her brother stood in the middle of the room with his shoulders slumped. She realized she'd made the right decision. He looked as if he were sleeping on his feet.

"I'll take the bed next to the window. Don't open the door or answer the phone." She dropped the Walmart plastic bag of clothes and two disposable cell phones onto the bed.

They'd bought them near the motel along with food for Damien. She handed over the white sack with a hamburger and fries, and pitched him a can of soda. As he dug into the food, she shrugged off her coat, tossing it on the bed. She pulled out jeans, a tee shirt, and a package of panties from the plastic bag and then picked up her backpack, heading toward the bathroom but stopped.

"When you finish eating, you can watch whatever you want." She took a step and stopped again. "As long as it's nothing we have to pay extra for."

He flopped onto the bed nearest the inside wall. "You're no fun. I used to watch Gramps's porn all the time."

"I guess you're just out of luck here. Think of it this

way. Do you really want to be sporting a woody with me in the room?"

"Shit, Sis! I need something to clean out my ears. Sick. Totally sick." His face crinkled up with his fingers in his ears as he pretended to gag.

"That took care of that," she murmured. Smiling, she shut the bathroom door behind her.

Chapter Seven

Angel looked into the mirror after swiping the condensation from the glass. She stared hard at her reflection, her face clean of makeup. When would the harsh things she'd been made to do show up on her face? Or maybe it did already and she didn't see it. For the last few years, she'd worn self-imposed blinders to get through each day. So who was to say they weren't still on? Since money was tight, and would become tighter as she avoided using her ATM or credit card, she had bought only the essentials. But she still had her makeup in the backpack and the gun in her coat pocket. She shook her head. Makeup and guns? When had she become that kind of person? Equating ownership of a weapon with beauty products?

Clasping the counter, her head hanging down to her chest, she inhaled. The shower dripped behind her. Her damp hair curled around her face and chin. The blow dryer had done a sorry job. She took another deep breath.

Was she wrong for running away with her brother? More like running scared. If she'd stayed, she could see herself becoming obsessed even more with Jake Whitfield. Obsessed with doing anything he wanted so he would marry her. How pitiful was that? It wasn't just for the money and property or even about her brother. The lonely semi-virgin consumed by a Whitfield, wanting his body, his cock, and his hand stinging her butt. A shiver tingled from the top of her head to her toes. Despite slashing him—truthfully she'd meant to warn him and nothing more—and throwing her knife and the letter opener, she wasn't a violent person, no matter how hard Mac had trained her. Anytime she'd hurt someone before, it had been in self-defense.

Jake made her crazy. Different emotions pulled her one way and then another. She wanted his touch, but felt ashamed by her quick and easy response. For years, she'd dreamed of his hands on her again, but she wanted more stroking and massaging along with slapping the fleshy part of her ass. And goodness, he'd done that. His mouth between her legs...she released a shaky sigh. The memory shot tingles to her breasts and pussy. But she knew he didn't really want her. Why would he? He could have any woman in Marystown, probably the whole county. Taking a deep breath, she straightened and shook off the feeling. She needed to concentrate on what she should do next.

From the sound of the TV, her brother had decided on a football game. Wonders never ceased. He was more of the typical geeky teenager who loved video games. Then again, he'd been changing and noticing girls more. She laughed silently. Between the Playboy magazines and Mac's porn, yeah, she could say that.

She tested the underwear hanging on the towel rack. Still damp. She'd washed the new panties and her old bra but the blow dryer did an even worse job drying the cotton than it had her hair. Yuck.

Brushing her hair back with her fingers, she refused to look in the mirror again. With a sigh, she jerked the over-sized tee shirt on and cringed as she slipped into the jeans commando. Then she carefully folded up her leather pants and corset and stuffed them into the backpack.

She opened the door and walked around the corner into the dim bedroom area. "Okay. It's your turn." Cigarette smoke hung heavy in the air. That little sneak. She bit back a grin. The boy had guts.

Opening her mouth to fuss, she snapped it shut. His bed was empty. Her gaze slid to the other bed. Her throat closed around her heart.

"How did you find us?"

Jake Whitfield looked at home as he leaned back against the headboard; his long legs stretched out down the bed and ankles crossed. He pressed a button on the remote and flipped to another football game. He blew out a stream of smoke into the air and then dropped the butt into a soda can on the nightstand. His gaze darted to her before returning to the TV screen.

Powerful and potent, his presence alone darkened the room and filled it with danger, floating above her head like the smoke from his extinguished cigarette. Each movement of his hard body captivated her.

"Easy. I tracked you down using the GPS." He continued to watch the game. His indifference worried her more than she wanted to admit. Similar to a tiger pretending to sleep until the prey came closer.

She needed to run for the back door, but a few things stopped her: her brother was missing and she was certain he'd stashed him somewhere, and he held a gun pointed at her.

"That's impossible. I disabled it." Was this it? No matter how she felt and how he treated her in his study, it didn't necessarily mean he cared a rat's ass for her. Would he kill her and leave her body for the maids to find?

"You disabled the one from the factory. All of my vehicles have an extra GPS. A few are rigged to lock the steering and stall the engine, and the Stingray is one of them. Since I didn't want to take a chance you'd ditch it for thieves to strip, I followed you." He clicked the remote and the room became quiet and pitch black in the corners. Light from the bathroom helped, but his face remained hidden in the shadows. "You look different, better without that white and black shit on your face."

"Where's Damien?" she asked, ignoring his comment.

The air conditioning kicked on and a chill swept over her. Oh, she wanted—needed to cross her arms over her breasts. With no makeup and no underwear, she almost felt naked. Standing in the light from the bathroom, he could probably see her nipples standing at attention against the thin cotton T-shirt. She looked for her coat and noticed it draped over a chair next to the small table instead of the bed. Had he checked her pockets?

"Don't even think about it. I put the Beretta out of reach, and your brother's on his way back to the house."

Was he as angry and lethal as his voice sounded?

"Then let's leave. Where he goes, I go." She stepped toward the plastic bag on the bed, and the muzzle of the gun followed her movement. "There's only clothing in it," she explained.

"I know." He motioned his gun toward her, his face still in the shadows. "Strip."

"What?" Her whole body flushed with embarrassment and hunger.

"You heard me."

"Is this how you get women in bed with you?" Her condemnation mixed with the need to comply puckered her nipples further into painful nubs. Her body had as little sense as she did when it came to Jake.

"This afternoon, I could've been sunk balls deep in you with your legs wrapping my waist and have you begging for more." His tone gave away his amusement at the thought. Asshole. "Strip, and don't make me say it again. It's time for your spanking. You've pushed me until I have no other choice."

"You have lots of choices, and you're not my dad or granddaddy for that matter. Besides I'm too old for whippings." Memory of the way his hands felt on her that fateful day had taught her something about herself.

"Spankings." He corrected her. "There is a difference you'll understand tonight." Then he said in a steady but cold tone, "I'm waiting. You wouldn't want to experience the consequences beyond what you face already."

Her pussy actually pulsed from the thought of being naked and over his knee. She'd never been so aware of a man in her life. The challenge he threw at her had sparked the roaring need she experienced whenever she remembered his hand on her tender buttocks.

A few seconds passed before she realized he said more after his initial threat. "What kind of consequences?"

"I can easily say no to marrying you and handle the fallout with your grandfather's people. But I'd rather have them work with me because I'm your husband and your brother's guardian, though I'm sure I can convince them it's in their best interest, even without your cooperation and my ring on your finger."

Her hands fisted. No way would she let him take control of her people. Not that she had any worries, they were loyal to the Tallys. Besides, she didn't have a problem with him having control of her body. She'd fantasized about his touch for a long time and what he desired meshed with hers. She exhaled.

"Marrying you isn't my big dream either," she lied. No need to make everything too easy for him. She'd dreamed about him for so many years. Dreamed about having him to herself and the two of them repeating that fateful day in the classroom.

The mattress squeaked when his long legs scissored off the bed, and he stood in front of her. She jumped and stared wide-eyed up into his face.

"Let me explain it this way," he said in a near whisper. "If you don't obey me, I'll be sure the next time you see your brother he'll be over thirty-five." He sounded more threatening than if he had hollered.

That pissed her off. She bit her bottom lip and nearly snarled. What would ranting solve?

Traffic noise peppered the room as they stared at each other.

She straightened her shoulders. "Listen, I understand where you're coming from. You're being dictated to from the grave by your old man. You hate it. It's the same for me. Mac never made my life easy either. Let's come to an agreement."

"I'm listening." His voice was deep and rough with restraint.

"You have me at a disadvantage. I have a feeling you can ignore Mac's will and still come out on top. For me, I'll get nothing from no one, and I can't even be around my brother unless I marry you." He growled with frustration at her repeating what he already knew. "So what I offer is, I'll marry you, take control of my people, and look after my brother. That way you won't have to change your lifestyle. You keep the funds from Mac's will for being Damien's guardian, and I'll work with you. Treat me as an equal in business, and in the bedroom, you'll be in control." She paused for emphasis. "Fully." If he agreed, could he tell she would get everything she ever wanted, including him, naked, in her bedroom? She wanted it so badly she could taste…no, feel it. Her whole body tingled and heated with a full-blown, lust-filled ache for him.

To prove her willingness, she crossed her arms, grabbed the ends of her T-shirt and slowly lifted it. She told herself she could convince Jake this would be the best option, but deep inside, she knew if he said no, she would find a way to persuade him. She wanted his full attention. His hands on her. She was old enough to know not everyone was wired the same way, didn't get pleasure from the same actions. Some women wanted flowers and to be wooed. Not her. She wanted what he obviously wanted, too.

From the moment she'd seen Jake at the cemetery, she knew he'd grown not only into the broad shoulders he possessed when he was sixteen, but into the authority he inherited. Power was a turn on and when it was combined with good looks and smarts, it was a bigger turn on.

Another reason she agreed to marry him was no one else in her life had the presence and guts to wield the power Jake did. And Jake's power could protect Damien no matter what she thought about his family. His power in the community and beyond could be a big help.

Who was she kidding? His power was no more than the icing on the cake.

She wanted to see what he'd learned since becoming an adult. Along with not having the time or opportunity, no one had interested her or captured her attention the years after he'd laid hands on her. Life had been difficult since leaving school, but she'd learned if she wanted something, she had to take every advantage and grab it while she could. She wanted Jake.

She dropped the shirt on the floor and stood straight, her bare nipples begging for his mouth.

"I'm waiting." His eyes flared hot, bringing the warmth in her cheeks up a notch.

She thumbed the snap below her bellybutton and pulled on the zipper tab. With a push, the jeans circled her ankles, and she stepped to the side, kicking the denim out of the way.

"What now?" Her challenging tone caused his brows to lift. What was she thinking? She scarcely registered his hand placing the gun on the dresser before he wrapped strong arms around her. Every sane thought left her brain. She wanted to taste him again.

Her mouth met his halfway. The touch sucked her into a whirlwind of emotions she'd never experienced. His kiss in the study was nothing compared to the one he gave her now. With his big hands he clasped her tight. Her nude body against the roughness of his clothes felt intoxicating. His tongue stroked hers until she gasped for breath. He caressed her shoulders to the small of her back. Her hands followed the dip of his spine beneath his shirt to the waist of his jeans. She loved touching him and being touched. Loved the hardness in the right places, rubbing and thrusting against her.

With a tight grip on her upper arms, he pushed her onto the bed and crawled in next to her. Resting on his elbow, he looked down, dancing his fingertips up and down her body, between her trembling breasts.

"Shh, everything's fine. Damn, your skin is so pale and soft. Like a woman's should be." He tilted his head, his gaze skimming her face before dropping to her chest. "When you were wearing that getup earlier, your breasts pushed up, begging for my touch, your skin appeared almost luminescent." He cupped one mound and squeezed, lightly pressing his fingers into her flesh and releasing his hold. "Look how your skin responds, changing to a light pink. I bet with the right pressure it turns to a beautiful rose color. Close to the same color as your lips." His other hand traveled up and his thumb rubbed across her lower lip. As if he couldn't resist, he cupped her breast again, but this time gently rolled the tip with his index finger. "I hate the thought of others seeing so much of you. You're not to wear that anymore. That is, except for me."

"Corset," she whispered. Her desire to have him touch more brought out a hunger she needed satisfied and only he could sate.

"What?" He pinched the nub. She exhaled and pushed out her chest, begging for more. Every stroke caused her to clench her thighs, and moisture betrayed her desire for his stinging touch.

"Corset. That's what the top is called." she said, her voice barely above a whisper.

"Yeah. Corset. Nothing showing so much of your breasts. Only for me and only when we're alone." He bent down and sucked on the tender nipple. Finally. She'd been wanting his mouth on them again. Nothing felt so good, except one other spot. Oh, she hoped he would go there again.

He bit at the tip.

She released a long drawn out hiss, loving how he set them on fire. When he moved away she pushed up on her elbows, confused.

His back to her, he sat on the edge of the bed.

"What—" She worried her lip.

"Over my knees," his voice brooked no argument.

She swallowed, needing to clear her throat, not dry from fear but wet in anticipation. She climbed off the bed and stood near enough to feel his body heat.

His knees spread enough to provide support for her upper body. Even in the dim room, she could see his cock pressed full and hard against his zipper. She wanted to reach out and run a finger down the bulge, instead she looked into his face. The cold, harsh expression didn't frighten her away, it drew her nearer. She wanted to caress the sharp angles of his cheeks and stubborn chin. She wanted to see him go up in flames for her.

"Face down. Rest your breasts against the outside of my leg and your stomach on top of the other." Each word firm and precise. How many women had he spanked since high school?

Nervousness shook her limbs, yet a need clawed at her to the point she was afraid she'd start crying and beg him to take her. First, she wanted to feel the sharp slap on her ass, bringing back the memories of so long ago. Would the feeling be the same or more? Or were the memories just that, misleading ones? The difference would be they understood more of what they had experienced then, and now knew how to satisfy the desire the act created.

With trembling knees, she stepped to his side and bent

over, following his instructions. She felt his cock jump next to her hip. Taking a deep breath, the air heavy in her lungs, she expected the first smack to follow immediately, but nothing happened.

What was he waiting for?

Chapter Eight

Jake stared down at the heart-shaped rear he'd thought about often over the years. He'd worried for a short period after the incident in high school that he might be a pervert and needed to abuse young girls to get himself off. By college, he quickly understood he enjoyed women, not girls, all consenting and enjoying the way he dominated their time together in bed. That was why he carefully picked the women he played with. Not every woman loved having their ass spanked before sex or took commands well from a lover when they were alone. Though he could be dictatorial outside the bedroom, he understood the need for the independent woman to hide that part of herself in public. And he liked that a lot. Knowing that the woman lived her life self-confidently each day, would later that evening be screaming in pleasure after she presented her ass to him, begging on her knees for his marks, for his cock, and willing to do whatever he commanded.

He smoothed his hand over the soft globes and squeezed one and then the other.

"You do understand why I feel it's necessary to punish

you?" He didn't wait for her response. "I accept your offer of being a united front for everyone. But leaving without my permission and stealing my car, throwing knives and letter openers at me, I won't put up with insubordination from a wife."

Her body jerked in surprise when he said wife. She understood. He'd already thought of her as his wife, his property, his to command. Her present obedience assured him she wanted what he offered. While he tracked her down, he'd come to the realization he'd been waiting for her all these years. Every woman he'd fucked and played with had been a sorry substitute for her. He couldn't imagine anyone else in her place. Maybe it was partly from her being his first, the one who showed him his darkest desires. It had to be the reason he decided to meet the will's requirement. At the time he'd flipped her on her back after chasing her down and looked into her eyes, he knew something special had happened. He'd never been so turned on. Then again, from what he'd been told and seen, no other woman he ever bedded before would be as dangerous as her. That idea hardened his cock until he ached.

"Ten smacks. Each time you move, I'll add another. Do you understand?"

"Yes, sir."

A buzz charged through him. He liked hearing her acknowledge his dominance over her. Fuck, she turned him on faster with those two words than any woman had before.

He inhaled deeply and then his open palm came down with a slap on a cheek followed quickly by another to the other one. The fleshly mounds jiggled. The solid pink shape of his hand rose to the surface. Fuck, it fired his blood. The mark said *MINE*.

She squirmed.

"Be still. Now it will be eleven."

He braced her with an arm across the back of her knees while he spanked her using loud, firm strokes. As he continued the rhythm, he noticed his fingers digging into her thigh. He eased up. Though he delighted in marking her, he wanted her concentrating on her sensitive behind, a reminder of her punishment and who did it.

Not wanting to rush, he paced the slaps. Only the right amount of pressure with each hit guaranteed she experienced the sharp pleasure he craved to give her. The sound added to the experience.

His cock throbbed.

She wiggled again.

"That's another one. Do not move."

Her well-toned body showed how she could conceivably break his hold and move away. That she hadn't tried, proved to him she wanted it. As he resumed the punishment, her moaning became louder. She lifted her ass to meet his hand. Fuck, yes. She loved receiving them as much as he relished seeing his prints on each cheek. He loved her obedience and how she felt beneath his hands.

In subtle movements, her hip rubbed against his aching cock. He stopped and her movements ceased. He needed to regain control though he couldn't resist touching her. The fleshier part of her ass was red and hot to the touch. The heat beneath his palm felt so good. He leaned down and kissed one crimson cheek. She gasped and shivered. Wanting assurance she desired it, too, he slipped a hand between her legs. Yeah. That was what he'd thought. He allowed a satisfied grin to spread over his face when his fingers met wetness. His balls tightened even more, he was seconds from exploding.

Unable to resist, he rubbed her clit. She cried out and

arched her back. Then he thrust two fingers deeply into her. Damn, she was tight. She returned each thrust with her own. When he returned to that hard little knot, she fell apart, crying and gasping for air.

His hand moved to her ass and lightly stroked her warmed skin, giving her time to recover. He closed his eyes for a few seconds, taking deep even breaths to regain control of his dick. Then he continued to count the slaps to her butt until he came to the last one.

"Are you through, sir?" Her words airy as she tried to catch her breath.

"Yes. Stay still." He needed to get his dick under control. His length pressed against his zipper to the point it would leave an impression.

Her body shifted. Suddenly, his pants loosened and her warm fingers wrapped around him.

"Angel," he warned.

Her hand stroked his length.

He straightened his back, and his head fell back, gritting his teeth to stop the howl of pleasure. In a smooth move, she slipped off his lap. Her hot mouth sank down over the tip, slowly taking every inch until he hit the back of her throat. She felt so damn good. Where had she learned that? Fuck, he didn't want to know.

Her tongue swirled the head and glided to the root. He gripped her hair and rammed his cock down her throat. She hummed as if she was tasting the best meal of her life. He groaned low and long.

Angel savored Jake's moans, assured she was doing it right.

She started to back off, but he held her still, his hand twisted in her hair.

"Uh-huh. Stay there. Breathe through your nose." His gruff voice betrayed how much it cost him to talk. "Now suck on me as if you want to swallow me whole. Oh, yes. That's it. I needed that. Suck harder. Rub your tongue around the rim. Yeah, that's the way." He rhythmically pounded in and out of her mouth, down her throat. Then his hiss of pleasure followed by a release. He held her head, giving her no recourse but to take everything he offered.

She gagged but managed to swallow. His control thrilled and aroused her even more.

All the books and porn movies she'd absorbed over the last few years helped with the pretense of her being experienced. Since her granddaddy rejected her every request to have a normal dating life, she'd found erotica to be a good and safe outlet for her fantasies. She smiled. Being level-headed enough, she was aware that real life never imitated fiction, but damn, if she hadn't come close with Jake in her mouth.

She needed Jake to want her as much as she wanted him. Every time his hand landed on her tender butt, she'd nearly climaxed but something had been missing, something she needed to push her over the edge. When his hand rubbed over her clit, she'd lost it. So much better than anything she'd every done for herself.

Really, what the hell was a virgin truly to know? That was, a semi-virgin.

With all the rumors flying around about her after the incident in high school, everyone believed she'd done it with Jake and his brothers along with half of the football team. If she'd been from one of the nice families of Marystown, not a soul would dare say such trash about her.

Then again, here she knelt between his legs, with his

softening cock in her mouth as she licked the head, and loving the hell out of it.

What would he say if he knew the truth about her? A trained collector who had never been loved by a man, literally and figuratively.

Mac thought it all a big joke. Who would've guessed that little Angel Tally knew at least twenty ways to incapacitate a man? For that matter, she theoretically knew as many ways to bring a man to his knees sexually. She'd been preparing for both nearly half of her life.

With his thumb and forefinger, he clasped her jaw. "Be careful and open wide," he warned. "I don't need those sharp little teeth scraping me." He pulled out of her mouth.

She blinked up at him. Their eyes met. She'd dreamed for years about doing that to Jake, to seeing his lost of control as he orgasmed. Little did he know she'd practiced on a dildo until she controlled her gag reflex as much as she could without the real experience. Her body buzzed with need for his body to blanket hers. She craved to rub against him like a cat, and then swallow his cock all over again. As she inhaled, preparing to ask for more, someone knocked on the door.

Disappointment and unease sliced through her as she cut her eyes over toward the door. He'd locked and chained it. Using a fistful of hair, he pulled her to eye level, regaining her attention. Goosebumps popped along her arms. His firm hold didn't hurt; in fact, his aggression rekindled her desire for more of what he could offer. Only Jake Whitfield had what it would take to tame her lust.

"Who were you expecting? Were you meeting someone?" Anger thinned his lips.

The unexpected accusation was the same as dousing her with reality.

An answering fury chilled her tone. "No one."

Her narrowing eyes shot him a look that said he would need to sleep with one eye open for the next few days. She understood his distrust, but he needed to know she had her limits. He could spank her and be rough during sex. What he did was with her permission, but he needed to give her the benefit of doubt when it came to all else. He'd better tread lightly. She wasn't a rug for him to scuff his boots on just because she would love to sit at his feet.

His eyes searched hers. "Okay. I believe you." He leaned in close and kissed her forehead. "Later, you and I will talk about our little arrangement. I like how you're not cowed by me, but you'll know who the master is in this relationship, and it isn't you, darling."

Before she opened her mouth to protest, the person on the other side banged a fist several times on the thin door.

Ignoring the pounding, he carefully reached out, maybe expecting her to jerk away, and caressed her cheek. Unable to resist, she leaned into his touch. What could she say, she liked his attention.

"Yo, boss? You've got a visitor." She recognized the voice of the other guard during her time at the Whitfield house. If she remembered correctly, his name was Matt.

"Who is it?" Jake said to the guard while looking hard into her eyes as if he wanted to say something but wasn't sure how. He pulled back on her hair until she arched her neck. She didn't fight him. Instead her breathing sped up with excitement. His hand slid down her neck and over a breast and continued around swand down until he squeezed a warm buttock. "You respond beautifully to my touch, so responsive, so needy," he said softly.

Her body fired up again as a prickling sensation teased her tender butt-cheeks. She squirmed for more. He'd been relentless but she savored it. Nothing had been too much to handle.

"Hey, boss, it's—"

"Alex Carleton." A woman's voice interrupted the guard.

Angel didn't recognize the name or the voice, but she felt Jake stiffen and not in the good way.

"Fuck," Jake said under his breath as his gaze darted to the ceiling in frustration.

When he turned his attention back to her, he hesitated for a second and then kissed her. His mouth proved he had much more to show her. Practicing by kissing on a pillow didn't improve her technique. She loved how his tongue licked and caressed hers.

It was as if he wanted her to understand she belonged to him, and nothing that happened in the next few minutes would change that.

She had no idea why, but she felt certain the woman on the other side of the door was partly the reason. For the moment, she'd pick her battles. Besides, she wanted to know what Jake was up to.

Jake released Angel and stepped back, wiping away the taste of her mouth and his pleasure with the back of his hand.

"Get your clothes and go into the bathroom to get dressed. When you come back out, keep your lips zipped," he ordered.

He grinned in response to her eat-shit look as she scooped up her clothes. He needed to temper his tone. Maybe he was teachable, especially as they were about to be married. But he probably thought he didn't need to change a thing? She obviously was into what he offered. His grin became wider. Of course, his attitude had nothing to do with how she gave him the best blow job in his life after being punished.

He chuckled and watched her reddish-pink ass shift back and forth as she stomped to the bathroom, and slammed the door closed. What passion. He'd bet good money, with a little training, he could redirect those little fits to more productive activities. What he'd give to have a little more time with her that evening.

For the first time in a long while, his body felt relaxed, yet energized. Just thinking about her plump lips wrapped around his dick brought a rush of hot blood back into that region, and he'd learned years ago a hard-on interfered with business. So he shook his head in an effort to clear it and return to the problem at hand.

"Jake!" From the sound of the screeching, Alex's patience had come to an end.

He zipped and snapped his jeans, realigning his dick to one side, away from the zipper. With a chuckle, he looked at his shirt. Somehow Angel had unbuttoned it. Uncaring, he straightened his shoulders and opened the door.

"Aren't you full of surprises, Special Agent *Alex* Carleton?" For the last several months, he'd been corresponding with the special agent in Washington, D.C., via email after an agent from their Birmingham division hooked him up, but he'd never guessed Alex was female. Shame on his assumption.

"Hello, Jake." She knocked his shoulder to the side with hers as she walked into the motel room.

Damn. She almost looked at him eye to eye. Plus she was a looker. Blonde hair pulled back into a clasp at the back of her neck. Nice rack. Navy blue jacket and pants with a white shirt along with plain, black manly shoes finished her look. When his gaze met hers, the coldness in her blue-green eyes chilled him to the bone. This was a woman who hated men. If she didn't like playing with bat and balls that was her business, he couldn't care less as the badge made her sexless in his eyes anyway. But he hated being played for a fool, and he had no doubt it had been done purposely. Sure, finding out about her gender shouldn't make a difference, but it did. If she misled him on something so basic, what else was she holding back?

Then there was Angel. At first, he was unsure how to tell her about his future plans without her freaking out. The idea came to him while he'd tracked her down. He would continue to use her brother as an angle, no matter her reaction to the news. She wanted her brother to stay on the straight and narrow path, and Jake wanted to get out of the crime aspect of his businesses. Hard to believe a Whitfield wanted to go straight, but he did. With the legal businesses Whitfield Industries owned and the expansions he planned, they could live well on the proceeds and never worry about going to jail.

So what if Angel found out his secret sooner than he'd planned. He gambled on her wanting the same outcome. Then their families could become upstanding, honest people.

Only thing, going strictly legal wasn't as simple as it sounded. Too many people craved the easy money and power, and depended on the dirtier family businesses to make a living. And with the void of the Whitfields moving out of the less legitimate businesses, another predator waited in the wings to take over.

"What happened to us meeting in a couple hours down the road?" His gaze tracked the special agent's movement in the room as he casually walked over to the nightstand and pocketed his gun.

Distrust was a two-way street. As every law enforcement agency that had ever crossed his path relished bringing the Whitfield brothers for every minor traffic violation or suspected crime, he expected the special agent to lie, cheat, and plant evidence whenever possible.

"You're not going to comment on me being female?" She darted a look his way as she continued to eye the bedspread pushed to the floor and mussed sheets.

"I noticed." He hated playing games, but he knew how to participate when needed.

She lifted the sheet, bringing it to her nose to sniff.

What was she? A fucking bloodhound bitch?

With Angel leaving and stealing his car, he had already changed his appointment with the FBI special agent. No matter how many times he told her they could meet on his return, she refused to wait. So he'd agreed to later in the evening, but there she stood, intruding on his personal business.

With a shake of her head, she threw it back on the bed and then glanced at the bathroom door as she made her return trek with one finger running across the dresser. He detested how nonchalant she acted and how she took it on herself to change their meeting time and place. They were to meet at one of the large casinos in Shreveport, and he'd never said anything about the motel.

"Where's your girlfriend? Hiding in the bathroom?" The special agent leaned a shoulder to the wall near the door and crossed her arms. Her jacket opened, giving Jake a glimpse of the expected holstered gun at her side.

At that moment, Angel walked into the room. She once again wore her black leather pants and red corset sans the coat that remained over the chair. Damn, her legs went on forever with those boots buckled at her knees, but her breasts drew his gaze to their soft depths. How in the hell had he ever mistaken her for a man?

With the dark goop around her eyes, white makeup, and black-rimmed red lipstick back in place, he expected fangs to show when she opened her mouth. They were going to talk about the makeup. After seeing her without it, he hated that she'd felt a need to slather it on again. Maybe it was her way of hiding. He didn't have the time to analyze her particularities.

"I'm right here." The corner of Angel's mouth turned up in a sneer. She looked as if she wanted to jump the woman and beat the shit out of her.

"Special Agent Alex Carleton." The woman held out her hand.

"I know what you are," Angel said with no emotion, refusing the hand without offering her name.

Jake almost laughed at the expression on the agent's face. Had she expected the sisterhood to unite against him? Even without asking, he knew Angel also suspected any overtures from law enforcement. She'd been brought up in the same criminal world.

That was when it hit him why he found her so fascinating—besides the sexual quirk they shared—and he was so willing to go along with the will. He'd never met a woman who fully understood the world he lived in and why he hated it. For certain, she hated it as much as he did. If he hadn't remembered her earlier comments about what she wanted for her brother, his gut instinct told him that. And he always trusted his gut. Despite going legal, her distrust of the government went as deep as his.

"Well, then." The special agent's hand dropped to her

side as she turned to Jake. "You said during this face-to-face meeting you'd start providing contact information on those who brought you the untaxed liquor and work your way down the list."

Jake caught Angel's uplifted eyebrow as she looked his way. He risked a lot by letting her hear the conversation. What if he was wrong, and she'd been testing him with her comments about her brother and how she felt about the criminal life? Killing him would be easy, all she would have to do is tell the wrong person about his meeting and what he planned.

"I will. But you've already proven you cannot be trusted, and maybe I need a show of faith." He spoke in a deadly serious voice. The woman needed to learn she couldn't take his cooperation for granted.

Alex's face flushed and anger sparked for a moment in her eyes until she regained control by placing her hands on her hips and hanging her head.

Jake waited for her response.

"What can I do to show you I'm on the up-and-up with you?" Her words, sharp and filled with irritation, pleased him to no end. He'd made his point. She had to rein in her ambition. Otherwise, she wouldn't lead this march to the good side.

"I want a copy of all the evidence the locals have gathered on the old man's death including what's in the autopsy." He sensed, more than saw, Angel shift where she stood near the nightstand. Satisfaction spread across his body. She had probably hoped he'd left the gun there. With his hand in his pocket, he squeezed the gun's grip, being sure his finger stayed off the trigger. When he looked at her, she pleaded with her eyes, and it struck him hard. No one had questioned her grandfather's death. "And the same for Mac's."

"The local boys might kick up a fuss." When he turned his gaze to her, Alex gave in. "All right. I'll get it to you within seventy-two hours."

"Forty-eight or the deal is off. I'm sure the ATF would love to hear from me." Every government agency loved to claim they smoothly collaborated with other agencies, but Jake knew better. It was human nature to want to lay claim to the kill.

"Fuck you." The woman stepped toward Jake with murder in her eyes.

In the split second it took to pull his gun to check the agent's movement, Angel lunged in front of him.

"Stay back," she said in a low growl to the special agent. A wicked looking switchblade glinted in the dimly lit room. Where had Angel stashed that one? Did he need to search every piece of clothing she owned? And every orifice? For the future protection of vital appendages, he might just need to do that.

"Darlin', you go ahead and handle this. Just don't hurt her too bad." He chuckled as he returned the gun to his pocket and picked up his cigarettes. With long experience, he shook the pack and pulled one out. Lifting a lighter to the cigarette tip as it hung from his mouth, he inhaled. The nicotine hit his bloodstream while he watched the women eye each other with distaste.

They were like night and day: one so upright she surely squeaked when she walked too fast; then there was Angel, who was so different from anyone he'd ever met and different from the girl he'd known in high school. He had a feeling he'd only begun to see the many layers that made up Angel Tally.

"Fine. Forty-eight hours then. At that time, we'll talk, and without your feral girlfriend. I never would've guessed you to be the type to get into that goth shit." She looked up and down at Angel with disgust on her face. Then she spit out, "Kinky bitch."

"Yes, I am, and proud of it." The evil grin Angel gave the woman tugged at his cock.

The special agent stepped back when Angel growled again beneath her breath. Jake had to hold back his laughter. No one could say his soon-to-be wife didn't have guts and a wicked sense of humor.

"You might want to remind her I'm a federal officer and can throw her ass into jail for a long time." Resentment filled Alex's tone.

"We're heading back to Marystown in the morning." Jake stretched out on the bed and took another draw. As he blew out the smoke, he added, "When you place the papers in my hand, we'll meet up again, but on my turf."

The special agent stiffly nodded before backing toward the door, keeping her attention on Angel's shiny knife.

Angel waited until the door closed behind the female agent before she relaxed her shoulders and exhaled. There was something about the woman that gave her the creeps. As her brother would say, "The bitch be crazy."

"Hand me your knife." The deep voice came from behind her.

Deadly. That was how he sounded. The laid-back attitude gone and the stern man from earlier had returned. A shiver of need raced down her back.

She turned and looked at his hand, palm up. The calluses and the small scars were expected from how hard

Whitfield had worked his sons, but the crooked middle finger...looked painful. From the swollen knuckle near the tip, his finger slanted to one side. It appeared to have been broken and not set.

With a well-practiced, one-handed move, she swiveled the lock, closed her Italian switchblade, and grabbed his wrist as she placed it in his hand. Not sure why she did it, she caressed his maltreated digit before she let go.

Seconds passed as neither said a word.

"How did you break it?" She finally ended the silence.

"Time to get a few hours of rest before we head back to Alabama." He acted as if he hadn't heard her question, but she knew better. She let it go. They all had secrets.

Easing onto the edge of the opposite bed, head bowed, she gripped the covers. "You swear my brother's okay?" She looked up into his face.

"Yeah. Tick's taking him straight to the house. He'll be fine." Compassion softened his features. "Get in bed."

"Okay." Why did she take his word for the truth? People had lied to her over and over, one of the many drawbacks of her job as a collector. But deep inside, she felt she could trust him.

She leaned down and unbuckled her boots, dropping them next to the bed before slipping beneath the sheets with her makeup and clothes on. Stripping once for him earlier had been enough, even though heat swirled over her sensitive areas as she remembered his hand slapping her buttocks, touching her in ways that had nothing to do with punishment. She'd never felt so alive.

For that matter, her life had changed from the moment she lifted the rifle and shot at the sniper during Jake's father's funeral.

The hiss of his cigarette being dropped into the soda can warned her before he turned off the lights.

"Scoot over."

Angel jumped as much from his voice being so near her ear as from the touch of his warm hand on her arm.

"There's an extra bed in here. Sleep there." Mixed emotions shook her. She wanted him to go away and leave her alone, but at the same time, she wanted his arms around her, feeling his heat seep into her lonely, chilled body.

As if he read her mind, he slid beneath the covers and spooned her body, his arms crossing over her breasts and pulling her against him.

Oh my, his hard body felt so good. When had she felt so safe? Like never?

His hips undulated against her sensitized rear. The hardness brought an unexpected groan from her lips. He felt so good. She pushed back and rolled her hips as his hands cupped her breasts and squeezed.

"Shh, Angel. Tomorrow we'll head back home and then I'll arrange for you to see a doctor. Once we get you set up with birth control and cleared, we'll marry. Then you and I are not going to leave my bed for a week."

"Birth control and cleared?" Who in the world did he think he was? She tried to sit up but his arms held her against him. "I'm already on birth control, and I'm clean." Mac had insisted. He didn't want to take the chance of his investment becoming messed up by pregnancy from a rape. Yeah. That was the type of grandfather she had.

"I had a checkup recently, and I'm all good," he said. When she remained stiff in his arms, he added, "Listen, I'm a stubborn, bossy asshole. Living with the old man taught me there's no room for softness or uncertainty in our world. Until I get my brothers on my side, we'll have to be careful in every aspect of our lives." He nuzzled her neck and inhaled. She felt his hand slide down her hair. Her body turned to mush. "But I'll protect you and your brother."

Her chest tightened as she turned her head and stared into his eyes, checking to see if he was being truthful or playing a game. For a Whitfield to say that to a Tally, well, it was unheard of.

Chapter Nine

Angel rarely felt comfortable with someone else driving, but Jake was different. Maybe it had something to do with the way he carried himself or the way he held her last night. This morning, he pretended as if nothing had happened between them. Instead, after they freshened up, he'd ordered her into the car, not giving her an option to stay or drive or walk. She wanted to protest his bossiness but his deep voice sent goosebumps along her arms, and her nipples perked up, begging for attention.

What caused her to fold like a house of cards where Jake was concerned? This wasn't the first time she'd been around a man who knew how to move, who felt secure in his own skin. Many of the men Mac had associated with were former military and took great care of their bodies. So if it wasn't his looks, and she really didn't want to think what his touch did to her. Maybe he controlled her by playing up to her greatest weakness: family obligation. He promised to protect her brother, but Jake had taken it one step further when he included her. No one had ever promised her that.

Not even Mac.

She wanted to push back the memories, but with the events of the last several hours, and with her guard down as she dozed in the soft leather seat of the Corvette, they came back with the force of a tornado.

Her transformation had begun the same afternoon after the incident in high school with Jake. When her mom picked her up, she'd cautioned Angel her granddaddy had demanded she be brought directly to his house. She'd also warned whatever punishment he doled out, she deserved it for being a slut. No one appeared to doubt Angel was guilty of lubricious behavior, and by her mom's relieved expression, she couldn't wait to leave her immoral daughter in someone else's hands.

The stupid screen door squeaked as usual when she let herself in the small foyer and then the large living room. Her granddaddy stood by the fireplace, staring into the empty hearth, his back straight and hands clasped behind him. He'd always been lean and stood military stiff. She'd heard he'd served with the Marines, in some type of special unit. He never talked about it, always turning the conversation away from his past. She'd often wondered if he missed the life. He treated everyone around him as if they were lowly privates by barking orders and expecting immediate obedience.

"Sally, what do you have to say about you and that Whitfield boy?"

"He had no right to touch me there."

Her fingers clutched at her school uniform skirt. She was afraid he'd order her to lift it to observe the damage. Her tender buttocks still tingled whenever she sat. She certainly didn't want anyone looking down there again.

The thought of having Jake looking again flashed

through her mind, bringing a flush to her face as warmth brushed her skin.

He cut his eyes over to her. "Did he hurt you?"

If she said yes, would one less Whitfield be in the world soon after? That would ensure the escalation of the long-time feud between the Whitfields and Tallys. No matter how much her ego had been bruised along with her rear end, she wanted to avoid having Jake's death on her hands.

"No more than my pride." Her face heated further with embarrassment. Jake had massacred her vanity and any thought of a mutual interest. Since the age of ten, she'd had a crush on him. She'd imagined they were star-crossed lovers similar to Romeo and Juliet. Only she preferred it without the dying at the end part. But now she no longer had to worry about such an ending, at least for her, for she preferred kissing a possum to ever touching Jake Whitfield.

Her granddaddy nodded, his intense gaze not leaving hers.

"Does school suit you?" he asked.

"It's okay, I guess." Forehead wrinkled, she hunched her shoulders. She actually hated it. The cliques and bullies made her life miserable. Her disability caused her more embarrassment than all of the taunts and insults from snobs and jocks combined.

After being left behind in one grade in elementary school, it took a kind teacher to discover she wasn't lazy or stupid but dyslexic. Her parents had scoffed at the notion that their child had a disability and refused to spend the money on a tutor. Thankfully, with help from a big-hearted teacher, who worked with her on her own time, Sally was promoted to the next grade level and managed to stay only one year behind over the following few years, but barely.

"That settles it. Starting tomorrow you'll begin your

training. My weak, good-for-nothing son sits his ass in prison for drugs again, and your mom's due to give birth to my grandson any day now. I can't have you turning up pregnant. Your family needs someone making a living." He stared at her from beneath his bushy eyebrows. "I'm no longer putting up with bloodsuckers who don't pull their own weight. I need a collector. It will be a hoot to turn those bastards on their ears when a female walks into their establishments to kick their asses for not paying."

She hadn't completely understood what he said until the next morning when she showed up after finishing her chores. He began her self-defense lessons. Yet it was more than defense. He showed her how to handle shotguns, rifles, pistols, and knives. Everything he'd learned in the Marines and elsewhere, he drilled into her over the next five years.

It was a lonely time. It was the time Granddaddy became Mac. He kept her busy whenever she wasn't at home cleaning and babysitting her newborn brother. In some ways she'd missed school, wondering what the other kids were learning. Of course, she didn't miss the bullies, though she didn't worry about seeing them elsewhere. She could easily teach them a lesson if they dared pick on her and her brother. Of course, within months of leaving school, the rumor about Jake raping her and then later about her little brother actually being their child spread like the flu throughout school and the small town. She knew if she denied the lies, they would only become bigger—no one ever believed a Tally—and for whatever reason the Whitfields never refuted them.

"Angel?"

Jake's voice brought her back to the present. No matter what had happened in the past, she'd made her bed and must lie in it. Only thing, she shared it with a big-ass-scary-but-good-looking Whitfield.

"Yeah?"

"When we return to Marystown, I'll set up an appointment with Judge Yancy. He can marry us this weekend." He squinted in the early morning light. "I'm sure you understand when we get back, not one word about Carleton better pass your lips. Got me?"

She looked at him. "I might not be the brightest bulb in the pack, but I get it. You need to keep your brothers totally clueless about your plans. I understand and don't care. Just as long you're telling the truth about going legal, I'm on board. That's what I want for Damien." She looked forward to telling Damien they would finally have a future, a real future away from generations of crime, but she was afraid it would sound too corny. Instead she added, "I'd marry the devil himself if he could make it happen."

"Damn, that's a step up from world's biggest asshole to the devil. I'm honored."

"You know what I mean." She fought a grin and looked away. Maybe he did.

The whining sound of tires on the interstate filled the car. She watched the scenery, trying to keep her mind off how her life would be with him, married to a man who didn't love her. But then again, was she really lovable? It had been years since she acted like regular girls, wanting to play with dolls or dress up. Proms and dates were events she watched on TV while babysitting her brother as she folded the never-ending pile of laundry. So much about a normal life she didn't understand.

A buzzing sound drew her attention.

Jake leaned to one side and pushed a button on the dash for a private conversation and then he lifted his phone.

"Speak."

Of course, answering the phone as a regular person would be beyond him.

"Uh-huh. You did right." His face darkened as he slammed his fist against the steering wheel, causing the car to swerve, but he quickly straightened it between the lines. "We'll be there in four hours. I know we're five hours out, but I'll make it in four." He pressed on the screen and tossed the phone into the cup holder.

"What happened?" Her heartbeat picked up speed with the Corvette.

"Damien."

She lost her breath.

"What about Damien?" she squeaked out when he remained quiet.

"He's okay."

She balled up her fist and hit him hard on the shoulder. "Start with that from now on. What did they tell you?"

The look he cast her way warned she better not strike him again or her ass would be staying red for a while.

"Someone shot at him," he finally added.

All the air left her lungs again.

His cruel lips stayed shut tight.

"What are you trying to do? Drive me insane?" She closed her eyes, spearing trembling fingers into her hair, and shook her head. "Save me from men who have terse down to an art," she murmured.

"There's not much to tell. Someone took a shot and busted out the window he stood next to. He's fine."

She let go of her head and glared at him. "So far you've told me nothing that would ensure me he's really okay. Where was he?" More questions scrabbled in her brain.

Was he bleeding? In the hospital? Oh, my God! She needed more information.

"At your place."

"What was he doing there?"

"Tick was with him."

Frustrated by his abbreviated information, she bit the side of her mouth and counted. She'd learned that trick after dealing with Mac for so many years. It kept her from opening her mouth, best way to practice patience. She hoped Jake would spit out the story. As the seconds passed, she eyed the phone just inches from her hand. The temptation to grab it and call Damien almost overrode her common sense, but she guessed they had confiscated his disposable phone, too.

Unable to hold back any longer, she decided pleading was called for.

"Would you please, *please* tell me the details? I'll imagine all kinds of crazy scenarios until you tell me the facts. Or do you get your jollies from doing this? Just because you couldn't care less what happens to your brothers, I love mine."

She heard his jaw pop. So what if he hated explaining anything to a Tally. How could she protect her brother if he refused to give her the facts?

"Tick said the boy wanted his own clothes and a few video games. They stopped at your home to let him run in for a minute after Tick checked inside." He tipped the turning signal, and they drove up an off-ramp. "While he stood outside, he heard a crack and broken glass falling. He thought your brother had done something until he heard squealing tires down the street. The white sedan turned the corner before Tick could get its tag. Your brother was unharmed, and he's at my house now. He's fine and so far has beaten Tick at Grand Theft Auto twice."

"Grand Theft Auto?" She'd ordered her brother to sell the game to the used video game store, but apparently he'd ignored her. What was she thinking? As far as she was concerned, knowing how close he'd come to dying, he could play the game all week long.

"Though I don't have to explain a damn thing to you, I do care about my brothers," he said, his attention on the road ahead. "In fact, I'd give my life to keep them safe." His voice sounded scratchy as if it pained him to voice his feelings.

"I'm sorry." She'd been unfair. "It's just that Damien isn't shot at every day. All of his life, I've been the only one to look after him. Patience is not one of my virtues."

"While we're talking about shooting, who were you shooting at in the cemetery?" he asked as he slowed the car, letting a big rig pull out from a gas station.

The question shocked her. She'd expected him to come around to the right conclusion, just not this soon. Yeah, he was smart, and she'd been certain he'd eventually put two and two together and realize her moral code wouldn't allow her to shoot at someone for a selfish reason. Now maybe they could work together and figure out who wanted them dead.

He glanced toward her and then returned his attention to the road. "If you're going to leave your mouth open, you might as well answer my question."

She swallowed. "You know, you really need to work on your manners."

"Would you *please* tell me the real reason you pulled out a rifle and placed a good dozen people's lives in danger?" His jaw popped again.

"You really know how to sweet talk a girl," she murmured and shook her head. She did like hearing him say please. She fought a grin. The subject wasn't one to let happiness bubble up and release.

"Angel?" The way he gritted his teeth saying her name, it sounded more of a warning.

Tempted to play the pulling-teeth scenario he'd pulled on her earlier, she decided against it as she firmly lived by the Golden Rule: *Do to others as you would have them do to you.* Hard to believe those trips to church Mac had insisted on had come in handy. He'd worried about his soul in his later years. By being plain-spoken, well, most times, she saved a lot of misery and misunderstanding. Those who dealt with her knew she was a straight shooter, figuratively and literally.

"Damien and I were at Granddaddy's gravesite, bringing some more flowers. I looked over at the crowd attending your father's services, when, I don't know, maybe a strong wind caused the tree limbs to sway a certain way or the guy moved, I really have no idea, but for a spilt second, the leaves parted and a flash of metal caught my peripheral vision. I continued to watch the spot and then I saw the sniper. He was closer to me, around two hundred yards from you. With the distance and the way the wind was blowing, I knew you wouldn't hear me, and there was no guarantee that you'd duck in time if you had. I've never known a Whitfield do what a Tally told them without an argument." She couldn't help the smirk.

Jake nodded, ignoring her dig. "He was in the trees?"

"Yes. Dressed in jungle camo with a mask."

"Damn." His jaw shifted a little more as he digested the info.

She guessed it was a lot to take in.

"If you're wondering, after I fired, the man dropped out of the tree and ran. I tried to follow, but some asshole t-boned Mac's van." She glanced at Jake, catching the brief smile on his face.

"It was necessary at the time. You know this means whoever killed the old man and your grandfather is now trying to kill me and your brother."

"That's what it appears like." What more could she say? In the last twenty-four hours, she'd realized that Jake and his brothers were her and Damien's only chance of living to a ripe old age. One worry constantly nagged at her. Was she letting her emotions blind her to the real Jake? Could she really trust him to help protect her brother?

Chapter Ten

Angel opened the car door after Jake pulled the Corvette to a gas pump and stepped out and pocketed his keys. She needed a break from his presence, if only for a couple of minutes. She needed to come to terms with what Jake had said about someone wanting to kill Damien.

"Fill the tank, and I'll pay inside while I get us some burgers," he said. People drove and walked in all directions at the huge truck stop, most appeared to go in and out the restaurant half of the building.

"I'll gas it up, but I don't want a burger. If they have salad, I'll take one with vinaigrette dressing on the side." With only a dry bagel that morning, her stomach had been protesting for the last few miles.

"You don't need to lose weight. I'll get you a burger and fries."

"I'm a vegan."

"A what?"

"I don't eat meat or any dairy products."

"No cheese?"

Why was it that was the first thing people asked? "No. No cheese."

He stared at her for a few seconds.

She raised her eyebrows.

"Shit. Okay." He shut the door behind him and stalked toward the restaurant.

Wow! She had to admit his easy acceptance surprised her.

Several minutes later, she'd twisted the cap closed on the tank and slipped back into the car. In no time, Jake exited the building with a couple of white bags.

"You didn't say what you wanted to drink, so I got you unsweet tea and some packages of sweetener."

Once again, he surprised her by not insisting he knew what was best, but instead handed her a sack with a plastic bowl filled with salad inside. Several small pink and yellow squares slid across the top of the clear lid along with a disposable fork and knife, and an unbuttered roll wrapped in wax paper nestled on the side.

After they hit the interstate, the sickening greasy scent of cooked beef filled the air. She rolled down her window a few inches before digging into the salad.

He tossed her a couple of napkins and then wiped his mouth in between bites of the largest hamburger he somehow held with one hand. The way he patted his lips and the corner of his mouth gave the scene a surreal feeling. How could Jake, after living with and growing up with a father who had a reputation of being the ultimate redneck, have such good manners? So strange and amazing.

"What?" He'd caught her staring. "Do I have mayo dripping off my chin?" He swiped with the napkin.

"No, no. I was wondering, from how you acted...that is, from what I've heard about your upbringing, I figured you would be...uh—" Before she could call him a heathen, he interrupted.

"Let's get something straight right now. Forget everything you heard about me, especially when I was a kid." Though he continued to eat, hamburger in one hand and the other with a napkin holding the steering wheel, he acted as if he cared little of what he'd revealed. She could tell her stuttering statement bothered him.

"I didn't mean anything by it." She had to admit that she'd barely stopped herself from saying she heard how Jake and his brothers had run wild, half naked, and coated with filth until old man Whitfield reined them in and put them to work.

He opened his mouth to respond when a loud bang rocked the car. She gasped and clutched the door armrest. The car swerved and vibrated as if it was about to fall apart. Jake turned the steering wheel, trying to regain control.

She squealed. The scenery swirled by as the car did a doughnut on the side of the interstate. Her salad scattered over her lap, around her feet, and over the console. Jake's hamburger fell apart as he squeezed it and the wheel.

They came to a stop with a jolt, heading in the wrong direction.

"What happened? Did the tire blow?" Her chest rose and fell as she tried to regain control of her panic.

"I guess you could say that. Someone shot at us," he said in a droll tone, his attention on the rearview mirror.

"What?" How many people were out there trying to kill them? It had been only thirty minutes ago when they received news about a bullet skating by Damien. Marystown was far away still. Unless the killers flew in a helicopter. No, that would be crazy.

"Hand me my gun," she demanded.

"Whose gun?" he asked, giving her a smug look.

Without a word, she cast an eat-dirt-and-die glare and then scooted down in the seat. She peeked over the door panel and looked around, trying to see who wanted them dead. Damn fiberglass car was no protection. Frustrated with Jake for keeping the gun, she could only claw the seat beneath her. She never felt more like a sitting duck.

A cloud of dust followed a brown truck flying backwards along the opposite side of the eastbound interstate. The same truck that had passed them seconds earlier, coming back for a second round. With a spray of rocks, it stopped and a flash of metal showed in the open window.

"Get down!" Jake pushed at her head.

The popping of bullets hitting the ground and the trunk foretold their ending. With amazing luck, a blue semi with a long, silver trailer drove by at a crawl. Probably the driver craning his neck to see what he believed was merely a wreck.

"Let's go! Stay on the shoulder." She pointed at the grass. "Keep the big rig between us and the shooter." Their only hope was to move alongside the truck until they could find an exit and hide.

He nodded and shifted the gearstick to reverse. Engine smoking and rear tire flopping, the car shook almost as hard as she did in fear. She wasn't sure if death was a possibility from being shot or Jake's driving.

They'd gone more than a mile, dodging road signs and mile markers when they came to an exit. Three gas stations with a handful of fast-food restaurants promised enough people to discourage the gunman. Witnesses came in handy, though Angel hated endangering anyone, but it was a gamble they had to take.

He shot up the on-ramp in reverse and cut the steering

wheel sharply. The thumping sound changed to metal on asphalt. The Corvette shot forward, pointing the correct way. She crossed her fingers, hoping it would work. The big rig had continued down the interstate, leaving them unprotected as Jake headed toward a little town off the exit. She scanned all of the lanes and overpass. No brown truck, but a creepy feeling warned her he'd be back.

"I don't see him," she said as she noticed Jake appeared a little pale. "Are you okay?"

"He didn't follow us. Not sure what's up, but we need to think of something fast before he backtracks."

He had ignored her question as he parked the car in front of a small garage he found. For the moment, they needed to fix the tire, repair whatever was smoking beneath the hood, and head back home to safety. Safety? She snorted. Home wasn't safe either, not after someone tried to kill her brother. Time would tell if Jake meant what he said about protecting her along with her brother. Her grandfather had always expected her to take care of everyone. The thought of someone looking after her would be a new experience.

"Grr! Give me my gun back. I freaking loathe being unarmed."

"Loathe?" He eyed her and then reached beneath the seat, handing her the Beretta. "As you know, it's my gun."

"Yeah, yeah. It's belongs to me now. Only fair since you still have mine." She checked the magazine in the Beretta. She wouldn't put it past him to unload the rounds. Nope. All the cartridges were there.

"Don't trust me," he stated.

She looked up. Did he sound a little bothered by what she said?

Before she could respond, he stepped out, slamming the

door behind him. Maybe she'd been around Mac for too many years. He rarely showed his feelings, and her dad only had one emotion: anger.

For what felt like forever, vehicles of every make and model zoomed in and out around her. She watched for the brown truck or anything suspicious but kept an eye on the yawning mouth of the garage door. An SUV sat on the raised rack and a man stood beneath it, hitting the undercarriage with a mallet. Then Jake and another man with grease-smeared jeans and T-shirt stepped into the sunlight. They shook hands, and the man stuck his hand into his front pocket.

Did he think they had time for the guy to repair the car before the shooter found them?

Jake walked to her side of the car and opened the door. "Let's go."

She grabbed her backpack and shoved the gun into the front zippered pocket, leaving it open and easily accessible.

"We don't have time to wait for him to fix it."

"I know. We've got a new ride." He led her around the building to an old pickup truck. "I've talked with Tick. He called in a rollback wrecker to pick up the Corvette and haul it back to Marystown."

For all its age, the red truck was in good shape and shined like a new penny.

"Will the guy keep his mouth shut if the shooter sees the Corvette and stops to ask questions?" She jumped into the cab. She raised her eyebrows. The interior smelled fresh. Not what she'd expected at all from the grease-smeared guy.

Jake balled the towel spread out over the driver seat and tossed it behind the seat.

"When I rented his truck, I threw in a healthy incentive to throw off our shooter."

That explained the cash the guy stuffed in his pocket.

"He's going to say we went the opposite way?"

"He'll keep it simple by saying we're in a black SUV. The shooter should realize we're headed back home."

She smiled. There were thousands of black SUVs. Though the red truck stood out like a pimple on the end of a teenager's nose, no one would imagine Jake would be caught dead in it. That sobered her. If they weren't careful, it was exactly what would happen.

As they headed back to the interstate, Angel hoped they would finally make it home. What were the chances of the shooter finding them a second time?

With that disturbing thought, she turned to him. "How did the shooter find us?"

"That's what bothers me, too. Only a handful of people knew where I was." His softly spoken words hung in the air. Someone he trusted had betrayed him.

The air conditioning struggled to keep up with the early June heat in the cab of the truck. Sweat beaded on her upper lip. She looked at Jake.

The view was more interesting than the passing one outside. From his golden skin to his sun-tipped hair, he gave off an outdoorsy vibe mixed with all-American boy gone bad man, a black hat wearing cowboy out of an old western. He even had the wrinkles at the corners of his crystal blue eyes. They interested her. Most men who possessed those little lines worked outside, caused by the sun and wind.

The Whitfield boys were known for all kinds of craziness and each were good-looking in their own way. Her mom used to say they had a ruthless, hungry look to them, the type to stay away from as they'd be nothing but trouble.

"Was it true that you and your brothers ran away from home at ten and lived for a month in the Cheaha Wilderness? With no adults, just you kids?" The story always sounded similar to a Huckleberry Finn adventure, and she often wished she'd been as brave.

"That's what the old man told everyone."

She fidgeted with her coat, ignoring the itch in her hand to touch him, to comfort him. The grimace crossing his face told how the story pained him. Instead she waited, hoping he indulged her this time.

"It all started innocent enough," he said while keeping his eyes on the road. "We wanted a snack. Only one problem, it was two in the morning. The cabinets in the kitchen are tall, even for some adults. Ethan dropped a bowl. Glass went everywhere." His tone started to change as his southern accent deepened, vowels stretched with each word, weaving a spell. Mac and his friends would do the same when they repeated a story from their past they'd told over and over again. "The housekeeper we had at the time harbored a fine distaste for kids, especially the male variety. She threw her clothes into her beaten leather bag and stomped out. When the old man came at us, we were sure we'd be seeing Saint Peter and those Golden Gates. Instead, he loaded us in the back of his extended cab truck and drove us down the interstate for what felt like hours. Once he turned off an exit in the middle of nowhere, he stayed on the little country road for a few miles more and then we found ourselves bouncing along a dirt trail that had to be no more than two trenches for the tires. It was mid-morning by the time he stopped. He dropped the tailgate and told us to get out. Seconds later, we were watching the rooster tail of his truck disappear in the distance. We were too stupid to be afraid. We pretended to be Tarzan."

A bitter grin crossed Jake's face. "Sen loved reading about Tarzan. Often, he snuck out the books, one by one, from the old man's library. So there we were, surrounded by tall trees, no adults, and each other to look after. We swung from the vines over creeks and built tree houses that tumbled down in a light wind. But standing in the middle of that forest, we thought it would be an adventure of a lifetime."

She rubbed her eyes and leaned back, her brain couldn't wrap around the thought. How could a grown person do that to his own kids? Just imagining Damien left alone miles from home at ten years old terrified her. "What did your mother say? Sen's mom was alive then, what did she do?"

He shrugged. "It was over a week before my mom noticed we were gone. She has a habit of not keeping up with time, and around those years, she often forgot to visit two to three weeks at a stretch. The old man gave her some cock-and-bull story of me being at a summer camp. It never crossed her mind, the old man barely bought us new clothes, no less pay for a camp." He glanced her way. "Sen's mom was too afraid to kick up a fuss. Being in the States illegally, she thought the old man would report her. I did hear later she tried to get the old man to tell her the truth."

"What about an Amber Alert?"

"The old man certainly wasn't going to report us missing or kidnapped. Mom believed whatever the old man told her. School was out for the summer. So the locals didn't worry about truancy. We starved the first few days until we realized there were fish in a stream we'd found. I happened to have a lighter on me for a fire, and Ethan had a safety pin and ball of string in his pocket. He claimed he had them because of the books he read about the apocalypse. He was such a morose kid. Sen found a great place to dig up some worms. I will say that first night we were certain bears would eat us or we'd be attacked by crazier old men than the one we lived with." He chuckled as he shook out a cigarette and cracked open the window before lighting it. After a long draw and blowing a stream of smoke out the window, he shook his head. "We had a run in with a skunk and the little asshole won. I'm certain they tracked us down by smell alone. None of us had bothered with baths or washing our clothes during those weeks. We probably looked like wooly-boogers."

While still horrified for Jake and his brothers, she couldn't help smiling at his description.

"Obviously you made it back home. How?"

"A couple hikers reported us to the forest ranger's office. Took two days to track us, and six of them to haul us back to the old man."

"What did your dad say?"

"Nothing really. He did warn us not to scare our new housekeeper." He flicked the cigarette butt out of the window. "That was when Jimmie Sue came to work for the old man."

"They didn't arrest him for neglect, abandonment, or anything?"

"Ha! You act as if you haven't lived in Sand County most of your life."

He was right. From what she'd heard from others, they lived differently from everyone else in the state. With all of the responsibilities she had along with dropping out of school, and not having a normal social life—thanks, Mac—she was a bit out of touch with even the simple things people took for granted.

She leaned her head back and stared at Jake. That month in the wilderness was only a small part of his childhood. She'd heard other rumors and just as bad. How anyone could be surprised he had been as wild as a buck was beyond her.

He was a handsome man, and she guessed he knew it and exploited it every chance. No one could call him pretty as he had a maturity to his face that spoke of hard times. Yet she would love to see those blue eyes soften as they had last night.

Closing her eyes, she bit her bottom lip to regulate her breathing. Just looking at him caused her to want to reach between her legs and relieve that ache. Thankfully, her white makeup hid her flushed face, but did little for the feeling washing over the rest of her body. Mercy, she craved his firm touch. Had she ever experienced such pleasure? His fingers delving into her hot, moist places had awakened desires she'd never known she had. Oh, sure, she'd satisfied the natural yearnings any normal woman endured, but nothing had prepared her for his forceful, mind-blowing domination. She often wondered if she had glossed over the truth about their encounter at school. She had wanted his attention so badly.

Truthfully, back then, she wanted anyone's attention, good or bad, but for a certain good-looking boy to grab her and touch her, there, even in punishment, and for her to enjoy it, showed how warped she'd been and still was in that way. To her, it felt thrilling and dangerous. And for her to want more? Her mind had to be bent.

Yet last night proved what she felt all those years ago had been real, and she wanted more. Only from Jake. The thought of someone else spanking her, touching her like Jake, didn't even appeal to her. She loved it when he made her lose control.

Guilt fed the blush as she remembered how Mac often

talked of reining in her baser needs and not to let them dictate her decisions. Angel closed her eyes to clear her mind of what Jake had done to her, and how he could fulfill so many of her fantasies.

Big mistake.

Instead of clearing it, a mental picture of what he looked like with his pants unzipped and open. The beautiful part of him. Firm, velvety, and hot. Oh, yes. He'd been hot and tasted so male. Not that she had anyone in real life to compare him with, but oh, yes, he was everything she ever dreamed of when he entered her mouth. She reveled in how he held her head and his hands shook. Yeah, she did that to him. Knowing how her hands and mouth made him tremble excited her even more.

"Hey, you okay over there?"

She jumped. Her eyes wide as she stared at him. "What?"

"You were moaning in your sleep."

Had she fallen asleep?

"Sorry. Bad dream." How long was she out? Her neck popped as she stretched one side and then the other.

"It wasn't that kind of moaning." His wicked grin warned her he'd heard more.

"You never did tell me how you broke your finger," she said, trying to get his mind off her licentious creaming.

He switched lanes and passed a long line of semis and RVs. The humming of the truck's engine shifted to a higher whine. Nothing in his expression said if the story was as painful as his finger appeared to be or if it was a stupid accident. Then why hadn't a doctor seen to it?

He obviously didn't intend to tell her.

She faced straight ahead, preparing to relax again and plan how to let Damien be a regular teenager while protecting him. No way would she leave the details up to the Whitfield boys.

"The old man broke it." He changed the station on the radio to classic rock.

A few seconds passed before it clicked in her brain that he'd finally responded to her prompt about the finger.

"I don't understand." She tilted her head. Surely he wasn't going to leave her hanging. What did he do? Slam it in a door?

"It was a week before Christmas. I was fourteen. At that age, I thought I knew everything and was a cocky little shit. The old man told me to help Jimmie Sue to take out the trash. It wouldn't have taken me but five minutes to do what he told me. But I thought *what I wanted to do* was too important. A group of us boys were going to the basketball court at a local church and dunk a few balls. I told him to fuck off and shot him a bird." He raised the finger. The tip leaned to one side. "I didn't even know the old man could move that fast. He picked me up and dropped me to the ground. I saw stars. I never knew until then the cartoons had it right. The stars, that is. But when you land on your head, you see everything including the truth of how you screwed up. The crack sounded as if it came from far away but the pain assured me it wasn't. He grabbed my finger and pulled it back between his thumb and forefinger. He snapped the tip like a twig. He said he'd break a joint each time I pointed one at him again."

She was surprised he told her so much. Another glance at the finger made her winced as she imagined the pain. The handful of times she'd been close to him when they were younger, she'd never noticed it, and he never favored it.

"Was it damaged so badly the doctor couldn't fix it?" She suspected the answer but hoped she was wrong.

"The old man refused to take me. I never told Jimmie Sue what he did. He would've denied it. I tried wrapping it, but it didn't heal right. Most the time it doesn't hurt, only when it's about to rain or if I jab it. The last couple days I've hit it a few times."

He passed a stream of cars and SUVs and then sighed. "It was a long time ago. Go back to sleep. If I hear you make any noise, I'll wake you."

"But—"

"Enough talk." He shook his head as he softened his tone. "Listen, we have plenty of time to get to know each other. Hell, I've got questions for you, but I need to keep an eye out for the shooter."

His bossiness didn't bother her. At some point during their impending time together, she'd need to make an issue of it, but for the moment she'd let it pass. Besides, most of the men in her world loved ordering people around, especially her. She'd learned to pick her battles. It made life a little easier and people tended to respect a person who controlled her temper. She had to admit the last few days, she didn't have anything to be proud of in that department. Maybe it had something to do with being so wound up around Jake. She wanted him in her bed.

Suddenly she ached all over. As if her body knew she could let go, not to be on guard twenty-four-seven as she had for the last several years. She closed her eyes and pulled her knees up in front of her. Turning her back to Jake, she leaned toward the passenger door with her cheek against the seat.

She thought about how his dad treated him. She and

Jake made a fine pair. Neither of them had lived an easy life.

For now, she needed him in her and Damien's life, and she would take advantage of everything he offered, including his body. She never looked a gift horse in the mouth. In his case, a stallion's mouth. She smiled at her pun.

Jake listened to the soft puffing sound Angel made as she slept on the opposite end of the truck's bench seat. Her horrified expression earlier, when he recounted his time in the wilderness, had been a surprise. Years and years had flown by since anyone had sympathized with the Whitfield boys.

He couldn't believe he'd told her that story. The brothers rarely talked even to each other about the things the old man did to them or made them do. Not that the old man was a pervert; instead he was more of what everyone knew him to be. An asshole.

With every word and deed, Angel fascinated him. When she stood between him and Alex, flashing her knife at the FBI agent, he knew she was something special. No one had ever done anything like that for him, except for his brothers, and certainly never his mother. The old man would've hated Angel. For any woman to stand up to him or refuse to use her sexuality to get her way, the old man would believe her to be unnatural.

Though few people realized it, he was determined not to be entirely like the old man. He was already on the road to being different. He was attracted to Angel. A lot. He knew of a way to show her how much.

Chapter Eleven

"Wake up, Angel."

Parked in front of Scene 69, a gentleman's club owned by the family, Jake waited for her eyes to open. Five miles outside of town, he'd received a call about a problem that had come up at the club, sending them on a detour. How would she react to the delay in returning to her brother?

He shook her shoulder. "Hey, wake up. I'm going in. So go with me or stay in the truck. Up to you."

Pale makeup smeared the truck's passenger window.

He had a love-hate relationship with the pasty stuff. He admitted he enjoyed how exotic she looked with her black and red lipstick and hair. Her personality even changed according to her wearing makeup or not. With it off, she was soft and feminine, a sultry kitten easily controlled. But as soon as she coated it on, she became all business and focused, even a little dangerous. Heat shot to his groin. Uncovering the many layers of Angel appealed to him in so many ways that it bothered him. He'd never been so drawn to a woman, especially like her.

She hummed and stretched and a part of him stretched, too. Hell, he had a meeting, and being hard in front of an employee wouldn't cut it.

"Where are we?" she asked as he stepped out of the truck.

Blinking, she looked around owlishly and twisted her back, loosening more stiff muscles.

"I've had a problem to come up and need to talk with someone first." He started to close the door.

"Give me your keys."

He stared at her. "Why?"

"I need to see my brother."

"I told you he's okay."

"Why should I believe you?"

"Are we back to that again? I told you he's fine. A few scratches and no more."

"What? You said he was unharmed." Her gaze fired darts in his direction.

"I said he was okay and he is. When some of the glass shattered, it cut his cheek and ear. Nothing to worry about."

"Nothing to worry...cut cheek and ear are not okay!" On her knees, she scrambled across the bench seat and reached for the keys in his hand.

He lifted his hand. "It stopped bleeding before Tick got him out to the car."

"I bet Tick didn't even take him to a doctor."

"Quinn looked at him."

"He's a freaking mortician. He's not qualified to give medical aid to anyone."

With Angel on her hands and knees, and spitting fire at him, thoughts of how he could help her control that temper almost pushed him back into the truck. Hell, her breasts appeared barely sitting inside that tight red lace and silk getup she wore.

"Listen, the longer I stand here and argue with you, the longer it will take for us to leave. So come with me or stay here without the keys, it's all up to you."

She shoved him to the side and jumped out of the truck. Her determined steps led away from the truck and the club.

"You're going the wrong way. The club is over here."

"Idiot! I'm walking to your house."

"It's almost ten miles away. We're on the opposite side of the town." His tone showed who he thought was the idiot.

"I know. I plan to hitchhike. A whole lot faster than waiting for you."

Jake gritted his teeth. Dammit, this was all he needed. He could sling her over his shoulder and force her to go into the club. No matter that it would make conversation a little hard with her kicking and screaming.

Mulling over his options, he decided the clubs were normally Ethan's territory to handle, and he could just get his ass out there and take care of it. He pulled out his cell phone and pressed Ethan's number.

"Hey, come over to Scene 69 and see what you can do for the manager."

"What the hell? Why didn't Karma call me, and what could be so important for her to bother you?" Ethan bit off each word. Jake knew his brother hated it when his own people didn't trust him to take care of problems.

"No, she didn't tell me anything, but that it was urgent, and she couldn't get a hold of you."

"I'm in the middle of something."

The murmuring Jake heard in the background said it was the female kind. Women appeared to be the bane of

Ethan's existence more so than Jake's, though at this point they could be tied.

"The club's your problem. I have one of my own to straighten out." He cut off the call and looked over to Angel.

Stand on the edge of the road, she stood with a hand on one thrust-out hip and her thumb pointing down the road, hoping for a ride. Wearing leather in the heat and with her outlandish hair and makeup, no normal driver would be brave enough to pick her up. And the person who was brave enough to do so would have only one thing on their mind. And hell no, he wouldn't let anyone touch her.

He cranked up the truck to ease it behind her. Just in time. A large, blue sedan had stopped, and the driver leaned over the front seat, talking to Angel with the passenger window rolled down. He probably hoped he found himself a good-time girl outside Scene 69.

Jake parked, jumped out of the truck to nudge her from the window. "Hi, Tom. How's Marcie doing?"

"Uh, fine, Jake." Tom Leaky had a reputation of liking underage girls. Not that anything illegal had come to light about his particular taste, but everyone watched their daughters around him.

"Tell her hi for me."

"I sure will." Tom's eyes jerked from Jake to Angel and then he shifted his car into drive and headed down the road with gravel spraying the asphalt.

"Asshole," Angel muttered, brushing off the dirt from her pants.

"And you were about to ride with him." Jake knew who she meant, but he couldn't help picking at her. "Get in the truck, and we'll go to the house."

She looked at him and then back at the road. "Maybe I'd rather take my chances with another stranger."

"Are you trying to push me into spanking you again so soon?" He admired how she straightened her shoulders and stared him down. The woman didn't act afraid of anything unless it involved her brother. But he did catch the flare of desire in her eyes when he said spanking. She liked how he could make her feel.

Hell, it was mutual.

Angel wanted to deny it. Not that she provoked him on purpose, but knowing if he became angry, the thought of him spanking her in punishment excited her. All he had to do was say the word and her nipples tightened and her clit throbbed with anticipation. What little self-respect she had left where he was concerned caused her to hesitate.

"Angel?"

"Fine." She stomped over to the passenger side of the truck and hopped in. He hooked a finger in the strap of her backpack before she could protest. She scooted over and watched him toss it in the bed of the truck. With a huff, she moved as far as she could from him. Sure, she acted like a little spoiled kid sitting against the door with her arms crossed over her chest, but she refused to let him know how much she wanted his touch. She needed to feel as if she had a little control over her situation. More importantly, she needed him to hurry up so she could check on her brother. Even if he let her use his cell phone, she wanted to see her brother in person, ensure he was all right. "You're wasting daylight."

After slipping into the driver's seat, he shut the door and gave her a heated glance filled with a warning. She figured she wouldn't like what he planned to say.

"Come over here." He motioned with two fingers.

"Don't argue with me. I'm taking you to your brother as you wanted. When we get there, you'll see for yourself he's okay, and then you and I are going to have a reckoning."

His no-nonsense tone didn't bother her. The Whitfield boys hardly took orders from the old man, no less a female. She was used to the attitude and often ignored it. Over the years, she'd worked hard to show Mac and his people that her gender had nothing to do with her success or failure at being the family collector.

Funny how the Whitfields and Tallys lived in the same small town—in neighborhoods on the opposite sides—but they rarely interacted with each other. She heard things. For one, how Jake and Ethan disappeared after graduation. She always thought they had gone away to college, but rumors said it had been for more nefarious means. The gossipmongers said they returned changed, still mean but quieter, more devious in the way they did the old man's business. No more wild parties with flashy women or drug-induced orgies. The night Dick Whitfield and Dewayne "Mac" Tally died, the boys were at another bar drinking but no women. They said they were laughing and playing cards, really enjoying themselves. Some even said they were cele-brating early, but after spending two days with him, she sensed there was more to the story. The only way she would find her answers was to stick around. As good of an excuse as any. It had nothing to do with how he interested her. How he made her feel. Oh, God, she was tired of making excuses for why she wanted to give in.

He frowned. Her silence appeared to bother him.

"Okay." They needed a reckoning on his public atti-tude, and they would talk about her terms. She slid next to him and pulled the belt across her lap to buckle.

For the next few miles, the thumping of the tires on the

rough road and the whistling of a loose window were the only sounds.

Why had he wanted her next to him? Was it a type of mind game? Be demanding at every turn and see how she reacted?

Over the years she'd learned to not fight the small battles. Energy wasted, better used for the important ones. Such as protecting her brother.

Anyway, she enjoyed being near Jake. The man oozed sex appeal. So it hadn't been a hardship, just the principle of it.

She jumped when he rested his hand over hers. Then he threaded their fingers together. She glanced over to his face. There were a couple of times in school she'd held a boy's hand, but it had been years ago. Holding a man's hand was a different experience. Rough with calluses, his large hand enclosed hers entirely. She felt the strength and appreciated how gentle he held hers.

A few more miles passed and then he moved their clasped hands to his thigh. Last night, she'd stretched her torso over those hard thighs, the taut muscles shifting and adjusting to her squirming as he spanked her.

She bit her bottom lip, hoping to drive her attention from where the back of her hand rested. This simple touching experience felt odd as if her body was outside herself. Unsure how to act, she stiffly sat beside him. Ironic, considering what they had done yesterday, and during their time together, she'd never second-guessed her actions.

Was this how other women felt with men? Was this something everyone took for granted? Time for her to quit analyzing it. She needed to enjoy the uncomplicated nuances to handholding.

• • •

Jake grinned. When he grabbed her hand, her eyes had flickered in surprise. Her look told him she suspected his actions. Instead of jerking away, though, she remained still, waiting to see what he planned to do next. He loved keeping her on her toes. He wanted to unzip those sexy leather pants and touch her tender moist heat. Chances were he could bring her to climax in thirty-seconds flat. Yesterday, she'd responded to his touch like a wildfire. Instant combustion. That excited him more than she could ever imagine.

"Why are we going the back way?" she asked.

He almost lied to her, but the narrowed glare he received said she expected it.

"I think we need to be careful. The fewer people who know we're coming in, the safer it'll be for us."

"I need my backpack."

"It's in the bed of the truck."

She twisted around and looked. "Did you take the gun out?"

"Yes."

"I want my gun back."

"Your gun?" Teasing her had become his favorite pastime.

"For goodness sakes! Not that again. Okay. Your other gun. You're armed. It's only right that I be, too."

The woman was observant. He'd slipped both guns beneath the driver's seat, hoping she hadn't noticed. And damn it, he understood her need to be armed, but it was time for her to become accustomed to being protected.

"No."

"Then give me my knife back."

"No." He had it in his pants' pocket.

She moved her hand and before she could unbuckle the

seatbelt, he slammed on the brakes and pulled the truck to the side of the road.

"What the hell do you think you're doing?" He clutched her arm.

"I've been armed for the last ten years of my life, and I demand you give me a weapon. Either the gun or my blade." Her chest rose and fell as she waited for his reply.

Did she really believe giving him a choice made her ardent demand acceptable? Her miscalculation brought a grin to his face. From the worried look she gave him, she understood his smile wasn't from humor, but more from his anticipation of what would happen next.

"Sit back," he said, keeping his voice even. "Loosen your seatbelt and be quiet." Time for her to understand a thing or two about him.

"Loosen?" Angel asked.

"Pull the belt to give yourself more room. It'll be okay. We're on the back roads, and I know every curve and hill. You'll be safe." His gruff voice stirred a heat in the pit of her stomach. Before she could ask what he wanted, though she suspected, he commanded, "Open your pants and push them to your knees."

He shifted the truck into drive, and they headed down a two-lane road.

A part of her wanted to say, *hell no*, but another became excited at the thought of his touch, out in the open, traveling down a small country road. She wanted his large, rough hands on her, touching, probing, and drawing heat and desire for more.

She unsnapped and slid her pants down, leaving her plain white panties. A pair from the package she'd bought yesterday. Hard to believe only one day had passed. So much had changed.

He groaned.

She darted a look up. Painful hunger flickered across his face. He liked what he saw, but he didn't make a move for a few seconds. She felt a little silly when his fingers moved over her thighs, up her stomach, and reached the elastic at her hip. She inhaled sharply at how wonderful his gentle touch was against her skin. His hand slipped beneath the thin cotton and one finger followed by another parted her moist folds.

"You're moist for me," his said so softly she almost didn't hear him. She wanted to say he had nothing to do with it, but the effort to lie wouldn't be worth it.

His middle finger dipped into her and came back to rotate over the hard nub begging for his attention. Her nails dug into the fabric at her knees. Without thought, her senses taking over, her legs opened until her pants stopped her. She released a shudder.

"Roll your hips against the tips of my fingers," he whispered.

Without hesitation, she followed his orders, releasing a moan.

A car zoomed past. She stopped. Embarrassment flooded her face. She looked down at his hand beneath the material and the juncture of her legs. Every bit of what he was doing to her proved what she watched on the Internet didn't fully prepare her for the true experience. This was real and way hotter with Jake caressing her.

"No," he growled. "Don't stop those little sexy sounds and movements. They can't see us. We're too high off the ground, and the windows are tinted."

He was right. She could easily see inside cars and most

SUVs from where she sat, but the passing automobiles sped by with the occupants in too much of a hurry to check out the cab of a truck.

Two fingers massaged her clitoris and the soft folds, bringing her nearly out of her seat. Her hips began to move again, thrusting for completion. When he stopped, she grabbed his wrist and forced his hand to continue. She arched her back as the small knot jerked with each wave.

His deep chuckle brought her back to what she'd done.

"Let me go, Angel."

Her hand held his wrist so tight she doubted his blood could reach his fingers.

Opening her hand, she took in a deep breath.

He cupped her for a few seconds, and then with a small pat to her sensitive mons, he removed his hand. Lifting his butt off the seat, he reached into his pants and adjusted his hard cock to a more comfortable position. She almost came again.

Surely her makeup would melt from the heat on her face. Embarrassment didn't stop her from staring at the bulge along his zipper while she straightened her clothes. She remembered the taste and texture of his length. Without caring about what he thought, she carefully reached over and smoothed her hand over it. Such wonder filled her. Just knowing he became hard from touching her excited her even more. A sense of heady power caused her to be bolder. She squeezed and stroked. The way he undulated his hips beneath her hand proved he wanted more of what she was doing.

She wanted him in her mouth again.

"You like touching me as much as I do you?"

Unable to voice her thoughts, she nodded.

Regaining control of her senses, a little, she answered,

"Yes. Nothing better than feeling how hard you get, how you grow longer, the hot silky feel of your cock. The way it changes is like magic." She bit her lip. She sounded stupid, but told the truth.

"Magic, huh?" He chuckled. "I bet you drove your grandfather crazy with all the boys following you around and sneaking into your bedroom in the middle of the night."

She moved her hand away. No surprise that he wanted to broach that subject. Most men claimed they cared little about their girlfriends' prior love life, but start talking marriage and then their history becomes all important. Would he be pleased with a nearly virginal wife? Or would he wonder what was wrong with her?

"How much longer before we arrive at your place?" She forced her gaze to look ahead.

He grabbed her hand and placed it back. Then he pushed a lever on the column and the steering wheel eased up. "Time enough. Unzip me."

For a moment, she closed her eyes. It was as if he read her earlier thoughts. She wanted him in her mouth again. So badly.

Without further hesitation, she leaned over and opened his jeans. She lifted his cock carefully out of the denim. With a confident grasp, she rotated her hand slightly along his length and stroked up and down.

"Oh, yeah. Firm hold. That's the way." His hips rose to meet each thrust of her hand. How was he keeping the truck on the road? If she'd been driving when he touched her, she'd gone off into the ditch.

Unable to resist, she bowed her head over his lap and sucked him in.

"Jesus H. Christ!" His long intake of breath could mean

pain or pleasure, but when his palm held her head down, she grinned. Pleasure was the winner.

Unable to take him as deep as she wanted, she pulled back and ran her tongue around the head and then sucked him in again. Her other hand dived in and cupped the tight sac beneath, squeezing slightly. He jerked and the unique flavor of Jake Whitfield shot down her throat.

"Fuck!" His hand smoothed her hair down the back of her head. "You have a talented mouth. I've never come so fast. I have a lot to thank the boyfriend who taught you that."

She licked the length of him as he softened. "No boyfriend. Books." Afraid that he thought she was crazy, she peeked up. His lazy grin reassured her.

"Books? I guess I need to see some of those books you're talking about." He tipped up her face and brushed his thumb across the bottom lip. His gaze fought with looking at her and keeping an eye on the road. "Close up my jeans and tighten your seatbelt. We're coming up to a very curvy section of the road."

Angel zipped, fastened his pants, and quickly placed her belt back in place. Her hands began to shake. Opening and closing her eyes as if it would help stop the trembling, she grimaced. What was up with her? Too much stimuli for the last twenty-four hours?

Seconds after the latch clicked, a big roar filled the cab and her shoulder slammed into the door as metal on metal screeched. A large white delivery truck rammed them from the side, barely missing Jake's door, as it pushed them into a utility pole. The person shifted gears, trying to either move the truck back or continue to drive through the bed into the cab. When she looked at the driver and caught only dark eyes in a black ski mask, she knew, first, it was no accident, and second, they didn't have much time to escape.

"The son of a bitch!" Jake looked her way. "Are you hurt?"

"I'm fine. We need to get out of here. He hit us on purpose and will ram us again." She pulled at the door handle. It swung open with a loud pop and hung crookedly above a ditch about six feet deep. Their only way out.

"Give me the knife," she screamed as she fought with the buckle. The stupid seatbelt had saved her but she needed out before their attacker charged again.

With no trouble, his belt released. He reached for hers. No matter how he jerked on it, it wouldn't give.

The delivery truck struck again. Gears shrieked in protest as it attempted to flatten the pickup truck.

"Shit!" He jammed his hand into a pocket and pulled her knife out.

"Give it to me! Don't press the button, it's tricky, it'll cut you!"

Without argument, he tossed her the knife. As she sawed at the thick material, he leaned over and scooped up the guns that had slid into her side of the floorboard.

The grinding of gears stopped, giving them a few seconds of warning that their attacker was backing up to plow into them once more.

Just as Angel cut her way out of the belt, the big truck smashed into them again. The pickup tilted, spilling them out into the ditch. Jake's arms wrapped around her a second before they hit the ground and rolled to the deepest part. Then three tons of metal landed above their heads with a loud crunch, and the tinkling of glass showered them, but the pickup's body was wider than the ditch. It stopped its descent, giving them room to scramble out of the way.

Jake held her away to scan for injuries. He nodded, satisfied she was unharmed. Without a word, he scrambled up the embankment, and she followed on his heels. As soon as he reached the top, he pulled a gun from his waistband and another from a pocket. No different from an old western, he fired in rapid succession. The *ping, ping, ping* of bullets hitting thin metal echoed around her. Then the squeal of tires and smell of rubber filled the air.

Chapter Twelve

Jake stood on the side of the road, staring as the plain white delivery truck with one working taillight disappear around the curve and out of sight.

"What is it about you that make people want to kill you?"

He turned to see Angel at the edge of the ditch, hands on knees, panting from the steep climb. Blood and sweat ran down her temple, smearing the white goop on her face. One side of her upper lip was already swollen. The throbbing near his left eye told him he was in no better condition.

"I'm a Whitfield," he said simply.

"Well, there is that." She slapped at her pants and coat. How in hell could the woman stand wearing leather in this heat? Yet, it'd probably stopped some of the glass from cutting her. His arm and cheek began to sting. Yeah, she most likely had fewer cuts than he did.

"Here. Put this in your coat pocket." He handed her one of the guns.

A black eyebrow quirked up. "You trust me now?"

Disbelief obvious in her tone. "Or you going to take it away again in a few minutes?"

"I trusted you before. Anyway, it's unloaded. I needed to replace the ammo in my gun." He turned and slid down into the ditch, trying to keep his feet under him. She'd followed to the top edge of the drop.

"Of course. I guess I could throw it at the asshole if he comes back." She mumbled some more, and he grinned as he stooped and scanned the area beneath the overturned truck. "What are you looking for?"

"Cell phone." Chances were it had tumbled out with them. Yep. There it was stuck in a pile of dead leaves. He skittered down the embankment and picked it up. One corner of the screen had a spiderweb crack. He rubbed the phone against his shirt and pressed a button to see if it still worked. It flickered and then lit up. Hot damn. He hadn't been looking forward to hitchhiking or walking back home. On returning to the top of the embankment, he hit Home under contacts. "Tick!"

"Is that you, boss?"

"Yeah. Send Matt down 82. We're about five miles from the house on the left." Jake continued to watch Angel.

Picking up the knife stuck in the ground—luckily it hadn't cut either of them—she closed it and slipped it into her coat. Then she flipped her red-tipped black hair behind a shoulder and stretched.

Unbelievable to imagine it, but he hardened.

"Whatcha you need him for?" Tick's breathless question caught Jake's attention. What was his employee nervous about?

"Matt had plenty of time to return." The guard had left the motel an hour before Jake had rounded up Angel. As far as he knew, Matt hadn't experienced any problems, unlike his and Angel's adventures. "Have you not seen him?"

"Well…"

"What the hell do I pay him for?" Tired, dirty, and inconceivably—considering the two soul-sucking blow jobs he had in the last twelve hours—horny as a teenager after prom, he couldn't keep his gaze off her. Just looking at the woman, no matter what was going on around him, heated his blood. Instead of catching the asshole who was making his life a misery, he wanted to return home and take her to bed. He contemplated the woman sitting a few feet away in the grass as she watched the road. He wanted to find out what other tricks she'd learned from her books.

Maybe it was the adrenaline of nearly being killed twice. He remembered the knives and letter opener in the study. No, nearly being killed five times in twenty-four hours had pushed his libido into overdrive.

He turned as the crunch of gravel beneath tires caught his attention. All thought of having sex quickly dissipated as a Sand County Sheriff's car pulled over with its light-bar flashing.

"Tick, be sure they send a cherry picker to lift a truck out of the ditch. Got to go. The law pulled up." He ended the call and waited.

Dammit, police interference was the last thing he needed.

Angel stood as the deputy exited his patrol car and walked with the typical swagger of a man who was armed and dangerous and knew it. Kind of like the way Jake moved.

"Hey, Sam." She'd dealt with the deputy before and knew as long as she talked straight, he wouldn't give her any attitude. "We had a little problem with a white van side-swiping us and running for it."

Out of the corner of her eye, she caught Jake glaring at her. Then he looked away, as if he didn't want the deputy to see how pissed he was at the moment. Had he expected her to lie?

"Everyone okay?" The deputy looked into the ditch.

"Yeah. Just a few bruises and cuts. Nothing big."

"I see. Whitfield, you need to take a field sobriety test?"

Angel stepped in front of Jake, redirecting the deputy's attention to her. "How are you so sure he was driving?"

"Come on, Angel. A Whitfield letting a female drive? I don't think so." Sam nodded toward Jake. "Walk back to the car with me."

A couple of seconds passed without Jake moving, not even with a look in the deputy's direction. His full gaze centered on her. Would he refuse just out of principle? As he had a soda with lunch and nothing else, she knew it was a given he'd pass without a hitch. So why the intense stare?

Finally, he broke the standoff. "Sure." Then he walked back to the patrol car.

She tapped her foot as she waited. The urge to move a little closer to hear what was being said had her body strung so tight she walked stiffly closer until she stood a yard from the sedan's grille.

Sam held an instrument near Jake's lips. "You know the drill, Whitfield." Jake leaned over and blew into the small plastic tube. "Harder." When the deputy moved it away, his eyes narrowed at the numbers on the small screen. "Well, it appears you've had one too many."

"What the hell?" Angel moved around the door and glowered. "All he drank was a plain Coca-Cola. How did he fail it?"

"Angel," Jake warned, shaking his head.

"Sam, I've always thought you were one of the good ones." She crossed her arms. What was going on?

Unable to see the deputy's eyes behind the dark sunglasses, she nevertheless glared his way. He pointed to the side of the road. "You go over there and sit down. I don't want to hear another peep out of you or I'll take your ass in, too."

Frustrated but with no other option left, she did as he ordered.

Sam pulled Jake by an arm to the end of the car and then pushed him face first over the trunk. After handcuffing him, he patted him down.

Panic washed over her. His gun.

She edged over to the ditch, hoping to find an opportunity to toss hers into the tall grass. Once he found Jake's, he'd be searching her. As she sat on the shoulder of the pavement, she slid the gun out of her pocket and pushed it over the small lip of the steep embankment. It tumbled down and stopped next to a clump of weeds. In plain sight. She closed her eyes for a second and sighed. There was nothing more she could do.

"There's your ride, Angel." Sam walked over to the black SUV that stopped a few yards away. Behind it was a large tow truck, sporting a cherry picker on the back bed.

What happened to Jake's gun? Had he dumped it before the deputy checked him for weapons?

The SUV's driver's door opened and Tick stepped out, glancing over to the patrol car as he spoke to the deputy. Angel followed his stare. Jake sat in the back watching with half-closed eyes.

When she pulled her attention to Sam again, he'd returned to his car and was on a cell phone. Who was he talking to? She'd never seen Sand County use a cell phone to communicate with headquarters. The county was too small and poor to invest in anything fancier than CB radios and walkie-talkies.

Tick hunkered down next to her as the beeping of the tow truck vibrated around them.

"What did the boss do?"

"Nothing actually. Then again, maybe being a Whitfield is enough. The deputy claims Jake's been drinking, when he hasn't." She felt so helpless. For now, Sam appeared satisfied with arresting Jake and ignoring her. Thank goodness for small favors. It had been one hell of a day.

"I'll call Dad and have him head over to the jail." Tick stood and moved away as he tapped the screen on his phone.

For the next half hour she sat on the side of the road. She calmed down somewhat after Tick loaned her his phone to talk with Damien. A few cars traveled by, all of them slowed to a crawl as the drivers stared. Not until a large white pickup eased by did she recognized a face. The man behind the wheel was Jake's cousin, Theodore Whitfield, also known as Teddy Bear. His grin spread wide as he spotted Jake in the backseat of the deputy's car. When he caught her watching, one eyebrow lifted as he puckered his lips. A second later, he hit the gas, his cackling drifting in the wind behind him.

"The deputy said you can go." Tick nodded toward the SUV as they watched the deputy's car do a three-point turn and head toward the next town. Sand City was the county seat, and the jail was located there. Jake twisted in his seat to look out the back window, his cold gaze on her as they drove away.

Did he believe she had something to do with the deputy showing up?

"So your dad's going to help him?" she asked without taking her eyes off Jake.

"Yeah. He's waiting at the courthouse. It'll be a few more hours before he can get Jake released. Dad'll insist on them taking a urine sample. If they demand a blood one, it would take too long. So Jake should be home by nightfall."

She looked into Tick's dark eyes. "You're so cool about all this. Does it happen often?"

"Enough." Tick opened the door for her and waited until she settled into the passenger seat before closing it behind her. When he was seated and cranked the engine, he added, "After Jake got out of the Army, he'd expected everyone to respect him. Hell, he'd fought for our country. You'd have thought it would be a given. First week back, he was picked up for suspected breaking and entering. Every week, it was something. The last year or so, they've eased off."

"Army? Jake?" Her world shifted. Not once had she heard a word about Jake serving in the military. She'd heard rumors of Ethan being sent to prison for eighteen months.

"He doesn't talk about it much, but his dad forced him to join. The choice was go into the Army or go to jail."

Color her confused. "How could he send his son to prison when he broke the law all the time?" She knew for a fact Dick Whitfield had been the biggest criminal in Sand County.

"The story is that Jake and Ethan had beaten up a store owner for no reason. The store owner was a good friend of Mac's." Tick glanced her way when they turned onto the Whitfield driveway. "Your granddaddy turned them in. Mr. Whitfield worked out the deal with the assistant D.A."

When they came to a stop outside the garage next to the house, he lightly touched her arm, keeping her from leaving the SUV. "Only thing is, about eight months after they shipped the boys off, the police get a 911 call to the store owner's house. His fourteen-year-old step-daughter was messed up bad. The guy had been banging her and slapping around her mother. The girl had reached her limit and shot him. He lived but all the bad crap came out. That's when the old man figured out what had really happened."

"Jake and Ethan had been trying to stop the store owner," Angel said as she shook her head in sorrow. "Why didn't they tell everyone what was going on? Why not call the police in the beginning?" The store owner was lucky she hadn't heard about it first. He would be in prison once she sicced the cops on him.

"The wife begged them not to say anything. She still loved the creep, and she'd made them believe it had happened only one time and the step-daughter had mental issues. When they were arrested, she never confessed. It would've been their word against hers. The daughter refused to talk, too."

She shook her head. "It's a sick world out there. What happened to the store owner?"

"He got sent to prison. Funny thing, the same one Ethan was in. A couple months in, the guy was found shanked in the showers." Tick opened the door and waited for her to follow.

The obvious answer was Ethan had killed the man, but Angel knew the easiest answer wasn't always the right one. Mr. Dick Whitfield was known to be a dangerous man to cross. Chances were he took care of the situation himself. She imagined he wouldn't like to be set up.

And she thought her family was scary.

Later that evening, she and Damien sat at the kitchen table with bowls of steaming cobbler. The scents of cinnamon and apples infused the cozy feeling Jimmie Sue easily created with her legendary cooking. The wonderful housekeeper had even bought almond milk and vegan butter, declaring the dessert was better for it.

Angel dipped her spoon into a mound of apple cobbler and savored the buttery taste, but even the sweet dessert didn't occupy her mind. Instead the memories of clear blue eyes flashing with heat and desire before she lowered her mouth to his cock, and the long groan of surrender when he came in her mouth filled her with a need to experience the sensations again. How was he the only man to invoke such wildness from her?

Jimmie Sue and Damien laughed, bringing Angel's attention back to the present. She averted her hot face, not taking the chance they could see, even through her pale makeup. Keeping her attention out the window, she scooped up another bite.

Earlier, the sun had disappeared from the horizon, and the security lights surrounding the house lit up the drive as bright as midday. With the spoon hovering near her mouth, her gaze followed a black sedan with dark tinted windows glide by the house, heading toward the back. Even without seeing who rode inside, the hair on her arms lifted, warning it was time to pay the devil.

Jake was home.

"Jimmie Sue, Big Judd said he'd drive you home." Jake hugged the housekeeper after she expressed her concern about local law enforcement needing more to do than harassing Whitfields. He could always count on her to support "her boys" when she felt someone treated them wrong.

"Have you heard where Matt disappeared to?" Jimmie Sue grabbed a sweater hanging on a hook near the door. Even at seventy degrees outside, she became chilled easily. "He is the most undependable boy I've ever been around."

"Sen's gone looking for him. He's probably holed up with one of his buddies playing video games." Not wanting to worry the older woman, he smiled and patiently waited as she said her goodbyes to Tick, Angel, and her brother.

One large hand cupping a bowl of cobbler, Tick moved around the table and sat next to the teenager. They started arguing which version of Warcraft they believed to be the best. Jake caught Tick's eye and nodded before he turned to Angel. He needed the teenager's attention elsewhere for a couple of hours. Time to teach his wife-to-be another lesson.

"Come with me," he quietly said to Angel and headed toward the back stairs. He reached the first landing before he heard the scrape of a chair being pushed back and then murmuring as she made her excuses to her brother and Tick.

Without waiting, he continued up the staircase and turned left toward his suite of rooms. As the oldest, he'd taken over the master suite. Jimmie Sue had cleared out all of the old man's personal effects a couple of days before the funeral and donated most of it to a local charity. Then he had a new bed delivered and set up yesterday. The housekeeper understood his need to move forward and take over every aspect of the old man's life and property. With his takeover of that room and the study, it wouldn't be long before the citizens of Marystown knew about it. People talked. Furniture dealers talked. Charity organizers talked. He needed them to spread the word. The more people who knew he was in command, the easier it would be to control those who worked for him.

He opened the door to his suite and stood to the side.

Angel reached his side and hesitated. She looked into his eyes. Whatever compassion she'd hoped to see wouldn't be there. He couldn't afford leniency at this point. Her chest rose and fell as she breathed in deeply, lifted her chin, and walked into the room.

"Kneel," he said in a level, firm voice after he closed and locked the door behind him.

Chapter Thirteen

Angel remained standing. She wanted to fall to her knees, craving the release his harsh voice promised, but they needed to clear up a few facts.

He leaned back, resting his shoulders on the door. With his arms and ankles crossed, he showed her that he had all the time in the world. Her gaze traveled over his broad shoulders and chest in his button-up shirt. Why was it everything about him appealed to her?

"Jake." Her voice cracked. Desire to touch him closed up her throat.

"Angel." His lips tightened as he waited for her to comply or explain. She did catch a mixture of impatience and anticipation in his light blue eyes.

"As you know, I've accepted that I have to marry you, but we need to come to terms about our relationship in and outside the bedroom." So twisted up inside, her lungs felt as if they would explode any minute, she inhaled long and deep.

He pushed off the door and walked a tight circle around

her. His fingers played with the red tips of her hair. "Go ahead." His hip brushed against her. She balled her fists.

His big presence swallowed the air in the room as desire swept over her. She wanted to lean against his hard body and soak in every bit of his heat. How wonderful would it be for his arms to hold her again as he had last night when she fell asleep? With a mental shake, she forced the words out of her mouth.

"Whenever others are around, I'm your equal." She closed her eyes as his hand dropped and skimmed over her collarbone. Her breasts lifted and fell with deep inhale and exhale as she tried to regulate her breathing.

"Is that so?" His smirk lit her temper.

"Do I have to prove it?" She tried to regain her composure, hating his condescending tone.

"Yeah."

She grabbed his wrist, shoved her shoulder into his ribs, and flipped him. He hit the floor with a grunt. The next second, he pulled her down, pressing her back to his chest and rolled to the side with her. Before she could struggle, he grasped her arm and twisted it, pulling up her numb hand to her shoulder blades. He quickly released his painful hold, and his arm hooked her neck to roll her over, face first, to the floor. His heavy body pressed her into the rug.

Panting, she remained stiff and on alert. What did he plan to do next?

"Nice move. We'll talk about what I believe equal means," he whispered into her ear.

She shivered. The reaction was more from how his body rubbed against her and his other arm pressed against her breasts and not from the threat in his tone or the pressure to her throat. All that maleness centered on what she said, his body wrapping her in his strength, brought a weakness to every joint in her body. She sagged in his hold and inhaled the scent of Jake: leather and the faint smell of tobacco.

Hadn't she wanted his arms around her?

No, not exactly in this way. She grinned knowing he couldn't see it as she decided she would take what she could get.

He released her and stood. Then he tugged her to her feet. With her facing away, he wrapped strong arms around her once again.

"Equals means I'm in this with you. Finding who killed our family," she said, ignoring his hiss, and then added, "and stopping whoever it is trying to kill Damien and you. I want to be involved in the decisions." He squeezed her as she continued. "Decisions that pertain to the investigation and anything that has to do with my brother." She relaxed into his embrace, if a person could call what he did that. He tightened his hold a little more. She could barely breathe but she felt safe and secure. Something she never remembered feeling.

The silence in the room didn't bother her. She felt his body tensing and a certain area pressed to the small of her back becoming hard. Jake's body said he had other things on his mind.

His hands covered her breasts and lightly squeezed. Then without warning, he jerked the corset down. She breathed in deeply, enjoying the freedom from the stiff material and letting him see how much she wanted his touch. He looked down and thumbed her taut nipples. Then he molded his hands over the soft mounds and tightened his thumbs and forefingers on the tender tips.

Releasing a sharp intake of breath, her eyes almost rolled in her head as shots of electricity raced from her breasts to clit. The pain-pleasure reminded her of how he made her feel when he spanked her. She threw her head back and pushed into his hands.

"You have beautiful tits." He released her nipples and cupped and lifted. "I agree but with limitations." He nipped at her ear. "Alone, I own you, and you do whatever I say. Out there," he nodded to the bedroom door, "I'll consider your opinion." He rolled his fingers and tugged the flesh between them.

"No," she croaked. Later she'd wonder how she held up against his sexual lure. Swallowing hard gave her a couple of seconds to clear her mind. "Partners out there. I'll let you lead, but partners still the same," she said in a near normal tone.

"Alone. You're mine to command?"

"Yes." Thank goodness he held her as her knees had turned to goo.

"Your mouth, your pussy, and your ass are mine."

"Yes." She closed her eyes and shuddered when need overwhelmed her.

He moved his hands down and wrapped his arms below her breasts, lifting her off her feet as he licked her neck. "Damn, you taste good, and I like how you stand up to me, and look after your brother. Your loyalty tells me a lot."

"Like how you can use me?" She blinked open her eyes and immediately bit the side of her mouth in an effort not to say more.

"Yeah. I already knew that. You proved that in the limo the other day." Before she could protest, his body's heat disappeared in a blink. He stepped back. She barely caught her balance. "Kneel," he commanded.

When she lifted her hands to tug the corset back in place, she hesitated at the shake of his head.

"Nuh-uh. Your breasts are mine, too. Leave them bare."

His dark tone melted any self-preservation she still possessed. Her nipples ached, they were so hard.

She slowly went on one knee and then the other. Her back straight, she waited with fists clenched at her side. Staring at the wall ahead, she tried to ignore the man behind her, but her body zinged in excitement.

Each heavy footstep warned her of where he was headed. She heard a slight creak from the large poster bed.

"Angel. Come here."

She started to stand.

"No. Crawl."

On her knees, she turned and glared. "That's carrying—"

"Then get out," he said, cutting off her complaint, daring her to not play the game.

"You're a real bastard. I had heard it, but always thought they didn't understand you the way I did."

Maybe Mac had been right. She'd watched too many romantic movies. Had she romanticized Jake and their interlude in high school? Interlude? Ah, hell. That confirmed it. She had. He'd proven to her already they had a business deal and nothing more. She'd provide sex, and he would give her orgasms, and they would be partners. Possibly partners. She had no illusion on that. Why she even trusted him was beyond her.

She looked at his long taut body half-sitting, half-stretched out on the edge of the bed, his eyelids heavy with desire as he watched her. No one had ever looked at her as he did. She'd been dreaming about being with him for what seemed forever. Life sometimes provided what you needed, instead of what you dreamed. She knew that better than anyone. She needed Jake in her life and not just for protection. She needed him to feel alive. She'd been dead since Mac had pulled her out of school. Maybe to her, this was love. No. Not love. Whatever it was, she desired it with all her heart. She would take it and enjoy every second. One thing she'd learned a long time ago, nothing good lasted.

"You don't know me," he growled.

"True."

When one masculine eyebrow lifted as he narrowed his eyes, she sighed and started crawling toward him. Truth be told, his bossiness turned her on, but he would learn the limits he could push her. He would regret pushing her. Two could play at this game.

Jake gritted his teeth to keep him from drooling down his chin. The woman didn't just crawl to him, she moved like a wild cat, slowly and gracefully. No way could he look away. Her breasts, full and tight, swung with every movement. She stared pointedly at his groin. An alarm sounded in the back of his head, screaming *manhood in danger*. But he couldn't resist enjoying the sight. His cock lengthened and hardened. Fuck. She was damn sexy all riled up. He may have to keep her on her knees every time they were alone. He trusted she loved his cock as much as he did, and she wouldn't do permanent damage. If he stopped her in time.

When she reached the bed, she looked up. Anger and hunger burned in those dark chocolate eyes. "What now?"

He managed to keep the grin from his face. He could easily guess her look was from being turned on in such a helpless way.

"Strip."

"Can I stand?"

"No."

Yep. He would be dead if her eyes shot bullets and wasn't filled with need.

She struggled to unhook her corset and then unlace her boots and slip off her socks. After she unzipped her pants and started wiggling it and her panties down her body, his cock and balls began to hurt. He'd been hard from the moment he entered the house and met her gaze across the table. His balls were so tight to his body he wasn't sure they would ever drop again. All he could think of was hammering into every hole in her body along with between her ample pale breasts.

Only the soft hum of a ceiling fan broke the quiet in the room. Then he realized he'd been staring at her for a minute or more without saying a word. Sitting back on her heels with arms akimbo, knees spread, she waited for his next instruction. Her pussy lips were slick and shiny with her need. He fucking loved that. A lot. She didn't try to hide her body from him.

He leaned down and cupped one pebble-tipped breast. Was there any material in the world as soft and silky as a woman's skin, especially her breasts and labia?

The purr from her throat jarred him back to his objective: punish her for saying too much in front of the deputy. Had she done so on purpose?

"Angel, how did you know that deputy?" She didn't say a word, just continued to stare at his heavy cock outlined in his jeans. He snapped his fingers in front of her face. She blinked several times as if drugged. When she looked into his face, the heat in her eyes had overrode her anger.

"Damien and a couple of his buddies set an old abandoned house on fire that was out in the middle of nowhere, but in Sand County. The same deputy caught them, and they had to call the fire department out. He made the boys apologize to each of the firemen. The men had to leave their family during Fourth of July celebrations to come and put it out. Since the Marystown police would've thrown him into jail with drunkards and psychos, I thought he was one of the nice ones."

What would she say if he told her she was right? The deputy was one of the good ones. Deputy Sam McKenzie had been following orders. Special Agent Alex Carleton had become impatient and wanted to talk to Jake especially after hearing about the trouble they had on the interstate. The deputy did have a mean streak as he didn't tell Jake about the agent until they were down the road a piece. He'd suspected something was up when the deputy hadn't patted him down all the way. His gun still hidden in his boot even when he was placed into the patrol car. If not for the handcuffs being hooked into the seat, he could've killed the man and gotten away if that had been his intent.

He almost told her but stopped. Maybe later. For now, she needed to learn a lesson.

Her hand slid across his thigh toward his zipper. He grabbed her wrist and pulled her over his lap. She whimpered. Not from fear, but need.

"Next time a law enforcement officer asks you a question, act as if you don't understand English. Tell him nothing."

"I know how to handle—"

Jake slapped one round cheek. "I said, tell him nothing." He slapped the other, leaving bright pink handprints on her ass.

Her body stiffened and then as he continued to redden her bottom, she began to squirm, rubbing her nipples against his leg as she held tight onto his ankle. Her little gasps mixed with moans betrayed how much she enjoyed the punishment.

Da-amn. After a couple more swats, he lifted her and threw her onto the bed facedown. Her red buttocks stuck out, either from wanting to be spanked some more or wanting to be fucked.

As soon as he unzipped, his cock jerked in anticipation from what would come next.

"I've wanted to do this for a long time." He smoothed her ass, feeling the heat before he slipped between her legs and checked for moisture. Oh yeah, soaked. She lifted and dipped her hips on his finger.

"More. Deeper please."

Her begging ramped up his need. He ran her wetness up between her folds and over her rosebud shaped anus. As small as it looked, she'd never taken a man that way or it had been a long time ago. That would be later. At the moment, he wanted as deep in her pussy as he could get and from the back was the best way to go deep.

He pushed his trousers down enough to give him the room he needed. Grabbing a condom from the nightstand, he opened the packet and rolled on the thin sheath.

"Hurry. Please, Jake." Her plea almost sent him over the edge, and he hadn't even entered her yet. He loved how she wanted what he planned to give her.

Slipping a finger into her, he rubbed the moisture around her pussy before placing the tip of his cock in her. With short jabs, he worked his way in. Tight. Fuck. He never remembered a woman ever being this tight. Could it be something to do with how she was built? Not that she was small, but some women's mouths were too small to give good head. Remembering her expertise in that area, that wasn't it. She whimpered, and he hesitated. Was he hurting her? Then she pushed back with all her weight and groaned as his cock finally slipped the rest of the way in. The snug fit was almost more than his cock could handle. How embarrassing would it be if he shot his load before he started pumping? She pulled away, and he grasped her hips and thrust into her. He was in control, and he planned to ride her hard.

"Oh, that feels so good," she said with a purr at the end. She appeared to handle it and want more.

"Yeah, it does." He continued thrusting as he adjusted his hold. Her breasts felt good in his hands. He squeezed with each full plunge into her. Each time his stomach pressed her butt, the heat from her spanked bottom drove him wild.

No matter how good of a battery-operated boyfriend a person owned, it hadn't prepared Angel for the real thing. Warm flesh pressed against her back, large rough hands tightening, squeezing her hips and then her breasts. His fullness thrusting into her most sensitive folds was an experience she wanted to repeat as often as possible.

She reached behind her and dug her nails into his ribs, wanting him closer, faster, craving to touch every inch of his hard body. She loved how he felt so different from her. His body varied from leathery skin to bristly and soft hair and then between his legs hot steel covered in silk. There wasn't an inch of him she wanted unexplored.

For her first time, it wasn't bad at all. All her preparation had paid off. She'd felt only a tinge of pain when he entered her.

His fingers moved over her stomach and farther down. Seconds from exploding, she held her hand over his to be sure he finished the job by rubbing her clit. As the waves burst through, she felt him jerk and follow her. She felt as if the room shook and the walls lit up with fireworks. He groaned as he came.

Then they heard shouting.

"What the hell?" Jake pulled out of her and jumped from the bed. She rolled over, and followed. He pushed the curtains to the side. A bright glow lit the evening sky in the direction of the garage.

"Son of a bitch!" He scrambled to throw away the condom, pull on his clothes as she reached for hers.

"Stay here. I'll check it out," he said as he buttoned his shirt.

"I'm coming with you." She drew tight on the strings lacing her corset. Had he so quickly forgotten their agreement? No way would she stay behind. Time for Jake to remember they were partners outside the bedroom.

She was seconds behind him. Several of the Whitfield guards were pulling out water hoses, while others moved the few cars and trucks sitting outside the garage. There was no hope for the huge building. It was in full flame.

The sirens of a fire truck, an EMT vehicle, and five law enforcement vehicles, two from Marystown and three from Sand County, echoed along the long drive as they came to pitch in and keep the fire from spreading. Who had called them? And how had they arrived so fast?

Angel rolled her eyes at the number of officers. She doubted any other house in the county would rate more than two officers, but they always hoped to find the Whitfields, as they did the Tallys, had been up to no good and maybe even to gloat a little.

She hollered at Tick to get Damien away from the fire.

"Anyone hurt?" one of the EMTs shouted at Jake.

"There's an apartment over the garage that's not in use. We've been a little busy and haven't had a chance to account for everyone yet." Jake wiped his forehead with a sleeve, smearing the soot.

"We'll stick around until everything is put out and you're sure no one is missing."

"Suit yourself."

"What about your brothers?" Angel quietly asked as the EMT ambled away. "They haven't returned home."

"They had errands to do. They'd let me know when they return. Besides their cars aren't here."

He didn't sound concerned, but he stared at the still-burning building. Two more explosions rocked the night from half-filled gas tanks in some of the classic cars Jake had mentioned. Such a waste.

"Mr. Whitfield, I need to ask you a few questions." One of the Sand County officers stood with a hand on his pistol handle as if waiting for Jake to draw. From his solemn expression, Angel was unsure if the officer had won or lost the decision in who would interview the eldest Whitfield.

"Yeah. Sure."

Angel walked up and stood next to Jake. The officer gave her a look over but didn't protest. Smart man.

"Where were you when the fire started?"

"In bed."

The deputy looked at Angel and back at Jake. He nodded as if coming to the conclusion they were together at the time. "What was your first clue that the fire had started?"

"The explosion."

"Explosion?"

Angel looked down and wiped her eyes as if something had stung them. She was trying her best not to laugh. Jake was an expert at saying what was needed without anything extra. His two-word answers were perfection. True, she could learn a thing or two from him. She listened for little while longer until she worried a giggle would escape. She even felt a little sorry for the young deputy. So she decided to move around and listen to what others were saying.

Taking her time, she walked the perimeter, staying out of everyone's way. She was strolling through a wooded area not far from the garage when she spotted something shiny in the undergrowth. A tassel with a silver tip. Something from a motorcycle's saddlebags, jacket, pants or fancy boots. She sniffed it. Gasoline. Was that what set the fire?

Without a second thought she stuck it in her pocket. Maybe she could find something else.

Two hours later they had the fire out and smoldering when the first shout told her they were in deep shit.

"We found a body!"

Chapter Fourteen

ngel watched the last patrol car disappear at the
end of the drive before she turned to Jake. His
face, lined and smeared with soot from the long
night, showed the anger he felt for what they found. The
police hadn't let up all night until dawn, questioning each of
them over and over again, suspecting someone held back
information.

"Do you think the body was one of your brothers?" she
asked gently. He had no word from Ethan or Sen.

"I have no idea. They'll let us know soon." The deep
wrinkles at the corner of his eyes gave away his worry.
"Matt's still missing, too."

"Who lived in the apartment?"

Jake lit a cigarette and released a stream of smoke.
"Until the funeral, me and Ethan. The old man wouldn't let
us back in the house when we returned."

"I heard that you enlisted in the Army after high school
and Ethan went to prison."

"What brought that up?" His crystal blue eyes chilled
her.

She ignored his question. "What happened to Sen? Did he go into the Army or prison?"

He took another toke and then blew the stream straight up. "Neither. He had to live with the old man for years alone. I can tell you it was twice the hell Ethan and I endured."

She wanted to know more but decided it was time to tell him what she'd found. "I've got something to show you."

His gaze drifted across her chest, and her nipples tightened. With only a look, he could crank her engine, and it drove her crazy. For the last two days, all she'd thought about was sucking him off or having sex with Jake or having his mouth on her pussy. Time for her to return to what needed to be done.

Ignoring what his leer revealed, she shoved the tassel at him. "This was behind the garage. It looks too shiny and clean to be out in the elements for long. I know Sen rides a motorcycle, and I thought it might've come off his equipment."

"His leathers are plain. He's not much of a showman. No tassels or silver. He says it makes it hard to hide if needed."

For some reason, Angel felt relief that his brother hadn't been involved. She wanted to trust them, but she had seen little of the two most of her life and especially the last two days. Even as kids, Jake had been more of the outgoing type in school. Ethan and Sen had appeared to be satisfied with staying in the background.

"Do you know of anyone else?"

"Yeah. My cousin, Teddy. The more tassels the better. He never was very bright." He threw down the cigarette butt and stepped on it.

"Let's go and find him." She started toward the cars.

"Whoa!" He grabbed her arm and headed to the back porch and kitchen. "We've been up for over twenty-four hours. We need to sleep and then we have other obligations to see to. I promise my cousin won't disappear. He's like a skin cancer, just when you think you burned it all off, he'll show up where you least expect it."

"Sick."

"But true. Come on." His big hand still held her arm as they walked up the interior stairs.

"You just want to get me in the bedroom so you can boss me around again."

He leaned down. "And you love every minute," he whispered. Then he slapped her ass as they entered the bedroom. "But I'm whipped," he chuckled at his pun, "and we need some rest."

Forty-five minutes later, showered, teeth and hair brushed, she sank into the mattress with the covers over her and Jake. His arms wrapped tight around her. The feeling was surreal. How had it happened so fast? It was what she'd dreamed about for so long, being with him. She glanced around the bright room, the sun shining in. The grays, whites, and blues blended in perfectly. A man's room. Despite the relaxing colors and furniture, and being in the middle of the morning, she doubted she could fall asleep. Her body refused to relax against his. Maybe she was too happy—no, that wasn't the word—dazed to be in Jake's bed, his arms, after so many years of imagining it.

His hand slid down her stomach. Chill bumps raced across her skin. That was another reason. Having all his muscle and hardness wrapped around her didn't induce sleep. Nothing separated them. He refused to let her wear a T-shirt. Yet having his bare skin against hers was heavenly. How in the world did he expect her not to want more of what they had done yesterday? Her body hummed with the need to rub and stroke.

"Shh, Angel. I'll take care of you, but we'll have more fun soon. We need a breather." Though she hated to admit it, he was right. They had all the time in the world.

Strong fingers rubbed between her tender folds and brought her off in seconds. She arched into his skillful caress and released a long hiss of satisfaction.

He gathered her closer with her cheek on his arm. The warmth from his body seeped into every inch of her. Her eyes became heavy with each second.

His hand stroked her belly. She smiled. A warm glow surrounded her, a feeling she'd never experienced before in her whole life. The pleasure of knowing she was wanted. That he enjoyed touching her as much as she loved touching him.

She drifted off as she felt his lips touch her hair.

Jake listened to her breathing even out as he smoothed her hair. He stopped and admired the strands against her neck. Damn, he loved how the black contrasted with her pale creamy skin. She surprised him at every turn. No one had ever flipped him over their shoulder and then early this morning after everything settled down and they prepared for bed, he had the biggest surprise ever in his life.

A couple of streaks of what looked like dried blood on the bed. To make certain, he'd checked the condom he'd thrown into the trash. Yep. More blood. In case it was something to do with her monthly, during their preparations for bed he'd asked when she expected her next cycle. "In two weeks," she'd said, curiosity evident. That told him what he needed to know.

When he'd entered her last night, she'd tensed. Her pussy had been so tight, and he'd wondered, but she hadn't shown any other sign of discomfort. So he had no idea until he saw the evidence.

Angel had been a virgin.

He'd been told that every woman handled it differently. She had mentioned reading books, and he suspected she watched some porn. She wasn't unaware. Had she tried to get rid of her hymen? He'd heard girls were doing crazy shit like that, so they could enjoy their first time.

None of it mattered. First time with him or a dildo, she was his and that would not change anytime soon.

He kissed the top of her head again. Releasing a deep sigh, he closed tired, scratchy eyes.

Images of the predawn morning hours flashed behind his eyes. Whose body was in the apartment? Deep inside, he was certain his brothers lived. With one other person uncounted for, chances were high it belonged to Matt.

Frustration pushed sleep back even further. He rubbed his eyes.

Fuck. He hated to tell the guy's aunt. Matt had been raised by her after his mom died when he was ten. His dad had never been in the picture. Shit. No one had seen Matt the last few hours, and the garage was part of his sector to guard. Most likely, he had been in the wrong place at the wrong time. Once the county medical examiner checked out the body, they would have a better idea of what happened.

He pulled Angel closer and nestled his nose in her hair. She smelled of vanilla and her own special scent, a mixture of leather and sex. Since he'd had his first woman, he'd never cared for cuddling. Yet it felt natural to do it with her.

When had his life become so different and complicated?

He chuckled. Since he tackled her in the cemetery.

Angel stirred and hummed with contentment.

"Shh. Go back to sleep," he whispered.

Truth be known, complicated started the day he was born and he'd never been afraid. So why worry now?

Chapter Fifteen

Angel reached the bottom of the stairs, relieved to hear Damien and Tick jabbering in the kitchen. When she turned the corner, her eyes widened. Jake's mom, Lydia, sat at the table with Jimmie Sue, smiling at the fellows stuffing their mouths between the commentary of their gaming the night before.

Jake was nowhere in sight.

She tugged at the gold-and-white corset and the decorative, matching short jacket with black lapels. She'd found them on a chair near the bed and guessed Jake had bought the set for her. Talk about glad she'd decided to wear the little jacket. She almost left it off. The corset was so beautiful that she hated to cover it up even a little bit.

Nervously, she stepped into the kitchen.

Jake's mom stared at her as if she were an alien. Angel smoothed her hands down the bare-there black leather skirt and tried not to breathe too deeply. Glad that her thigh-high boots with spike heels covered all but six inches of what the skirt didn't, she scooted into the chair next to Damien.

Even at barely fifty years old and five-one, Lydia Whitfield was beautiful with all her thick, long blonde hair and large blue eyes. Angel felt like a freak next to her.

"Hon, you want some chicken and dumplings?" Jimmie Sue stood, dipping into a large pot, preparing her bowl before receiving an answer.

"Sorry. I'm vegan." She hated inconveniencing anyone, she rather look after herself, but she was tired of apologizing for wanting to eat healthy. "A salad would be wonderful." Angel's stomach growled.

"That's no way to live, just on fruit, vegetables, and tofu." Lydia Whitfield's gaze dropped to her leather skirt. "And I thought that style of living included the clothes you wear."

Obviously, Jake's mom was more up on current trends than Angel would've thought. "I can eat a lot more than that. There are beans, nuts, and grains. And I buy old leather clothes and retrofit them."

Jimmie Sue waved them off. "Well, I never want anyone to go hungry in my kitchen. Give me a minute, and I'll get you fixed up." The older woman began pulling out all kinds of fresh vegetables from the fridge.

"Sis, you won't believe how sharp Tick is in the latest Grand Theft Auto. He's already several levels above me. And he's shown me some tricks on Warcraft. You wouldn't believe the stuff I missed. Tonight, he promises to teach me how to play Fortnite." Damien's whole body vibrated in excitement. Angel glanced at his large soda.

"How many have you had today?"

"Ahh, sis. Just a couple. I'm okay. School's out and we're just hanging." He darted a look at Tick in support. The big guy only shrugged.

"No more after this one. Water, juices, or noncaffeinated drinks only. You know it hypes you up, and you won't be able to sleep. You had enough craziness the last few days, you need to stay away from those games for a while."

"Aww! That's not fair."

"Boys will be boys. It won't hurt anything. Summertime. Boys need to let loose." Lydia added her two cents, and Angel really wished she hadn't. The woman didn't know anything about her brother.

"Mrs. Whitfield, Damien has ADD, and if I don't limit his intake of caffeine, he'll bounce off the walls and get in all kinds of problems."

"Jake never gave me any trouble at all when he was young. A perfect child." Her eyes got a spacey look as if she was seeing something no one else in the room did.

"Okay, Mom, quit telling people that. You'll make all of the other mothers jealous." Jake walked into the room and hugged her.

"Well, it's true," she said in a small singsong voice.

"Hey, Jake, you have time for a bowl of chicken and dumplings?" Jimmie Sue pulled out a larger bowl and began dipping."

"I believe I do. That will give Angel time to eat, too. Then we have people to meet."

Angel tucked her hair behind an ear. She politely gave a thank you to Jimmie Sue when she sat a strawberry and romaine lettuce salad on the table. Checking the label on the vinaigrette dressing next to it, she sprinkled it on and dug in. With a quick bite—she was so hungry—she then asked, "What people?"

He merely raised an eyebrow as he bit into a steaming dumpling. As he chewed, his gaze wandered over her face and down to her corset. He pointed his fork at her. "I knew it would fit you. Perfect in fact. You look beautiful."

Thankfully, her white makeup hid her blush. She never remembered anyone calling her beautiful. Pretty, one time by her mom. And she couldn't get used to his acceptance of her preferred style of dress. It'd driven Mac nuts. Her little way of being defiant.

"Thanks. It's different from my others." Her breasts still mounded for all to see, even with all the pretty lacing and beaded jacket. Considering what he'd said about her other corset, she was surprised he bought it for her. She wondered why.

He grinned and continued to eat.

As soon as she swallowed her last bite, Jake stood and held his hand out to her. "Time, darling."

She blinked and looked around. Everyone stood, smiling.

"Time for what?"

"You'll see."

Flowers and vines hung from everywhere in the front yard. A bridal bower stood at the end of a small path with a minister, Bible in hand, waiting beneath. Two fiddlers started up with the bridal march. Oh, no. The words "here comes the bride, big, fat, and wide" came to mind. The crazy childhood verses told her how nervous all of the attention was making her. Was she ready for this?

"What about your brothers?" Angel asked Jake, trying to keep her mind from what was happening.

"They'll understand the urgency." His grimness betrayed the worry about his siblings.

"Urgency?" She wasn't so sure she understood. The will had not placed a time limit on it.

He turned his gaze to her. "Whoever shot at your

brother and burned my garage had something to do with the old men dying. My gut tells me they don't want us to unite our businesses. So we need to make sure they don't get what they want."

She had the same feeling, too.

"So will you marry me today?" The warmth in his tone and eyes sealed her doom. How could she say no? Why would she? This was a dream come true. Whatever the next few days, weeks, months, or years held for them, she would take one moment at a time. All of it would be worth it to be with him.

"Yes." Such a simple word with so much hope wrapped around it.

He nodded and they walked down the stairs from the front porch.

With each step she took, the delicious tenderness in her thighs and ass reminded her what had happened between them in his bedroom. She wanted to experience more. Soon.

Without realizing she'd done it, her fingers grasped his.

"Good girl," he teased. He squeezed her trembling hand and then released it.

She'd almost reached for him again, when Damien slipped between her and Jake and hooked his arm around hers. She scanned the decorations and number of people standing around. Her dithering allowed Jake time to get in position next to the minister. Lydia hesitantly handed Angel a large bouquet of yellow and white flowers. From the way the woman cast a despairing glance her way, she really didn't want her son marrying her.

Talk about a strange wedding, though it explained his gift of her gold corset and jacket. When had he found time to pick it out for her? She imagined the guests thought they looked to be an odd couple. What with the bride wearing thigh-high boots and a short leather skirt, and the groom laid back and sexy in his black slacks and button-down white shirt sans tie.

She admitted that she felt lighthearted and excited by it all. Yet tears trembled on her lashes as she listened to the preacher recite the vows. She wished her mother was still alive to see this. She bet her dad had been invited, and he refused to come. She hadn't seen him in the two years he'd been out of prison. Not that she wanted him there. He'd only stir up trouble. She did see a few of Mac's friends and hoped they understood why she was giving in. Well, at least from a business point of view. She sure didn't want them thinking about how great Jake was in bed, and it was part of the reason she gave in so easy. Oh, God, why did her thoughts keep going there? She was obsessed by his cock and mouth. *Stop thinking about it!*

Another step brought her within inches of him. Her brother let her go and kissed her cheek before he moved away. Goodness, she forgotten how tall he'd become the last few months.

Jake grabbed her hands as if he sensed that she wanted to go screaming into the nearby woods. Dreams didn't come true for Tallys. She, more than anyone, knew that. Sure, he rocked her world when it came to sex and all the kinkiness she loved, but marriage required more.

What was she doing?

Rings appeared, seemingly from nowhere. For Jake, she slid on his finger a plain wide, dark titanium ring, and he, in turn, placed an eternity ring of diamonds on hers. She stared at it for a long time. She'd never owned a piece of jewelry so beautiful. And shiny.

"I now pronounce you husband and wife. You may kiss the bride." The preacher raised his hands. Everyone shouted. She glanced at her brother as he jumped up and down. Then she remembered why she was there. It wasn't just for her own selfish reasons. It was to protect Damien.

When Jake wrapped her into his arms and kissed her, no prissy smack either, she wondered if she'd made a mistake. Sure his kisses melted her into her boots, but he didn't love her. He lusted for her for sure. Most likely, he would break her heart.

She wanted to grab two handfuls of sun-tipped hair and hang on. The man could kiss.

Were her emotions going up and down because she was losing her mind?

A crack resounded in the air. Probably a redneck decided to celebrate by firing his weapon in the air. The crowd quieted as if searching for the culprit. When several more shots fired off and screams followed, she knew they were in deep trouble. She found herself on the ground with Damien next to her. Tick off to one side a couple of feet away.

Hoping everyone was okay, Angel looked around and spotted Jake with the preacher and Lydia squatting near some chairs.

"Who's firing at us?" Eyes wide, Damien scooted a little closer to her.

She pulled out a small Beretta from her waistband, glad she hadn't left it in the bedroom earlier. She waited for more shots to determine the direction. Jake ran low to a man's body and leaned over to pat the fellow's back. From the way the man moved, he should be okay.

Jake sprinted toward the thicker section of the woods with two of his guards on his heels.

"Stay here with Tick and don't move until he does," she said to Damien. She was counting on the big guy's well-known self-preservation to protect her brother, too. In case, she added toward Tick's way, "If I come back and see one mark on him, I can promise you'll be seeing the emergency room fifteen minutes later. Understand?"

Tick nodded and placed an arm around Damien.

Without a second thought, she jerked off her boots, stilettos were hell to run in especially over dirt, and running on tiptoes didn't help much either. She hoped the little socks on her feet could handle all the pinecones and straw spread over the ground.

Crouched low, she darted around the house to a section parallel to the direction Jake had taken. A couple more gunshots led her to Jake and the guards. They had the man surrounded. Throwing his rifle off to the side, he surrendered and stood with hands above his head. At the same time, a movement several yards away caught her attention. Dressed in camouflage, the other man leaned to one side from behind a tree, giving away his position, and aimed in the shooter's direction, probably at Jake. Without a second thought, Angel fired. The man in camo screamed and dropped, not moving any longer.

In seconds, Jake reached her. "Who did you shoot?"

She shrugged and pointed to what looked to be a pile of green leaves. "He was about to take out your shooter or shoot you. His camo made it hard to wing him. So I may have done more damage than I planned." Her voice sounded cold and distant, but inside she shook.

With his handgun pointed down, Jake stalked over and kicked at the piles of leaves. A man's body flopped over. Jake leaned down to check for a pulse. He squinted at Angel for a second and then he motioned for one of the guards and spoke in a low tone. The guard nodded and lifted the limp body, heading away from the crowd.

Somehow she remained standing as her stomach churned. She'd cut a few men and even kicked the crap out of one in the balls, but she'd never killed anyone. The Tally name put fear in most of her opponents and protected her more than she needed to be violent.

Trying to get her mind off the dead man, she turned her attention to the one being held between two big, angry Whitfield men.

Inhaling deeply, she nodded toward the man. "What are you going to do about him?"

Jake's eyes narrowed as he glanced down. "Are you okay?"

That was when she realized she held her gun pointed their way. She became more embarrassed when she noticed how her hand trembled.

She flipped the safety on and dropped her hand to her side. "I'm fine. I just never..."

What in the world was happening to her? Not once had her life as a collector affected her as the last few minutes. Had her feelings for Jake help drag down the wall of indifference she'd built to protect herself? Was worrying about her new husband making her weak?

"Take him to the pump house. I'll be along later," Jake said to his men.

Then the trees spun as Jake picked her up and started toward the house.

Breathless, she didn't protest as her arms automatically circled his neck. Her gun rested against his shoulder. His warmth seeped into her chilled body. She pressed her cheek beneath his chin, feeling his heart beat fast against her own chest as he took the steps two at a time. Was the fast thumping due to carrying her or because they were coming closer to the bedroom? His domain.

He stretched her out in the middle of the bed, taking her gun and placing it safely inside the top drawer of the nightstand. She pushed up, and he pressed her back.

"No. Don't move." His mouth was set in a grim straight line.

"But—"

"Remember our agreement?" He looked at her from beneath his brows.

"Yes, but—" She wanted to ask so many questions, wanted him to assure her that she didn't screw up. She needed...what?

"Shh! Relax." Jake pulled off the ruined socks from her feet and then dragged down her skirt, throwing it onto the floor. "Damn."

Instead of a thong, she wore a pearl G-string that rubbed against her clitoris whenever she moved.

He spread her legs and cupped her mons. She moaned. His big hand was so warm against her.

"Damn. You better be glad I didn't know you had this on." He leaned over and ran his tongue along the string of pearls. "We would've never made it to the wedding." The heel of his palm rotated, and she bowed her back. "Hold onto the headboard."

She stretched and grasped beneath the edge above her head. As she suspected, her breasts lifted out of the corset.

Jake noticed, too, and flicked, rubbed, and twisted a nipple, bringing more pleasure than pain.

"Oh, baby, you're a man's wet dream come to life," he growled and then his mouth covered her labia, with a dip of his tongue into the sensitized folds. His finger hooked the pearls, sliding them beside her hard clit as he licked the swollen nub.

She bit her bottom lip to keep from screaming. Another

new experience for her, and Jake was an expert. In no time, she arched, pressing into his mouth and wave after wave of pleasure strummed through her body.

"Feel better?"

Limp and satisfied, she watched Jake. Her eyes only partially open. He slipped off the little jacket and then unhooked and unlaced her corset, tossing it to the side. Without hesitation, he massaged her breasts and ribs where the corset had crushed her flesh. She moaned in delight. The man knew where to touch.

"Yes. Thank you," she whispered.

He slid his hand down her legs.

"Why did you keep quiet about it being your first time?"

As soon as she tensed, he began rubbing her left foot. She collapsed when his thumb rubbed the center, making her toes curl. She'd forgotten about running over pine cones and sticks with only socks to protect her. They stung from tenderness and little punctures and scratches.

"I didn't hide anything. You wouldn't believe me if I told you that I hadn't been with anyone else. Last summer, I got tired of waiting for you and decided to get rid of it myself. Really, who would believe I'm a virgin at my age?"

"Waiting for me, huh? Why me?"

The way he said it caught her attention, and she tilted her head. She wanted to say, *Why not?* But she stopped herself and cleared her throat.

"There isn't another man in my life that ever made me feel like you do. Besides, it's a moot point now."

He stopped and stared at her for a few seconds. As if he couldn't figure out her angle.

Had he not felt the same thing she had that fateful day?

Then he began rubbing her other foot. Never in a million years would she have guessed Jake Whitfield gave great foot rubs. After a few more minutes, she felt her body float. He released his hold and stood by the bed. Still boneless, she peeked between her eyelashes and watched him. He appeared to be analyzing her. After a long pause, he turned to the nightstand drawer, taking her gun out. As soon as she heard the bedroom door close, she drifted off to sleep.

Jake's cock ached like a son of a bitch as he strode downstairs. He moved it into the crease of his hip, hoping to find a little more room in his jeans until the son of a bitch calmed down. The woman he left in his bed had looked so feminine and soft. Those tiny pink pearls on her hips and dividing her pussy had brought a powerful throbbing between his legs. She was the most sensual recent-lustful-ex-virgin he'd ever been around, willing to do anything he wanted and continuing to surprise him at every turn.

I got tired of waiting for you.

Why had she waited for him at all? So she hadn't known about her grandfather's will. In any case, hadn't she told him the will had changed only recently? It didn't make sense. Finding out the reason she'd waited would have to be for another time.

He looked down at the gun in his hand. There had been no ID on the man who fired at the wedding party, but Jake had recognized him. While the man dressed in camo Angel had inadvertently killed, there had been nothing on him, too, but neither Jake nor any of his men recognized him. One of his men had dumped the body in the Sand County swamps about ten miles from the house. While it would probably take Jake most of the night to break down the gun and throw the pieces in different areas throughout the surrounding counties, it would be worth it to protect her.

Besides, he needed a little night air to clear his mind and come up with a solution for the shooter he had locked up in the pump house.

How was he going to explain to Special Agent Alex Carleton that he was holding one of her men? Hell, for that matter, she better have a good explanation to why he'd been firing into the wedding crowd.

Chapter Sixteen

Jake watched Special Agent Alex Carleton pull her navy blue sedan in front of the pump house. The frown she wore alerted him she probably had the scenario all wrong. No surprise there. Most law enforcement officials expected the worst from the Whitfields.

"If one hair is harmed on my man's head, I'll kick your ass to the nearest federal pen, do you understand?" She swiped at her forehead with the back of her hand.

The weatherman had said on the radio the high would be in the mid-eighties and the woman had pants, shirt, and matching jacket. No wonder sweat poured off her. What was it with these crazy women and their clothes?

"Considering he was hiding in the trees with a gun drawn, and we were looking for the person shooting at us, let's say he's lucky he only has bruises. I stopped my fellows from beating the shit out of him. But next time you want to spy on me, you might want to give me a heads up."

"That would defeat the purpose, asshole." She jerked open the pump house's door and walked inside. The temperature dropped ten degrees easily. Between the sound of rushing water and the noise of the pumps, they had to yell at each other to be heard.

"Where is he?"

Jake pointed over to a corner. "He's had plenty of fluids and food. I cleaned up his wounds the best I could. You might get someone to look at the cut on his forehead."

She strode over to her man and leaned down, asking the wounded man a question Jake couldn't hear. The man nodded. Then she faced Jake. "Give me the key."

He tossed it her way. With a nod to one of his men, a guard helped with the wounded agent, and they followed Alex out to the sedan's backseat.

"What happened to the shooter?" she asked.

Jake pressed his lips together and stared at her.

"Okay. I knew better than to ask." She leaned into the sedan and cranked up the engine. She then pressed the air-conditioner controls to lower the temp for the man in the back. "Don't forget you have one week, and if you don't follow through, I'll go to Plan B. You know you won't like it."

"Keep your men off my property, and I can provide what I promised. But if you send any more, our deal's off." He hated being jerked around, and she appeared to be the type to love taking a man by the balls and squeezing. "And don't *you* forget, you have only six more hours."

Her glare said she understood what he meant. The autopsy and evidence reports were due.

"Between being ran off the road and having someone burn down part of your property, I thought you could use the help." The grin on her face revealed how much she enjoyed his frustration.

"I'm handling it. Change of management can bring out

the bad side of people. You know, testing their boundaries. So don't you worry about me."

"Testing boundaries? I hadn't heard it called that." She laughed as she slid into her car and then spun the wheels as she headed down the dirt road and off his property.

Damn, time that he checked into where his brothers had disappeared. Sen had gone into Sand County to see what he could snoop out there. Ethan had scheduled visits with a couple of informants in Birmingham, hoping for confirmation on who they suspected of setting up a hit against the old men.

Special Agent Carleton couldn't bring the reports fast enough as far as Jake was concerned. An itch between his shoulder blades told him a clue would pop up and lead to the killer. Of course, he didn't expect the killer's name to jump out waving a flag, but something would show up. Something that the investigators would never pick up on.

He did suspect his old man's cousins had a hand in it, but neither one of them had the guts or skill with a gun to kill the two old men so smoothly. They hired someone. He needed the evidence before he could kick them out of the company. Then he and his brothers would have total control of Marystown and most of Sand County.

Chances were, the only reasons the cousins hadn't made their move when he'd been in the Army and Ethan in prison was their fear of the old man. Only for the last few years had Jake and his brothers been given the authority to run a few of the businesses. That was probably the time his cousins started planning the old man's death and takeover.

Was that it? Had the cousins become worried they would be cut out? Stood to reason. That was exactly what he'd planned, once the old man handed over the reins of Whitfield Industries. Then again, it was all speculation.

Maybe Sen or Ethan had heard. He leaned against the hood of his car and pulled out his cell phone.

Calling Sen first, voicemail answered. He waited for the tone, before he said, "You, bastard. Give me a call. I need some answers and I want to know you're okay."

Then he tried Ethen. When he was sure it was about to go into voicemail, too, his brother picked up.

"Yeah?" he croaked.

"Have you found anything out about who killed the old man?"

"I'm following a lead, but, Bro, I have to say things are getting complicated. It's not just homegrown trouble. We have an infestation from hotter climes and—" His brother went quiet.

"Ethan? What are you talking about?" Somedays, Jake was tempted to choke his brothers.

The silence continued.

He looked down at the cell phone. The connection had failed.

Damn it.

He called Ethan again. The voicemail recording came on.

"Call me back when you're sober, and you better sober up quick!"

Fisting the cell phone, he barely held back the urge to throw it. He didn't have time to go out and buy a new one.

From what he could decipher of Ethan's crazy words, it appeared they had trouble coming from the outside. Rubbing his neck, he looked around. His men stood off to the side, waiting patiently for their orders.

"Let's go into town. I have a meeting I need to get to."

. . .

At the back wall of the closed restaurant, Angel stood with arms crossed, glaring at Walter Finny. Over two-hundred-twenty pounds and six-five, Mac's right-hand man had always treated her with respect, but from the sound of his four-packs-a-day voice, he struggled to hold his temper.

"You and Damien need to come and live at Mac's house. You'll be safer there. That sorry husband of yours, he almost got you killed at least twice."

She didn't correct him by saying it was three times. Some things were best kept quiet.

"I've never lived at Mac's house, and there's no reason to do so now. I'm better protected at the Whitfields'."

"Where's your husband? He should be by your side. He can't even find time to meet with us. I'm not sure about merging with Whitfields." Another soldier of Mac's piped up.

She stared down the man. He nervously looked around and stepped back. Most of the men were a little afraid of her. Many believed she was as insane as her late grand-daddy. Maybe they were right.

A deep familiar voice near the back door spoke up.

"Her husband had a little situation of his own to take care of." The crowd parted as Jake walked to the front, his angry gaze taking in the crowd of men. "But no matter, I know my wife can handle this meeting without my help. Before we start a merger of certain Whitfield and Tally properties and businesses, it stands to reason that we need to find out who killed my father and her grandfather. That same guilty person or persons obviously got wind of the old men wanting to stop the feud and merge the families. And I believe they are connected with the attempt on Damien. If you have heard anything or suspect anyone, let Angel know. Until we get this solved, all businesses remain running as they had when Mac was alive, but for one change. You'll report to Angel or me. We'll give you the details later."

Before the meeting, she and Jake had agreed to split up the Tally businesses. She would remain over the collection agency and the restaurants. Jake would handle the convenience stores and the bait shops. He worried about her handling collection, but she refused to give in. Her guess was he planned to fight that battle later. Knowing how he liked to fight dirty, the bedroom would probably be the battleground. She actually looked forward to it.

Murmuring in the back of the room rumbled to the front.

"Speak up or shut up now." Angel had to be hard and blunt with the men or they would think her weak. She craned her neck to see if she could guess who still grumbled.

"When did we start taking orders from a Whitfield?" Bill Turner, the manager of the restaurant they met in, looked around for support. Several men nodded but remained quiet.

Angel placed a hand on Jake's arm to stop him from answering. When he looked into her eyes, he stepped back and nodded toward her. Her gaze went soft for a couple of seconds. She liked knowing he was a man of his word.

Squaring her shoulders, she turned toward the men.

"Since yesterday, when I married Jake Whitfield," she answered the man's question. "Mac's will said that he wanted us to merge with the Whitfields, and our marriage sealed the deal. He planned for Damien to take over one day, but he's too young now." She wanted to add she would make sure Damien *never* had anything to do with the illegal aspects of the organization. He was too good to put up with the hell. "The businesses need a strong arm, someone with experience, and Mac knew Jake had what's needed. I'm willing to do anything to keep M. T. Companies working smoothly. What about you? If you want to keep your position in the company, you'll continue to follow orders." She fought the urge to look toward Jake, but she gave in by saying, "Is there anything you want to add, Jake?" Unable to resist any longer, she glanced his way.

His smirk didn't bother her at all. For some reason, she had a feeling he was proud of her, probably because she said exactly what they had agreed on. Whatever She ignored the affection swelling in her chest. Sex and business. That's all they had between them.

The Tally holdings were in his hands now. She'd been Mac's collector, not his heir apparent. Mac had made that clear to her many times. No matter how much he taught her, she would never be good enough. She didn't have the right equipment between her legs. She actually didn't care. Releasing a sigh, she looked down at her feet. So what if Jake only needed to walk into the room to earn their respect.

"She's right. But remember those who normally reported to Mac will report to me now." The tone Jake used made clear that he expected no arguments. "Angel will continue to work the areas she held for Mac. Overall, she and I will be partners. When Damien turns eighteen, he'll start his training to take over at twenty-five just as Mac had intended."

What the hell? She hadn't agreed to anything like he described. Damien would be away at college at eighteen. Sure as hell not in Marystown. Jake knew that. Her eyes narrowed as she watched him. What was he up to? Was he planning to double-cross her? She hated being so unsure of him. He talked about her loyalty, but she was uncertain about his to her.

An hour later, they walked out to their respective cars. Two of Jake's men hung back, giving them privacy. She caught his elbow.

"What was that all about when it comes to Damien starting training?" The desire to believe what he'd been telling her all along ate at her.

He shook out a cigarette, narrowing his eyes at her as he lit it and inhaled.

"Are you going to do this every time I open my mouth?" His even tone assured her he wasn't angry, mildly curious instead.

"I can't risk misinterpreting anything you say. If I wait too long, it will be too late. You'll have it in your mind it's okay."

"Fine." He released a long stream of smoke. "You expect Damien to go to college, right?"

"Yes, sir," she said with a sarcastic tone.

When he stepped into her personal space, her breath caught. Instead of feeling threatened by his size and height, she thought of how he controlled her body in bed, brought out the feminine side she often forgot she possessed. Her nipples peaked, and she tried taking in her next breath without groaning. Being so near him, only carnal thoughts raced through her mind.

"I like that," he whispered in her ear.

"What?" Her voice sounded airy.

"You calling me sir."

"Oh." She released a shaky breath.

He leaned down and pressed his nose to her neck and inhaled. Then he slowly dragged his tongue over her rapidly beating pulse.

"Please," she whispered.

"Please what, baby?"

The sound of gravel under car tires snapped her out of his spell. She stepped back, expecting a smirk on his face. Forehead wrinkled, he stared at her as if he'd never seen her before. Then he looked down at his cigarette and flicked off the long ash.

"Damien will go to college." She dared him to say otherwise.

"Angel, I see no reason to change that. Makes sense that he learns all the ins and outs of being a legal business owner. Wouldn't you agree?"

"Yes." She turned her head, watching him out of the corner of her eyes in confusion. Where was he going with this?

"For the next eight years, we'll be working, strengthening our businesses. We'll see if we can weed out those who refuse to turn a new leaf. By the time he graduates college, everything should be sorted out."

"What are you planning to do? You know, when it's all over?"

"I don't know. I have money in several off-shore accounts. Probably buy an island and live out my days there."

"I can't see you lying around."

His gaze slid down her body and back up. "You'll be surprised what I'll do."

A delicious shiver trickled down her body. She wanted him badly.

"What about your brothers? One of them may want to run the Whitfield Industries."

"There's a good possibility Sen will stay." He tilted his head. "I don't plan to literally and legally merge the companies. Sen can run what's left of Whitfield Industries and Damien head the legal aspects of Tally Holdings."

"What about Ethan?"

"He hates anything to do with the old man, including the businesses. The only reason he stuck around and helped was for me and Sen. We stick together until everyone is okay. Anyway, he has a cousin from his mom's side who's been asking him to join his business in Nashville. I expect he'd take him up on the offer in the next year or so, if not sooner."

"What will I do?" Her tone soft, she felt a little unsure of what her future held. With the way Mac had changed her, and the way she'd lived her life the last few years, she wasn't fit for an office job.

Was he planning to go off to his private island and leave her behind? Probably run around on the beach nude with a bevy of beautiful native girls? What would become of her? She turned her head, not wanting him to see the fear in her eyes. She was always afraid of becoming the old cat lady of Marystown. As she didn't own a cat, or any pet for that matter, she knew she was being silly.

She wanted him to want her without her having to beg. She could beat off the women, but it wouldn't solve her problem. He had to need her for her.

A broad hand cupped her cheek.

"Baby, you'll go with me. You're mine now. Fuck, I even married you." His gruff voice brought her gaze up to his. "Besides, you're damn good at sucking my cock, and I haven't tried out that ass yet." She could tell he had spoken the crass words in an attempt to lighten the mood.

Her smile refused to stay hidden. Waves of electricity shot straight to her pussy. The man had a filthy mouth. She loved it.

He kissed the tip of her nose.

"You want to go with me?" he asked with a smirky, crooked grin on his face.

Afraid she would start crying—what was it about this man that made her so emotional?—she merely nodded. Could he see all the hope and desire in her eyes? Did he understand what she was unable to express?

She loved him with all her being. But she didn't want to be a burden. She'd been one to her family until Mac had taken her under his wing. She never wanted to depend on anyone else to take care of her, especially the only man she'd ever loved.

When the time came, if he still wanted her, she would go without any regrets and be whatever he wanted.

If he didn't, well, she could do many things. Oh, hell. Maybe she'd buy a kitten. But nothing would make her happier than being with Jake.

She rather buy handcuffs and try them out on Jake. A good way to make sure he didn't change his mind and leave her behind.

Chapter Seventeen

J ake leaned over and eyed the cryptic text from Sen.

For the last two days, he'd been waiting for his brothers to get their act together and return home. Ethan had called yesterday to say he and Karma were tracking down information in Nashville. They had been followed by Rat Boy, but they were able to lose him and would be in touch when they could. Why in the hell was the manager of Scene 69 involved with their personal business? And what in the hell was Rat Boy up to?

As Jake and his brothers' phones had tracking devices, he'd checked on Ethan a couple of hours earlier. The blue dot had slowly moved along Broadway in Nashville. The son of a bitch probably had stopped in Tootsie's and gotten drunk instead of doing his job.

Now he had a text from Sen with only a few words: wound, hiding, cabin, later. His cell phone was completely turned off or destroyed. No way to track. Ethan was right. They needed to place a tracking chip on their bodies.

What the hell? Was Sen somewhere bleeding to death and a year from now he would find his body? The northern area of Alabama had miles upon miles of rivers with rental cabins along the shore.

"Tick!" Jake stared at his ceiling.

"Yeah, boss?"

"Get six of the boys together out front in twenty minutes."

He wanted to go with them, but Luc had texted an hour before, saying he had info on the burnt body. Plus by nightfall, Special Agent Carleton would drop off all of the evidence the FBI had on the Marystown murders, as they referred to them now. She'd pleaded for another forty-eight hours to provide the information she owed him. He had to say, he'd taken pleasure in her begging. It suited his needs, anyway. There was so much going on, he hadn't felt like dealing with her.

So there he was, setting up a search party despite the possibility of angering his middle brother. Who knew what they would interrupt? If Sen hadn't been wounded, he wouldn't worry so much. Sending the men was merely a precaution. Otherwise, no matter who was coming by the house, he'd be on the road searching for his brother.

"What are you hollering about?" Angel glided in.

He loved watching her move. Those long legs encased in leather. She moved as if she was on the prowl, so cool and dangerous. To think of it, he'd never seen her break a sweat. Well, except during sex.

Jake stretched out a knee and reached down to adjust his hardening dick. The woman loved to play games in the bedroom. Experimenting never flustered her. Her sexuality had been bottled up for a long time. She loved to read the dirtiest books he'd ever come across and possessed the kinkiest collection of porn videos. Fucking-A, he benefited.

"Sen texted that he's hurt and then his phone went black. The tracking isn't working. Cell is dead."

Her eyebrows had lifted when he said tracking.

"Do you have something on me?" Her eyes narrowed.

Yeah. He liked it when she went all badass on him. No threat there. He was a bigger badass, and she knew who the master was in their relationship.

"Yes." He refused to say more. Let her guess where.

She pulled out her cell phone from her backpack. A simple flip, she thumbed off the back protective shell. On the other side was a small chip. She shot a furious look his way.

"I would suggest you leave it there. There's one on mine. I've already downloaded the app on your phone. When we're alone tonight, I'll show you how it works. Your brother has a tracker on his phone, too."

Her wrinkled forehead smoothed out. Damn, she was too easy. Maybe because she thinks the same way he did. It was a little frightening how they could read each other's thoughts. Marriage shouldn't be so effortless. If not for the murders and outside forces trying move in on the businesses, life would be pretty good.

Damn. Was he already pussy-whipped?

Nah. Never. But he enjoyed that beautiful pussy. And he loved teasing her with his cock.

Though he didn't have the time, he couldn't resist pushing away from his desk and scooting down in his chair a little and crossing one ankle over his knee.

Her gaze zeroed on the bulge beneath his zipper and then she looked away. In seconds, she stared again. She was so easy.

"In a few minutes, I'm going to brief the men on Sen's disappearance. I want you to be there with me. You okay with that?" Hell, he loved it when she stared at his crotch no matter how much she fought it.

The silence stretched out a few seconds. His dick lengthened, nudging toward his belt. She blinked, frowned, and looked up.

No way could he hold back a grin.

"See something more interesting?"

She opened her mouth and then as if reconsidering the consequences, she snapped it shut. Instead of looking repentant, she sashayed around the desk.

"Angel?" He held his breath as she kneeled and lightly pushed at his foot until both were flat on the floor. His knees parted as she moved between them and unbuckled his belt. The soft clicking of the zipper filled the room.

"Angel?" he asked again. He had no plans to stop her, but wanted to know what she was thinking.

"I figured if you're going to flaunt it, I'll bring it out to play." She shoved his flap to the side and clasped his dick.

Then her hot mouth swallowed him.

"For fuck sakes!" He arched his back and pumped. "You make the sexiest sounds when you're sucking on me." The humming and slurping was enough to drive him over the edge. He fisted her hair and held her as he shot down her throat.

"That's it. You're such a good girl." He released her and smoothed her hair.

She fell back, panting and grinning big. "And you're a good boy. Ten-second wonder." Her tongue swiped at her bottom lip as if she wanted to savor his taste.

He groaned. "Girl, you're going to be the death of me. I show you tonight how long I can last and see how you like it."

As he tucked his dick into his pants and zipped up, he looked her over.

"Come here," he ordered and patted his thigh.

"This isn't the bedroom." Her cheeks reddened.

He laughed. "I want you to sit on my lap. Don't be such a pussy."

"Considering how much you love my pussy, I think that's a good thing."

"Keep that smart mouth going, and I'll haul you off upstairs and tear up your butt good," he said, biting the side of his mouth to keep from chuckling. He loved her sass.

The flash of hunger in her eyes matched his desire to see her ass naked and red.

With that natural grace of hers, she rose to her feet and gingerly sat on his lap. His gaze almost even with hers reminded him of how tall she was for a woman.

He checked out her clothes. The lightweight T-shirt she wore beneath a thin leather jacket, instead of a forbidden-in-public corset, revealed her stiff nipples, even through her bra. She probably enjoyed sucking him off almost as much as he did having her do it.

"Take off your jacket and shirt," he ordered. His voice husky with anticipation.

"Yes, sir." Her pretty green eyes glittered. Yeah, she loved it when he took over. She immediately did what he said.

"Now don't move," he warned.

She held herself still. Fuck, she was made for him.

He unclipped her plain white bra and slipped it down her arms and away. He unsnapped her pants and pushed the zipper down. His mouth covered one perky nipple as his hand dove between her legs, thrusting a finger into her heat. She gasped from the duo sensations.

"Yes, sir!"

He chuckled.

Moisture lubricated his path up to her clit. A hard and needy elongated pebble. Maybe she'd trained it to sit up and take notice after all of the practice she gave it over the years. As he drew circles around the bundle of nerves, he sucked her tit, nipping and tugging after each strong pull. She bowed her body and squealed between gritted teeth.

Her sweet pussy undulated, and this time she didn't hold back.

"Jake, oh, Jaaake!" Her hips lifted, pushing her pelvis to his hand.

He released her breast and gave her nipple one last lick.

"I'm glad you understand I'm the only one who can get you off like that. You're mine and no one else's. Got me?"

Those soft green eyes hidden beneath heavy eyelids stared at him with satisfaction as she nodded. Her body was limp in his hold. He savored having her so sweet and giving in his arms. He cradled her to his chest and kissed her temple.

Jake shuffled through the file Quinn had just handed him. Ignoring the older man for a few seconds, he scanned the sheets inside.

"So two of his fingers were missing?" Jake's gut turned with the thought of the torture Matt had endured.

"Yeah. They looked to be a clean cut. Whoever did it knew what they were doing," Quinn said as he paced in front of Jake's desk.

"And you're sure it's Matt?"

"Yep. Dr. Kelly had been his family's dentist for years. He confirmed the dental records matched the body's."

Quinn continued to walk back and forth, every few steps he looked over at Jake as if he wanted to ask a question.

"What's got you so antsy?" Jake looked up from the paper in frustration. The man had to know he wouldn't let it out that Quinn had leaked the autopsy report.

"Have you seen Tessa lately?"

"Your daughter?"

Quinn gave a clipped nod.

"I haven't seen her since Christmas when I came by and left your bonus." Nothing was done for a Whitfield without a price. "Why? What's wrong?"

"She left a note a couple days ago saying she patched up your brother, and he needed her help again." Quinn stopped and glared. "I called her several times without an answer and checked her home. No one's there. I told you to keep him away from her."

Quinn never cared for Sen. Jake wasn't sure the why of it, but tried to steer his brother clear of the funeral director and his daughter.

"He disappeared a few days ago, and yesterday I received a message from him saying he'd been wounded. For the last year, he's stayed away from her, but you've got to know if he's hurt, he'd go by your place to get patched up. Listen. Do you think your daughter was there when he showed up? Did she mention where he was going?"

"That's just it. I haven't heard from her since she left the note. If your brother has done anything to her, I'll have him thrown in jail for statutory rape."

"Quinn, even I know that Tessa is old enough to give consent. So that's not an option."

The older man smoothed thin strands of hair over his balding pate.

"Right. Damn, it feels like she just turned fifteen last year."

He wasn't surprised by the man not knowing his own daughter's age. Hell, Dick Whitfield never remembered his sons' birthdates and often got their names mixed up.

"Hey, you were bragging a couple years ago that she'd changed from nursing to mortuary science. So she has to be what, twenty-two?"

"She'll be twenty-one next month. She's doing great in her classes, and she almost finished with the apprenticeship. My assistant embalmer agrees with me, that she's doing great. Of course, the apple doesn't fall far from the tree. How did the time go by so fast?" The bewildered, wild-eyed look on Quinn's face cooled Jake's temper. He didn't need an irate father getting in the middle of whatever was going on with his brother.

"If she's with Sen, I promise she's safe. He needed some medical care. She's helping him. You taught her well."

"Right. You're right. You know I don't really have anything against the boy. I just wanted more for her. Away from Marysville." Quinn headed toward the door. "Let me know if you hear anything."

Twenty-nine was nowhere near a boy, but Quinn believed anyone under forty to be a kid. And wanted more? Yeah. Only those after money believed a Whitfield was a worthy catch.

"Everything will be fine. I've got my men out searching for Sen now. I'll tell them to be on the lookout for Tessa, too."

"That will be good. Thanks," Quinn said before closing the door on his way out.

No more than five minutes passed before he received a call from the gate of Special Agent Carleton's arrival. He didn't worry what his men thought about his receiving an FBI agent. Considering how his father had many government officials on his payroll, he recently being dropping hints that the agent was on his.

A knock on the door brought him around his desk, waiting for her entrance. Not as a sign of respect; the woman didn't invoke those feelings. He barely tolerated her. But he knew how to play the game. At the moment, he needed her to believe she had an upper hand.

"Come in."

Tick opened the door and stood to the side. Alex strolled by him. Dressed in her usual navy blue jacket and pants with white shirt, she looked a little ruffled. Probably frustrated at the beefed-up security.

She could be annoyed all she wanted. Without a briefcase or papers in hand, his anger rose with every second that passed.

"Where's the evidence?" he asked as soon as Tick walked out and closed the door.

"Hello to you, too. Is that any way to treat a partner?"

"We ain't fucking partners. You're the devil I have to deal with until I accomplish my goals." He closed his mouth without spilling his end game.

Instead of making her mad, she tilted up one corner of her lips.

"The devil you know, heh?" As she did in the hotel room, she looked around, taking in the expensive art and heavy oak pieces left over from the old man's taste. "I wouldn't have pegged you as the type to do the classics in decorating your office." Without waiting for a comment, she added, "I figured you would be all glass and chrome with maybe a few whips on the wall."

That last stroked his interest, and he hoped without

showing any expression on his face. Who had been talking to her? Someone not too close as they had the wrong brother. Jake preferred the hands-on approach.

"Why do you not have the information you promised me?"

"Where's your lovely new wife? I heard she throws a mean knife."

What the fuck? Someone was blabbing big time. Then it came to him and made sense. Teddy Bear or Rat Boy. What was she doing talking with them?

"You're wasting my time. You have the documents I wanted or not?"

She narrowed her eyes. Her shoulders slumped, but her jaw remained rigid. He won the battle of wills this time. Her attempt to infuriate him failed.

"Okay, okay." She slung the large purse off her shoulder and drew out a file. It wasn't thick. He couldn't wait to get his hands on it. It wouldn't take much paper to type a name or two. That was all he needed. Who was responsible for his old man's death?

Chapter Eighteen

In front of a Sand City restaurant, staring blindly out of the driver's side window of Mac's old truck, Angel smiled. Her index finger rubbed her wedding band.

The last few mornings, waking in bed with Jake was nothing but a fantasy come true. Earlier, when she walked out of the *en suite* bathroom, the light behind her spotlighted the man sprawled over the mattress. Her heart almost stopped from the decadent view. The top sheet draped off the side revealed a muscular back, lean hips with taut buttocks perfect for squeezing. Powerful thighs any ball player would be proud of topped off long calves and feet. He groaned, and her gaze shot up. Her face warmed at the thought of being caught staring, but one eye partially covered by thick, blond-tipped strands remained closed. His hair stuck out in the way only men looked sexy. Brawny arms half hidden beneath the pillow he hugged reminded her of how he held her at night. Tight and shielded. The bristles on his jaw highlighted the overall impact of a dangerous man resting.

Why wasn't drool drying at the corner of his mouth? It

wasn't right. Was there nothing the man did that didn't turn her on?

No. Even watching him sleep made her release a deep sigh. She felt like a lovesick idiot.

A car door slammed nearby, jerking her out of the trance. She blinked to clear her mind of lustful thoughts about her husband.

She sighed again. Husband? Who would've thought?

In an attempt to salvage part of the day, she replayed her conversation with Walter, her second-in-command, during breakfast. He'd called to tell her one of Mac's restaurant managers had been skimming off the blackjack game in the back room. If she allowed one person to skim, others would quickly follow. She had a love/hate attitude about this part of her job. She hated hurting people. She loved punishing those who deserved it.

The county seat of Sand City had only one bar, six restaurants, and twelve churches. Southerns loved to eat and pray. The Catfish Fry, a family owned eatery, was managed by the grandson of the original owner. Bud Vinnie the third, called Trey to keep confusion down, was a self-involved little snit.

She pushed open the glass door and stepped inside. Her outfit for the day was her usual ankle-length leather coat and four-inch heeled, multi-buckle motorcycle boots, pushing her height to over six feet. Out of respect for Jake's wishes, she wore a red T-shirt with her black jeans, instead of a corset. She'd even reduced the amount of pale makeup, though she continued with the smoky eyes and black lipstick. She had an image to uphold. People wouldn't mess with someone if they looked different from the norm.

The stench of burnt oil and fish turned her stomach. Maybe she should have told Jake about the trouble with

Trey. Then again, she'd been handling situations similar to this on her own for a while.

"Hey there, doll!"

At five-foot-eight with rusty-brown hair slicked back from his face, he acted and sounded more like a fifty-year-old man than his thirty-plus years.

Angel narrowed her eyes when he gave her a once-over. She wanted this trip concluded as quickly as possible. So she ignored his ogle and nodded for him to follow her as she walked toward the kitchen. The game was always set up in a large storeroom at the back corner. She stopped outside the door and lifted her chin to the man near the door. The guard was Walter's cousin and could easily pass as a brother in size and temperament.

She turned her back to the loyal Tally man and crossed her arms, staring down at Trey. His usual smirk irritated her, but she was used to it. The man had an ego the size of Walter's cousin.

Not wanting to put up with any more of Trey's leers, she got to the point.

"I've been informed your earnings are down." A person never talked straight about anything illegal in a public setting. She regarded any place not her home—actually Jake's—or her office to be public. Why take a chance of someone overhearing and feeding information to the police?

Trey understood what she meant.

He pulled his head back. "Are you accusing me of something?"

She watched him for a few minutes. She knew he was lying. He knew she was aware of it, but she wanted him to stew for a little bit. Her gaze didn't waver.

His squinty eyes darted away and he cleared his throat.

"With the death of your grandfather, may his soul rest

in peace, a lot of people were afraid that the Whitfields would take over the games." He glanced down at the row of diamonds on her hand. "It looks as if someone did."

She stepped closer while she eased a knife from her coat pocket.

"You have another slow night, and I'll have to introduce you to my friend, butterfly," she warned.

Trey proved how stupid he was when one corner of his mouth lifted in a smirk.

"My name isn't Trey just because I'm the third in line of owning this dump. I do relish threesomes. I've always wanted to climb the luscious tree of Angel Tally," he said as he reached up to touch her hair, "and you're more than welcome to bring your little friend. Does she like black leather, too?"

In a flash, she grabbed the front of the man's shirt and slammed him into the wall. A clicking sound warned of danger before the cold steel of her butterfly knife touched his throat. Walter had alerted her about Trey needing visuals to make a lasting impression. Merely talking to him wouldn't do at all.

"So you want my little friend to kiss your neck. I need to warn you that she's like a vampire and loves blood. Oops. See. She's thirsty for a taste." Blood trickled down to his collarbone and soaked into his shirt. "Listen to me carefully. No more skimming unless it's the fry oil, understand?"

His Adam's apple bobbed. More blood seeped from the thin line.

"Yes," he whispered, trying not to move.

"Good." She lifted her knife and stepped back. "I knew we'd understand each other, and I didn't need to talk with your dad." After wiping the blood from the blade onto his shirt, she flashed the knife in his face as she clicked it closed with a twist of her wrist.

All the color leached out of his face. Trey didn't want his dad involved. Bud Junior was less of a pleasant man than his son.

"Yeah, yeah. Totally a misunderstanding on my part." He said each word as if he couldn't catch his breath.

The numbness she always experienced while working started to fade away. A queasy feeling jumbled her thoughts. She reached out to the counter to regain her balance. Her hand landed on a towel. To cover the weakness, she grabbed up the cloth and tossed it to Trey.

Then she walked out.

"Hey, Angel."

She closed the car door behind her and turned to smile at her brother. Damien trotted over and gave her a bear hug. When would she get used to seeing him so tall? He not only looked at her eye-to-eye, but may be an inch taller. As Mac and their dad had been over six feet tall, she expected he wasn't finished growing.

"Had fun?" She swiped at the green and blue paint smeared on one ear lobe and several strands of his hair.

"Hell, yeah."

"Damien," she warned.

"Sorry, sorry. Tick and I took some paint guns out onto this massive field—you have to see it. It's part of their property. There are bales of hay and wood cutouts set up in different places. They even have a couple buildings. Tick said they use the area to practice shooting, and the rest of the time playing with paintball guns. It was so awesome! I won. Tick said I was a natural. That I have a great eye. He promised to show me how to fire a real gun."

She disliked the last idea. Instead of arguing with her brother, she decided to wait and speak with Tick.

"Jimmie Sue said she'll take you to buy some clothes for this summer and a couple things for school this afternoon," she said. All of their clothes and a few personal items had been moved to the Whitfield's house some days ago.

"Can't Tick take me?"

"Do you really want Tick helping you pick out your clothes?" The man wore a tie with everything, including plaid shirts. It was crazy.

"I guess not. But I wanted to check out the arcade at the mall, and I thought—"

She held up her hand, shaking her head. "You know that Tick isn't your play buddy? He's one of Jake's guards."

"Yeah, I know, but he's a friend, too. We have a lot in common."

"How about calling one or two of your friends from school and see if they want to play video games or do paintball later?"

Her brother squinted at her. "You hate Tick."

The sadness on his face almost had her giving in. He was really such a good kid. "You know that's not true. You need to play with kids your age. Someone who doesn't carry a gun."

"You carry a gun."

"Not all the time, but we're not talking about me." She felt as if she was about to lose the argument if she didn't think of something fast. So she suggested a couple of names and finally Damien agreed.

They walked into the kitchen laughing as Damien recounted how he shot Tick so many times on his butt, he looked to have a multi-colored target painted on it. When Angel saw who sat in the room with Jimmie Sue, she hesitated.

"You got here just in time, Damien. I've saved you a few of my homemade chocolate chip cookies." Jimmie Sue uncovered a plate and revealed a half dozen. "Before you say anything, Angel, that boy is about to have a growth spurt. He's eating like a bear before hibernation. So it shouldn't ruin his supper."

Angel suspected Jimmie Sue loved mothering them. The housekeeper was so kind and considerate, going out of her way to prepare vegan meals for Angel and keeping up with a teenager. In an effort to show her appreciation, Angel let her have free rein in feeding her brother. Most of the time. His sweet tooth often got out of hand. Really, he needed fruits more than refined sugars.

"A growing boy needs a well-balanced meal and that includes meat." Lydia sat straight at the table and eyed Angel as if she'd rolled in the mud. "You'll understand when you have your own children."

Angel gritted her teeth. Though the woman had given birth to Jake, Angel had paid attention to the few childhood stories he'd shared. His mom played no part in how Jake was brought up. Of course, it wasn't Lydia's fault Dick Whitfield had been an asshole and restricted her custody, but Angel felt if it had been her kid, she would've found a way to be involved big time.

"I've left it up to Damien to decide if he wants to be vegan or not. Jimmie Sue does a good job making sure he has a well-balanced diet." In no way would it pay to attack the woman. Jake was very protective of his mom. She admired him for it, and she'd rather not test whose side he would align with. Coming up with the short stick was a common enough occurrence in Angel's past that she didn't expect it to be any different now.

Lydia looked up and down the length of Angel. "While Jimmie Sue takes Damien shopping, I'll take you to some of my shops. Time for you to dress as a Whitfield."

Again, Angel gritted her teeth, certain the back ones would crack at any minute. Considering old man Whitfield never married Lydia, she couldn't be the example to follow *to dress as a Whitfield.*

"Thank you, Lydia, but I—"

"We have business to attend this weekend, Mom. You'll have to plan it another time." Jake walked in from the hallway and leaned down and hugged his mom before going over to Jimmie Sue to fold her into his arms and squeeze. "We'll be back Sunday afternoon."

Darting an appreciative look his way, Angel blushed with the memory of how Jake looked asleep and naked. Funny that the thought of their having sex didn't embarrass her. Why should it? The last three nights, he'd been late coming home, even later than her. Too many people demanding their attention. He'd woken her up and tenderly stroked to a fever pitch and made love to her before they dropped off from exhaustion.

With all the sex, she hadn't fully recovered from the soreness between her legs. She dipped her head so no one would see her grin. For all she cared, he could fuck her raw if he wanted. She craved his touch that badly.

Oh, she wanted to bury her red face into her hands. How could she be such a wimp and pushover?

One thing she'd learned from Mac was to enjoy every second with the one who made you happy. In the last year, he'd become rather nostalgic and even talked on occasion about his wife, her grandmother. From the way he spoke about her, he'd loved her deeply. Once, he'd admitted he should've been a better husband. Her grandmother had hated the feud between the two families. Maybe that was why he'd conspired with Dick Whitfield and wrote their wills the way they had.

"Angel?" Jake asked, breaking into her thoughts. He lifted his chin toward the kitchen's open back door.

This afternoon he dressed in gray slacks and a button-down shirt with the long sleeves rolled up to his forearms. His hair, brushed back from his face, glistened from a recent shower. She wanted to press her face to his neck as the scent of clean man drifted over her senses. The man easily sent her heart racing. Why couldn't she be as cool and put together as he did?

"Sure." She inhaled, pulling herself together. "You behave," she said to her brother and leaned over to hug him. He squeezed her back. She loved how Damien never pushed her away in mortification as so many other teenagers did their siblings or parents. She was so grateful she had someone to love her back. She briefly glanced toward Jake. He watched with one eyebrow lifted.

"I always do." Damien waved as he stared at his new mobile phone. She shook her head, smiling in fondness. In her brother's case, she probably rated second or third in his heart, behind his phone and Jake's gaming system.

She hoped this phone wouldn't drop calls like the cheap one she'd brought him. Lydia had given it to Damien, and her brother had promptly thanked her for the unexpected gift. Her heart melted with the thought. Mischievous with a bit of a temper he needed to learn to control, overall he was a good boy with pretty decent manners.

Angel smiled at Jimmie Sue. "Make him put it up while you're shopping. If you don't, I have a feeling you'll be talking to the top of his head most of the afternoon." Angel would set some ground rules soon.

"Don't worry. We'll be fine." The housekeeper gave Damien a tender look.

Her brother never had so many women doting on him. She wasn't sure if it was a good thing or not.

She picked up her coat and started to ease by her patient husband.

"Leave that here. You don't need it." He grabbed her elbow for a second.

Looking at the old leather coat, she hesitated.

"Baby, relax and be yourself for the weekend," Jake said in a whisper as he brushed her hair to the side, gazing deeply into her eyes.

The coat was part of her persona. The badass goth girl determined to show the world she wasn't afraid of anyone. She could tell by his tender look, he wanted her to trust him. Whatever he planned probably wouldn't require her to bring her bitchy collector-self. She hooked it on the peg near the back door. He was right. Lifting her backpack from the wooden chair's finial, she discreetly moved her small Beretta from her coat to a side pocket and zipped it up. She nodded to her coat. "I'll put it up when I get back."

She didn't want to cause any extra work for Jimmie Sue than she and Damien did already.

"No. No. It's no problem for me to drop it off in Jake's room. I mean, your room. Heck, you know what I mean." Jimmie Sue laughed, shaking her head. "Things are changing so fast around here my poor brain can't keep up."

"Okay. Thanks." Angel nodded at Jimmie Sue. The housekeeper slid another cookie over to Damien.

The corner of her lips lifted slightly. Nearly every time she looked at the housekeeper happiness filled her, and she smiled no matter how often she fought it. Lately, she'd wondered what her life would've been like if Jimmie Sue had been her mother. Her chest tightened. Nothing could be changed. It was what it was.

Angel headed toward the open door and dipped her head toward Lydia. "Good day."

The woman narrowed her eyes at Angel but didn't say a word in return.

What had Angel expected? The woman had issues. Just as long as she didn't mistreat Damien, Angel could handle her. Otherwise, there would be an in-your-face discussion at the Whitfield house.

Chapter Nineteen

J ake turned the SUV off the main highway they'd been traveling down for the last ten minutes. He cut his eyes over to Angel. She'd been quiet since he started the vehicle.

"You okay over there?" Why had he asked her that?

Normally, he preferred the quiet. Sure, her husky voice warmed his blood. Though he would never tell her, he did respect her opinion. She had a knack for reading people and the situation, like Special Agent Alex Carleton. Of course, it hadn't taken much to figure out the agent was a crazy bitch.

"You haven't told me where we're going." Angel fingered the backpack on her lap as if she was nervous about something.

"In a minute. First, let's talk about your visit to Trey Vinnie. I heard you went to take care of a problem and you went alone." He felt her gaze on his face as he continued to watch the road.

"Yeah. He'd been skimming the games." She sighed and leaned her head back.

"He's a mean son of a bitch. Not many people dare to reprimand him."

"Maybe, but this is part of my job."

"Even Sen knows with certain people he should bring a backup. A couple of his people have a reputation for testing the boundaries. Instead of taking a chance they would use the opportunity to stab him in the back, he takes someone to guard his it." Jake had to make her realize that she was no longer alone. "I believe a couple days ago I asked you to start taking one of the men with you."

"I don't need a babysitter."

"Babysitter. No, but backup, in case the shit hits the fan." His jaw popped from frustration. "Angel, it's a simple request, one I shouldn't have to repeat."

"Fine." Her tone said she really wasn't.

"You and I will discuss it more in depth when we reach the cabin."

"You just want an excuse to beat my ass again."

The heat in the vehicle shot up. He sensed her anger, but it was mixed with hunger for his firm, hot touch.

"No." He flashed a grin her way. "Do I really need an excuse?"

Her beautiful green eyes lit up with anticipation. That was his girl. She loved their bedroom fun as much as he did. The discipline merely spiced up their relationship.

After a few minutes, he glanced her way again.

She looked relaxed in the plain top and black pants. No leather coat. He couldn't help but feel satisfied with how she hadn't argued with him about the damn coat. He would find a way to hide or throw away the thing. He liked how every day she dressed more like an average young woman. Not that he thought of her as anything but extraordinary. He suspected Jimmie Sue and his mom had a lot to do with it. He'd noticed how Angel used the goth crap as some type of shield. He didn't want her to be that way. If she wanted to wear it because it's her style, fine. But not to hide who she was. Her granddaddy suppressing her sexuality hadn't been good for her. Every person needed to be desired, wanted. What he knew of Mac, the man probably kept a firm thumb on Angel, and in turn, his grandson. She rebelled by changing her name and dressing like a vampire.

Remembering her earlier question, he said, "The trip is twofold. I have some of the men looking through the cabins around Smith Lake for Sen. I wanted to check in with them personally. Though most have been loyal to me and the old man for years, I can be missing something. Seeing what I want to see." He looked her way for a few seconds. Her gaze still remained on her backpack, but her hands rested on top, unmoving. She was listening to every single word. "It's a beautiful day and I thought you'd enjoy going with me and being, you know, my second set of eyes."

She lifted her head, nodding. "Oh, I see."

Unable to hold it back, maybe he was drunk on sunshine, he chuckled.

"What's so funny?" She tilted her head, staring at him.

"Your answer."

Her face went blank and then lightened up. She laughed, too. "I guess it's a good thing I see, since you want me to be your second set."

"Yeah." It was a good feeling to have a woman with a sense of humor. Knowing they would be spending a lot of time together was sounding better every day. He chuckled again.

Sure, he worried about Sen, but he kept reminding himself of how much sense his brother had, and Sen knew how to handle any situation. He was probably holed up somewhere. Damn. He hoped to hell it wasn't with Tessa.

Jake shook his head. Whatever happened between Sen and Tessa, his brother could handle Quinn.

"That was only one part? You said two, or did I miss something?"

He lightly hit the brakes and turned onto a small paved road. In between the trees, the sparkling water gave away how close they were to their first destination.

"Nah. You're right. I thought after we took care of business, we'd stay at one of the cabins I keep on reserve."

When she slanted him a knowing look, he smiled big.

"No. The cabin was used to decompress after the old man rode our asses—" He stopped his explanation on seeing her head snap back and horror widen her eyes. Holding up one hand, he chuckled and then tried to regain control, to sound serious. "Don't worry. I was referring to the old man chewing us out for doing or not doing something. Really, woman, you need to quit watching porn." He was relieved when they finally reached the lodge's parking lot. His howls of laughter caused his sides to ache. He couldn't remember the last time he'd felt so carefree.

Hell, looking for Sen was merely an excuse. If anyone could take care of himself in the wilderness, it was his middle brother. Even as a kid he'd proven that. Jake guessed he needed some time away from all of the crap in Marystown.

"Like you don't watch them with me. Are you high on something?" Her concern brightened his day even more.

"No. I'm just more tired than I thought. It felt good to laugh. Let's go and see what the guys have found and then we'll head up to the cabin. Some of the men are staying here, and I need to pick up the key at the front desk." He parked the car in front and stepped out. Reaching behind him, he checked on the holster at the small of his back. Frightening the staff wouldn't be the way to go. His Glock was secure.

Checking in took a little longer than he'd hoped. While they waited, he made sure Angel met each of the men. After their impromptu meeting, the men dispersed, some headed out, starting their search, a few would hang around and watch the perimeter of the lodge, and the last two men would follow them to their cabin. If anything strange happened, they would immediately notify Jake.

After giving final instructions, he walked along the wide porch, passing the dozens of rocking chairs, looking for his wife. When he reached the end, he stopped in his tracks. Angel had stepped onto the lawn in front of the lodge to make a quick call to check on Damien.

The afternoon sun rays scattered over the section of grassy area she stood in. Eyes closed, she lifted her face with a wide grin, enjoying the warmth and light breeze.

He liked seeing her so relaxed, and the crimson top he'd bought her accented creamy skin along her neck and across her collar bone. Her slim, long legs, encased in black pants, ended in motorcycle boots. Female and savage. He found the view sexy. Not exactly beautiful, she was an exotic temptress by far. Just what he needed.

His possessiveness could stem from knowing she had never belonged to anyone else. Or that when she was in his bedroom, the wild woman turned into a sex kitten who loved doing whatever he wanted. Fuck, he was hard just thinking about spanking her perfect ass and having her suck his dick.

He needed to buy her red more often. Maybe he'd get her to wear the red corset again and nothing else. The thought of her bending over and his hand slapping a rosy globe made his breathing quicken.

Damn, he needed to keep his mind on business.

Regaining control of his senses, he tapped the old-fashioned key he held against a post to draw her attention.

"You ready?" Without waiting for her answer, he headed toward the car. Just as he reached for the handle, a loud crack resounded behind him. "Everyone get down," he shouted. As soon as he dropped to the ground, he pulled out the Glock and looked around for Angel. He blinked in surprise. Hands fisted her own gun as her gaze searched the trees nearby, she was stretched out beside him. How had she moved so fast? "You good?"

"Yes. Just surprised to be a target way out here. Do you think whoever wounded Sen is looking for him and spotted us?"

He grinned. He liked how her mind worked. The same as his, calm and appraising the situation.

"Chances are good. We must be getting in their way."

"I guess so."

Pride swelled in his chest. Her awareness as she continued to check out the surrounding landscape once more reminded him of how much they had in common. She fixed her stare on an area across a small slough. His gaze followed hers. A thick stand of trees ended on a cliff. The uppermost limbs swayed with the breeze. Then he noticed one limb closer to the ground shake. Not close enough to be a deer. Whoever hid in the tree was unused to working in the wilderness and revealed their location. They were probably preparing to run for it.

Jake waved over one of his men. "Did you see him?"

Dan nodded. He'd been raised out in the middle of nowhere by his grandmother. With no grocery store nearby and poor, he'd grown up on game. So he was familiar with tracking.

"Go and get him. Alive. Pick two men to help. Take him to the barn. Let me know when you have him talking."

The tall blond man nodded again. In seconds, he disappeared into the tree-line with two men trotting behind.

"Come on. Whoever was shooting is on the run now." He helped her to her feet and slapped at the dirt on the back of her pants. Being shot at was becoming a daily thing.

"What are you doing?" She stepped away.

He looked up and then straightened. "What?" His mind hadn't really been on what he was doing. How long would they have to worry about being shot?

Her eyes twinkled in a flushed face. "You're so funny." She brushed his lips with hers. "Keep the spanking to the bedroom," she whispered.

What was she talking about? "I have no idea what you mean. Come on." He opened the car door for her.

Before she ducked inside, she leaned over and said, "You better finish what you started."

He laughed. Then he realized she referred to his hands slapping the seat of her pants a moment earlier. Unable to resist, he leaned down and took her mouth. His tongue slid inside and licked along hers. She groaned as his hand cupped a hard tipped breast. The thin bra didn't hide her reaction at all

She arched into his touch. Damn, he loved her instant responsiveness.

"Jake, please, not in front of the guys," she said against his lips.

He threw a glance over his shoulder. His men stood around, guns hidden at their sides, but their gazes everywhere but toward the SUV. Smart men.

"Let's go." He closed the passenger door and walked around.

Never had a woman made him forget himself as often as Angel did.

Angel watched the line of cars break up as they came to a four-way stop. Some traveled to the other side of the lake, others along the same side, while the last car followed the SUV to provide security for the weekend.

She glanced over to Jake.

"Did you pack a change of clothes for me?"

"Nope."

That was it? No explanation?

"I can wear this outfit back home, but what about tomorrow?"

"What about tomorrow?"

Why was he being so obtuse?

She narrowed her eyes, trying to figure out his game. If the cabin had a washer and dryer, she could easily launder her clothes each night. For that matter, she could wash them out in a sink. Wouldn't be the first time she'd done it.

"Is this cabin one your brothers used often?"

"Yep."

Good. It could have all types of clothing left behind. Then again, with three men, it might not even have running water. Oh, no. She hoped it had most of the modern conveniences.

Jake turned the car off the main road onto a small paved one. They continued to climb through an open gate and then passed a large barn. She'd been afraid at first it was the cabin. Talk about relieved when they continued on, and then cut to one side as their car leveled out. The cabin didn't look like a one-room shack, but not as fancy or huge like others she'd seen before. Mid-sized, it looked plain, but well-maintained. Trees blocked the view of the water on both sides.

She stepped out of the car and waited for Jake to give the two men instructions. Once the men got back into their car and drove back down the hill to the gate, he unlocked the door.

"Stay behind me. I need to check inside before we can relax."

Who was he talking to? She could handle an intruder as efficiently as he could. He knew that. Instead of protesting, she stood back as her gaze followed his movements. Hand at his back, ready to grab his gun, he carefully hugged the wall, being cautious as he entered each room. He looked so sexy being the big, bad protector.

Her chest lightened, and she knew her grin was lopsided. Yes. She kind of liked it.

The cabin had the expected large living room–kitchen combination with floor-to-ceiling glass windows facing the valley. A loft above their heads held a pool table and air hockey table. The large bedroom on one side came with a large jet tub. What she hadn't expected were the four bedrooms below with a media room in the center, cool and dark, and two more baths. A wide deck jutted out from the living room and a smaller one downstairs had a huge hot tub that took up one end and hung over a cliff above the water. The entrance of the building had been misleading as to how big it was inside.

"This is great," she said as they returned to the main room.

"The best part is that we have it to ourselves for two nights. Alone."

"Alone? With guards outside?"

"They're halfway down the drive. With orders to not disturb us unless it is life or death." He lifted his eyebrows. "The place is wired with cameras around the exterior along with motion detectors. Most of the time, animals trigger the cameras. No one can see in unless they're a bird and can fly into the top of the trees."

"And that's important, why?" Oh, he was a little devil. She knew what he was about to say, and she had no problem with it. To have him alone. No responsibilities to tend to in a moment's notice. No one to walk in unexpectedly, no knocks on the door, no one to hear her scream with the pleasure-pain he loved to inflict, and besides, they loved to experiment. Just the two of them enjoying their time together.

He merely grinned.

They deserved the time to get to know each other. Sure, sex was important. A person could learn a lot about a partner with the physical act, but they needed to talk, too. What better way to build on a relationship than to be alone together.

She closed her eyes for a second.

Truth be told, did he want to know her? Really know her? Was she interesting enough for him? She'd never felt comfortable talking about herself, especially anything positive. She was more apt to tell about her goof ups. How would he react when she finally did or said something stupid? Would he regret marrying her even more than he already did? When they solved their current situations, would he leave her?

She shook her head. That wasn't the way to think.

Worrying never stopped things from happening. Taking one day at a time, enjoying what was offered, tomorrow could take care of itself. How many times had Mac said that to her?

With a deep breath, she followed him over to the kitchen area. He opened the fridge. Lifting his hand to the top of the door, he gazed into the upper section. Several beer bottles and soft drinks lined up waiting to be taken. The muscles on his back shifted as he reached for one.

Goodness, she looked forward to running her hands over each shifting muscle. Her fingers curled.

"Want a beer?"

"Sure," she said in a breathless voice. Reaching for the bottle, he pulled back.

"Wait. Is Bud for vegans?"

"Yes." Not once had he teased or acted put out by her lifestyle. He needed to do something to piss her off before she found herself totally and deeply in love with the man. It would kill her if he left her behind.

She took the offered beer and turned away. Looking at him hurt too much. She wanted him to love her too much. Tilting the bottle, she groaned. Her eyes drifted closed as she savored the cool liquid, stopping after several swallows. When she opened her eyes, facing a window, she caught Jake's reflection behind her. He stared back at her.

She wished she could read his mind. Was he disgusted by her unladylike manners, guzzling down half of the bottle?

"Sorry. I was so thirsty."

"Nothing to be sorry about. That was sexy as hell. I've never seen a woman do that."

Her face warmed. "I like beer."

In two strides, he stood in front of her and his mouth took hers. When he pulled back enough for his breath to mix with hers, he said, "I do, too, especially when it's on your lips." He licked her mouth and slipped his tongue inside to caress hers. "So much better than from the bottle," he said, his voice low and husky.

She blinked up at him. The bottle disappeared from her hand, and she heard a thud as he set it on the nearby counter. His nimble fingers slid beneath her T-shirt and unclasped her bra. She inhaled deeply. He cupped her breasts. Her back arched as he massaged their fullness.

Oh, that felt so good. Bras were a classic Catch-22. To not wear one, her breasts would sag before she was thirty, but to wear one properly, the support restricted her breathing. The way he handled her breasts and rubbed her ribs showed how much he knew what she needed. She found out so much about her own body every time he touched her.

"Go and strip completely. Get on the bed, stomach down with your feet on the floor," he whispered into her ear.

The orders in his husky timbre sent a fabulous thrill through her body. She understood he planned to punish her for handling the restaurant manager without backup. He didn't care that she'd done it alone for years now. Mac had trusted her to be careful. Jake wasn't as sure of her skills.

Just as well. She would've found something for him to punish her for, if not for that.

By the time he'd entered the bedroom, her heartbeat had picked up speed. The air-conditioned room wasn't the solitary reason for the goosebumps popping up on her arms and legs. Hearing his footsteps tightened her nipples to the point of pain. Her breathing quickened.

"Spread your legs." His deep voice washed her with need. "Wider." He tapped the inside of her thighs.

Shifting her feet to the desired width apart, she closed her eyes and sank her teeth into her bottom lip. She wanted to say hurry, but her dry mouth refused to let one word out. Anticipation tightened every muscle in her body.

His large warm hand stroked down one cheek to thigh. She jumped.

"Easy, sweetheart. You know you want this. Wasn't it just yesterday we talked about us looking out for each other. You need someone bigger and stronger to take care of you."

One part of her still wanted to protest his assumption she couldn't take care of herself. While another part loved knowing he could be counted on to look after her. She was tired of being alone. Her brother would be leaving for college in a few short years, and even at home, he had his friends. He wasn't much for hanging with his big sister. Actually, when he was around, she worried he would offer to help or become involved in the work she handled.

Jake's fingers skimmed over her folds.

"Please, Jake."

"Yeah, baby. We're two peas in a pod, heh? We love control. I love controlling you and you love how I do it."

She gasped when his palm slapped her fleshy rear end. No gentle tap, but a good bit of his strength behind the smack. Her shocked nerves shot pain direct to her pussy. A long moan escaped her lips. Why did she enjoy this? She didn't know or care.

"That's my baby. You can't get enough."

Warmth seeped into her bones and her clit throbbed. A few more smacks, spread over both cheeks, had her panting. Her nails dug into the comforter. With each jolt, her nipples rubbed against the material, and she yearned for more. Her soft pleading changed to whimpers. She craved his body on top of hers, entering her with the forceful strokes exhibiting his wild desire for her.

"I love hearing your moans mixed with whimpers. My dick is so hard for you, I'm sure I'll burst."

"Please, please, please." She whimpered again.

"Shh, we're almost there." Several more rained down on her butt until she had a hard time breathing. He stopped. "Promise to take a backup on future collection runs."

"I promise."

"That means you wait until someone is available or I go with you. I'll give you a list of my men who you can trust, if yours aren't available. Understand?"

"Yes."

"Yes, what?"

Confused for a split second, she searched her memory for the correct response. Then it came to her.

"Yes, sir." She licked her dry lips. Mercy, she craved more of his touch. The man was driving her insane with lust.

Something touched her butt. She realized he'd pressed a kiss to an abused buttock and then quickly did the same to the other one.

"Move up and turn around. On your back and head off the edge of the mattress."

She already figured what he wanted. In seconds, she had her mouth wide open and Jake feeding her his long, thick cock. Her tongue swirled around the head as more slid down to the back of her throat.

"Swallow. It will help," he instructed.

Before she thought to gag, he pulled back and started over again. Breathing through her nose, she continued to suck him down, and he picked up speed until he hammered toward completion.

"Damn, you're so fucking sexy. The view is so carnal, a fucking turn on." His voice sounded so husky and deep. She liked how much her submission aroused him. "I'd love to let you take everything I offer, but I miss that sweet pussy." He backed away, his cock slipping out, still hard.

Sitting up and twisting around, she started to lay back.

"No, no. On your stomach again."

"My butt is so sore." Surely, he wasn't going to beat it more. "I learned my lesson."

"It's okay, sweetheart. Your punishment is over. Yeah, that's it. Your knees beneath you, spread them, head on the bed. Yeah. That's a good girl." He lightly rubbed the sore flesh. "You're so pretty and red with a little pink surrounding each one. So warm. Perfect." His gruff voice turned her on as much as his touch. "Now let me see if you're as eager as I am." A thick finger swiped between her legs. "Oh, yeah. Hot and moist. Even swollen. You'll be so tight, just the way I want it."

She gave a small mewl, wanting him to hurry. He chuckled.

"Fuck. You are so hot."

His cock pressed against her. She wiggled.

"Be still." He slapped a sensitive cheek.

Her body shivered. She wasn't sure how long she could be still.

Then he shoved his cock all the way in. She screamed. Not from pain, though there had been a little, but the sheer pleasure of having him in her. Over her. Taking her. The man took long deep strokes with a rhythm that called to her soul. With each inward slide, the forceful thrust pushed up her butt and the angle touched a part of her she didn't know existed. She squealed when her orgasm hit. He plunged in several more times.

"So damn fucking good." Then he became still.

The bed trembled. She opened her eyes and noticed his arms shaking.

"Jake. Hold me."

He fell to the side, taking her with him. His cock remained in her as he wrapped her in his arms.

"I got you. And I don't plan to let you go anytime soon."

She kissed him on his arm. *Anytime soon.* If only it was forever.

Chapter Twenty

Angel woke a few hours later with someone slamming their fist to the door. Jake whispered for her to stay under the covers as he slid out. Tugging up his jeans with one hand, he picked up his gun from the nightstand. Lazy, and feeling sure he was safe, what with guards outside and...well, it was Jake. The man could handle anything. Including her.

Earlier, they had gotten out of bed and showered, making love with her back to the tile and Jake holding her legs as the warm water beat down on their surging bodies. They decided to laze away the day in bed, only moving to kiss or fuck.

She heard murmuring, but she recognized the voice. It was Dan. Jake's man who had been sent out to track down the shooter.

By the time Jake returned to the bedroom, she'd dressed and sat on the end of the bed.

"Did he catch the person?" she asked as soon as he entered the room.

"No. But he found a cabin on the other side of the

mountain broken into. Someone had spent a couple days there. Bloody bandages found in the trash. Canned food opened and eaten. It must have been where Sen holed up after he'd been shot." The concerned look on his face told her there was more.

"What makes you think it was your brother?"

"He left a note."

"A note?"

"Yeah. He knew I'd be looking for him around the lake. He always hung around here whenever the old man came down too hard on him or just the normal shit he had to put up with."

"I see. Did he mention in the note where he was going next?"

"No. But I know he's okay. He has Tessa with him. They'll look out for each other."

"Tessa? Quinn's daughter?"

"Yeah. You know her?"

"No, not really. I've only seen her whenever I needed to see her dad. She's fascinating to watch her talk with her hands. It's amazing how much emotion she can show without saying a word." Angel felt sorry for the girl though Tessa always had a smile on her face and never let her disability hold her back.

He began pacing back and forth in front of her.

"You have something else on your mind?" she asked.

"Yeah." He continued moving.

"Your other brother okay?"

"Yeah." Then he proceeded to tell her about Ethan's trip into Nashville and having Rat Boy tracking him. Then he gave her info about Matt's missing fingers, but he continued to look away, his face cold with anger. Why didn't he spit it all out?

"What has you wound up?" She wished they lived a normal life, but years ago she'd come to terms with all of the drama. Besides, they probably didn't deserve peace and quiet. Too many sins committed in the name of family business, creating various types of turmoil while taking care of the people they loved. All her life she'd been dealing with crap, the kind regular people only saw on TV.

"I have news the bullets that killed the old men were not from the same gun." His gaze darted her way as he continued walking the width of the room and back.

"So two shooters," she stated.

"Or the shooter had talent and could shoot two guns real fast."

"What are the chances of that?"

"Slim to none."

"So two shooters," she repeated. "Now, not only do we need to find one killer but two. Well, shit." She wanted to scream at the top of her lungs, but Mac had taught her the importance of restraint. After taking a couple of deep breaths, she measured each word she said. "What do we do next?"

"There's one more thing."

Her stomach sank. How much more would they take?

"Go ahead. Let's get it all out so we can do what's needed. I may yet send Damien to military school up north."

"Military school. He'll hate you for it."

"Better that than me burying him in the ground. So far we had two shooters who killed the old men." She raised two fingers. "One on the highway"—another finger up—"two at the wedding and one at the lodge"—a whole hand opened wide and one finger popped up on the other hand. "We have no idea how they are all connected, if they are connected at all. Are they someone close who hates us? Or are they coming in from the outside, wanting to take over our territory? Do you think your cousins could be planning all of this?"

"There's a good chance they are involved, but neither one of those assholes can shoot worth a damn. The old man used to talk about how they couldn't shoot the side of a barn." Jake finally stopped and sat beside her. "I've known this for some time, kept hoping it was rumors, but a group from Atlanta has decided to move into our area. They've been spotted sniffing around Birmingham."

"What are the chances they're part of our troubles?"

"That's my girl." He grinned and her heart sped up. His handsome face nearly pushed her to grab him by the neck and wrestle him to the floor. "I don't think they had a hand in the old men's death. I do believe they are behind the trouble with my cousins and the current shootings. Something deep inside tells me the old men died because someone close had a grudge. You and I know the old men were nowhere near paragons of virtue."

They laughed, shaking their heads.

Then he stopped and stared at her as if he'd never seen her smile.

Feeling uneasy by the depth of his stare, she shook her head.

"Don't look at me. Despite being a mean bastard, Mac helped me protect Damien and bring him up to be a good boy. Killing him has never crossed my mind."

He nodded. "Same with me. I've plotted the old man's death many times, but I never would've done it. Ethan and Sen wouldn't have either."

"It appears we're back to square one."

Out of the blue, Jake draped his arm around her shoulder. She liked how relaxed he acted around her. When had anyone, besides her brother, acted that way?

"Is that why you never reported your grandfather for his abuse?"

"Ha! Like anyone would believe me. Or if they did, they'd most likely ask him to beat me more, I deserved it. You probably don't remember, but I was a bit of a troublemaker in the day."

"You? Nah. Not you." He chuckled. Though his face turned serious, his eyes twinkled. "Why did you steal my wallet? You knew I'd catch you."

Trying to hold back her grin, she raised her eyebrows. "Yes. I knew."

He stared at her for a moment longer and then burst out laughing. "You have always been after me, haven't you?"

"Yes. It was the only way I could get you to look at me. I've had a crush on you since I was six years old."

"Six? A little young, isn't it?"

"Maybe. But you probably don't remember—"

"You said that before."

"Well, this time you won't. I was six and hiding in the middle of a rack of clothes while Mom shopped. You came in with your mom. In minutes, you ducked into the same rack. Before I could scream for you to get out, you pressed your finger to my lips and smiled. I thought you were the prettyish boy in the world."

"Prettyish?"

"Hey, sue me. I was six."

"What did you do, kiss me?"

She couldn't help rolling her eyes at him. "Quit. Kids then, remember? We giggled and watched everyone until my mom started threatening to kill me if I didn't come out of my hiding place." She had waved and been so sad when it was over, and she rarely saw the boy again. Then she was told to stay away *that* Whitfield. Then in her first year of high school she saw him daily, while he never looked her way. "Do you not remember that?"

Though it was silly, it bothered her to think he didn't remember.

"I remember one time hiding in the racks and coming across a little girl, but nothing else."

"Hey, you were older than me. You should remember more."

He looked away. "I had a lot going on at the time," he said.

"Weren't you seven when you found out about your brothers?"

"Yeah. One day, it was me and Mom living with the old man in the big house. Then the next, I come home on the bus, and Ethan and Sen were there and Mom wasn't."

She pressed to his side and slipped an arm around his waist. Resting her head on his chest, she held him to her as he squeezed her tight by the shoulder.

"Oh, that sucked."

"We had fucked up childhoods, heh?"

"I guess so. I'll say I had it a little easier than you and your brothers."

"How's that?"

"I don't know. Maybe because no matter how much Mac treated me like a grandson, he never forgot I was a girl. He wasn't gentle in no way, but he never abandoned me in the middle of the forest or broke my finger and refused treatment. Your old man went a step too far several times. I think he was a self-centered son of a bitch." She said the last in a heated tone.

In a swirl of movement, Jake picked her up and tossed

her onto the middle of the bed, covering her with his big body. His mouth took hers, and before she had time to think, he stripped off her clothes.

She loved his aggressiveness. Whatever she'd said to rile up his testosterone, she hoped to do it again. And often.

What the fuck?

Jake's eyes opened. Staring at the ceiling, unmoving, he waited for a repeat of whatever disturbed his sleep.

Angel's breathing, tickling the hairs on his chest with her dainty puffs, and the churning of the fan above were the only sounds. Then he heard it again. A creaking of a board near the French doors that led out to a long back porch. With careful movements, he eased from beneath her and out of the bed.

Damn it, one knee ached like a son-of-a-bitch. He limped a step and massaged it. He was sore all over. It had been years since he'd had so much sex in one night, and at the time, it had been three prostitutes he'd purchased when he turned twenty-one. With a shake of his head, he looked back at the woman he now called wife. He couldn't have asked for one who suited him better. She met him stroke for stroke, ready to try anything, and demanded more.

He picked up his mobile phone from the table next to the bed. Holding it close to his chest and hunched over, not letting the light brighten up the room, he clicked over to the cameras situated around the cabin. Nothing. Had he imagined the sound?

Another creak outside had Jake sliding the phone underneath a pillow and then palming his gun. In a wide stride, ignoring the twinges in his knee as he rolled his foot from side to heel and then toe, he quietly moved to the doors. No alarm had gone off.

"Need help?" Angel asked in a low tone.

The "shh" he released barely pierced the silence.

He fingered open an edge of the curtain covering one side. A shadow wavered at the other end of the porch. The moon hidden by the clouds confirmed the shadow wasn't from the surrounding trees. He'd left a lamp on in the huge central room. His men had instructions to stay in the surrounding trees and road, no touching the cabin, and it included no walking across the back deck. Whoever was out there knew the cameras' blind spots, or had looped the transmitting views.

Behind him, he heard the faint rubbing of the mattress against boxsprings followed by soft footsteps. He looked down as Angel peeked out of the curtains. She wore his shirt, opened to below her belly button. Mentally, he groaned. The woman was going to get him killed.

Reining in his libido, he nodded when she jerked her head toward the living room.

They made their way toward the bedroom door and through a short hallway. Jake held up his hand. They stopped before crossing the threshold into the large living area.

Out of the shadows a barstool flew toward Jake's face. In a smooth move, he knocked it to the side with his forearm. *Fuck, that hurt.*

A knife sliced through the air, just inches from Jake's nose, and landed in the large attacker's chest. The man screeched like a little girl and grabbed at the handle.

"I wouldn't do that," Angel said in a matter-of-fact tone to the man. As soon as the man pulled the blade out, he crumpled to the floor. "He should have listened to me. I had suspected it hit his heart." She shuddered and turned away.

"Are you okay?" He carefully touched her shoulders and pulled her to his chest, pressing her cheek to his rapid heartbeat.

"I don't think there is anyone else here. They would've pounced already." Her voice was strangely level and cold. She'd acted the same way at the wedding when she'd killed the shooter. He knew how hard it was on her to take a life. Hell, it would be the same for any normal human.

"You are one crazy, dangerous woman," he whispered into her hair as he kissed the top of her head.

"Crazy, huh?" She pulled away and her gaze dropped. "You're the one standing there buck-naked with a hard-on."

"What can I say, adrenaline and you creating havoc does something to me." He wrapped his arms around her and squeezed. All of that soft womanly body pressed to his harder one made him want her, but there was more. A peacefulness enveloped him unlike anything he'd ever experienced before. He'd found a woman who was more than a bed partner. He'd never believed in soul mates, but he was beginning to understand why men wrote ballads and poems to the women they loved. His eyes blurred. What was he saying? Now wasn't the time to have such insane thoughts.

She squeezed him back and sighed.

"I guess we need to get our clothes on and check on your guards. Oh, no. I hope the idiot in there didn't kill them." Her voice cracked at the end.

He picked her up and carried her into the bedroom. "You stay here. I'll call and check." The intruder appeared to come from the thicket at the end of the porch. Jake guessed he would be chopping down the trees near the water before long. "He was probably the shooter Dan lost."

He was also the shadow spotted moments ago. If only he could figure out who sent the man. Too many people gunning for the Whitfields and Tallys.

After he checked on his lax security, he would discover who in hell messed with the camera images and where the man came from. "I doubt the men even know we've been attacked."

As soon as her butt met the mattress, she scrambled to her feet. He appreciated the flashes of rounded ass and sweet pussy.

"No, no. There's no way you're leaving me. I've proven to you over and over again I can help." She pulled on a scrap of material for underwear and then the pair of black jeans she'd worn earlier. "Quit gawking and get dressed, unless you plan to go naked."

He reached out, grabbed her hand, and tugged her toward him. Unable to resist, he cupped her breasts. "Did you forget where we are?"

Her forehead wrinkled. "In a cabin with a dead man in the next room." She tilted her head, staring at him, and then her eyes rolled upward. "In the bedroom."

"My cabin. My bedroom."

"Your bedroom," she said in a sarcastic tone as she rocked her head side to side with each syllable.

Damn, she was cute.

"That means per our agreement, I'm the boss here," he said, making sure she understood his seriousness.

"Yes, sir."

He leaned down, spread open the shirt, and sucked on the tip of each nipple. A smile tugged at the corner of his lips when she whimpered. With a satisfying smack, he stopped. "Finish dressing, and I'll call down to the gate."

She grinned, and his heart did a weird flip. He growled,

and she laughed.

Fishing his phone from beneath the pillow, he punched in the speed dial number and waited for the lead guard to answer. A familiar gruff hello assured him what he'd guessed had been correct.

"Call Tick to arrange for a clean up crew."

Silence reigned for a couple seconds on the other end until a sigh echoed through the connection. "Fuck, Mr. Whitfield. I swear we've been patrolling the area."

"We'll talk about it later. We're leaving in about fifteen minutes to head back to the house. I want to pass the cleanup van on the other side of the interstate and know it left when I asked it to." No matter there were few cabins nearby, he didn't want to take a chance of anyone eavesdropping on their phone conversations. Too simple to do with all the gadgets available on the Internet.

"Yes, sir."

Jake cut off the connection.

"I'm glad we're leaving. There is so much to be done back home," Angel said.

"Home?"

She hesitated in hooking her bra beneath his shirt she still wore. "I guess I consider your house as mine, too. That's okay, isn't it?"

Her question was unnecessary as the will had given her the big monstrosity, but he could tell she wasn't thinking that way, and his answer was important to her.

"Yeah. It's good." He clasped the back of her neck and eased her closer, his lips hovering over hers. "I like knowing you're comfortable enough to think that. Plus, I like having you in my bed," he said in a low, rough tone.

Her eagerness was obvious when she covered his mouth with hers, taking his breath away.

Chapter Twenty-One

ngel awoke with a start, sweaty and anxious. She reached out for Jake. Her hand met cold sheets. Feeling desolated by the empty part of the bed, she covered her head with the sheet. Why was it whenever she sought some comfort, the person she needed wasn't there?

No. That wasn't the way she wanted to think. She was a grown woman and didn't need coddling.

Trying to shake off the uneasy feeling, she said beneath her breath, "It was a silly little dream."

In her mind's eye, she saw the man she'd killed. He'd worn a hoodie and his crooked finger pointed at her like in a Charles Dickens story. Awake and eyes open, the dream should be laughable, but her thumping heartbeat said otherwise.

After returning to the Whitfield house yesterday morning, she'd struggled to unwind. Jake had taken off to meet with his brother, Ethan. His youngest brother had left Nashville with the cops on his tail. Ethan and the woman traveling with him had given them the slip and now holed up at her place. News came back to her the man she'd killed had been part of the organization in Atlanta trying to take over Jake's family's business.

Determined to block out the memories last night, she hunted down her brother—of course, he sat at the kitchen table eating another wonderful smelling dessert—and asked about the clothes buying trip. Damien had entertained her with the craziness of shopping with Jimmie Sue.

All was good while they had picked out clothes together, but once he'd trekked back into the dressing room area, he knew he was in trouble. She'd been on his heels. He'd freaked out when she continued into his dressing room and insisted on helping him try on the new jeans. When he politely told her to leave, she'd claimed he didn't have anything she hadn't seen before.

Without missing a beat, he'd said, "Then it is only right I help you try on your clothes."

The seventy-plus woman blushed so deeply he'd been afraid he caused her to have a stroke. Flustered and good humored about it, Jimmie Sue remained outside of the room the rest of the afternoon.

No one could ever say her brother didn't speak his mind. He and Angel had inherited that trait from Mac.

Turning onto her side, she checked the clock on Jake's nightstand. Three in the morning.

Where was he? She needed his warm body. His deep voice. He'd help to keep her mind off the dead man at the cabin. If Jake's arms had been around her when she woke up, the dream would have been much different. She was certain of that.

Unable to tolerate the lonely bed, she jumped out and slipped on her old cotton robe. Jake had made fun of the tiny blue kittens printed on it. She hadn't cared. Her mother had given it to her before she died. Angel wore the ratty robe whenever she needed a little comfort.

Alone and early in the morning, doubts always assailed her from all sides. Was she wrong to give in to Mac's wishes in marrying Jake? Could he betray her to the FBI agent? Or was he with another woman? Should she trust him with her heart? All her insecurities bombarded her. Why had he agreed to the marriage? He could walk away from everything and disappear. Men had done so to many women over the centuries. Why should he care what happened to her brother? Or her? She didn't even want to think about how she compared to any of his ex-girlfriends.

She shook her head. Too late to torment herself about any of that foolishness. What was, was. She had to deal with the here and now. No more concerns about yesterday or anything she couldn't correct.

In the kitchen, a dim light beneath the cabinets softly lit the countertops. She opened the refrigerator and drew out a bottle of water. Twisting off the cap, she chugged down half of the cool liquid.

"Fuck, that's still hot," a deep voice said behind her.

She choked. With a nearby towel, she dabbed at her chin and chest. "You scared the shit out of me. Next time let me know you're there." She closed the fridge.

"Yeah, good thing you don't have a knife," Jake said from the shadows at the opposite end of the kitchen table.

Without hesitation, she dipped her hand in a pocket and pulled out a switchblade, flipped it open. The sharp edge glinted even in the low light.

"I should've known," he said. His derisive chuckle gave her chills.

Her eyes adjusted enough for her to see Jake holding a half-empty tumbler. He lifted it and swallowed the dark contents. The smoky smell of bourbon wafted to her side of the room.

With a flick of her wrist, she closed the knife and dropped it into her pocket.

"What happened?' She eased closer to him.

"Everything. Nothing." He chuckled again. She didn't like the sound of it. Something had happened.

"Why are you sitting down here in the dark?"

"Come here." The squeak of wood scraping against tile echoed in the room. He slapped his hands on his thighs. "Right here."

"This isn't the bedroom."

"I just want to hold you."

That sounded...odd. He was in a strange mood, as if he was tired beyond measure.

Deciding to play along in an effort to find out what had happened, as she did want to give comfort and maybe receive it in return, she placed the bottle on the table and carefully walked to his chair. When she started to sit sideways on his lap, he grabbed her waist and changed her direction. Knees parted to clasp each side of his hips with her butt on his lap, she faced his sexy lips and hooded eyes. She liked this position. She wiggled, feeling a hard ridge rubbing against her clit. How long would it take him to realize she was naked underneath her robe?

He untied the sash of her robe and pushed it off her shoulders.

Obviously, not long. She grinned.

His calloused hands covered her ass cheeks and squeezed, pulling her closer to his body.

"Fuck, you feel good," he said with a groan in his voice.

She sighed. Feeling his clothed hard body next to her

bare one was so sensual and freaking erotic. Her taut nipples brushed against the cotton of his shirt.

"Someone could walk in on us," she whispered.

"Let them." One big hand cupped the back of her head, keeping her still for him to ravage her mouth. His tongue stroked, forcing her mouth to widen and take his kiss.

She reached for the buttons on his shirt, but he quickly grabbed one hand and pushed it down to his zipper. Without hesitation, she scooted back a little, unfastened his pants, and lifted his cock. Just like his body, hard and hot.

Without being told, she raised her hips and smoothly brought them down, centering his cock in her heat.

He jerked his mouth from hers, arched his neck as he released a heavy groan. "Damn, just what I needed. You feel so fucking tight."

Times like now, she was glad her legs were so long. Using her knees, she pushed until he almost came out and then she began pumping up and down. He clasped her ass again and helped to steady her rhythm. As if it had been days instead of hours, he came in no time. Hearing his chest rumble with pleasure and feeling his cock pulsate helped nudge her over the edge. He moaned again when her body rippled with her orgasm.

Seconds ticked by while she regained her breath and her heartbeat settled. Unable to restrain her impulse, she leaned up and nipped at his earlobe.

"What the hell?" He growled. His eyes twinkled though no smile appeared.

"You never answered me. What happened?" She started to worry something horrible had happened to one or both of his brothers.

Jake urged her to rest a cheek on his shoulder, holding her firm but gentle.

"I told Ethan about my meetings with the FBI agent."

"I thought you were going to wait."

"He'd recognized her in town and went ballistic."

If only she'd been there to soothe things over between the brothers. Then again, would they have listened to her?

She leaned back, stroking his cheek. He pressed against her hand. "Were you able to calm him down?" She stared into his eyes. The poor guy was as starved for her touch as she was for his.

"No."

"Wait. How did he know she was FBI?"

"She'd visited Holman while he was there."

"Oh, hell. That was where he served his time?" Everyone knew about the overcrowding and horrible conditions. It wasn't called Slaughterhouse for nothing.

"Yeah. What little he's told me, it was a living hell there." He rubbed her arms up and down. "While mopping a corridor, he'd watched her attack the inmate she'd been interrogating. Took three guards to drag her off the man. The warden had her kicked out. Seeing an FBI agent act crazy inside a state prison is something a person never forgets."

"I can imagine that scene would stick. So what are we going to do?"

"We?" One corner of his mouth perked up.

"Yes. We." She lightly brushed her lips against his. "We're in this together."

"Yeah. I guess we are." He kissed her hard, laving every inch of her tongue, and pulling and licking her bottom lip. He took her breath away before easing back. "He did promise not to do anything and give me time to check on a few options," he said as he rested his forehead to hers.

"Like what?"

"He'd heard she'd been fired recently and was only pushing her own agenda or the Atlanta organization's."

From what Jake had told her, it was the same Atlanta organization that was headed by Mikolas Savalas. A dangerous man who Mac had established a treaty with years ago. Since her granddaddy's death, she suspected Savalas thought it would be okay to move into Tally and Whitfield territory.

"Holy crap. What a way to go about taking over the businesses. What with the inside information you would provide."

"Right. Chances are I've been fucked over big time."

Sitting on the front porch, Jake watched the trees change from black to green bathed in gold as the sun peeked over the leafy tops. He loved the land surrounding the old house. A great place for kids to play and be carefree.

With the right parent.

He inhaled on his cigarette, savoring the biting smoke and how it calmed his thoughts. After a couple of seconds, he blew a long stream, even adding several rings to float over the railing.

Yeah. Some aspects of the old homestead and town would be missed, but he had too many bad memories. Leaving for good would not be a hardship. Especially having Angel by his side. Shit. He never thought he would feel that way. The woman had gotten under his skin and all in good ways. She surprised him every day. Open-minded and willing to listen to what he said about running her family's organization to trying new positions, she pleased him at every turn.

"Hey, Jake, is it okay for me to ask you a question?"

Jake leaned back in the rocking chair and looked over his shoulder at Angel's brother standing next to the open front door.

"Sure. Close the door and have a seat." The cool air from the house's interior reminded him of how the humidity built during the early morning hours. "Must be important to get you up this early."

"I was wondering if you could take me to the store to buy Sis a present." The teenager grimaced.

"That's pretty nice, bro. What's the occasion?" Jake took a last drag off his cigarette and then pinched off the fire, letting it drop to the cement floor to step on it. With a flick of a finger, he shot the stub into the shrubbery.

A few seconds went by without a sound from Damien. Jake glanced over. The teenager stood staring at him with a mixture of confusion and anger.

"What?" Jake pushed off the chair and towered over Damien. If he was going to be attacked, he'd rather stand.

"Today is her birthday," Damien said between gritted teeth.

"I see." Jake nodded. "Birthdays are important to you." The last more of a statement than question.

"Yep." Damien's eyes narrowed.

The teenager had an attitude he needed to work on if he planned to stick around Jake and his brothers for any length of time. He better be happy Jake's old man wasn't alive. Dick Whitfield never hesitated in slamming him face first onto the porch railing for the show of temper. Damien was lucky Jake refused to follow his old man's footsteps.

"Listen. Let's go back inside and eat breakfast. Your sister is still asleep." Jake wasn't about to say what happened earlier in the morning, causing Angel to be so exhausted.

"From what I remember, most of the stores do not open until ten. We'll each find her something."

The teenager's jaw unclenched, and he released a couple of huffs.

"You really didn't know?" Damien tilted his head. So much like his sister with the same color of eyes.

"Nope, but I should've found out." He placed an arm over the teenager's shoulders. "So she's twenty-nine."

"Nah. Twenty-seven."

Math had always come easy to him. Jake stopped. "Thirteen years ago, in April—Christ! That means your sister was fourteen when—Jesus H."

"When what?"

Jake looked down. Damien was truly a good kid. Hell, how many teenaged brothers worried about their sister's birthday?

"The last time we saw each other in high school," he said simply, not sure of how much the teenager knew about what happened all those years ago.

"Oh, you're talking about when you...you know..." Damien twisted his lips in an attempt to stop from grinning. "When you whipped her butt."

"Who told you?"

"Like Mac didn't bring it up anytime he wanted to embarrass Angel." Damien rolled his eyes.

"He did?"

"Yep. Mac loved teasing people until they lost their temper. Only the last few years, Angel learned to ignore him. I guess he overused it."

"Sounds like it." Jake's jaw popped. It sickened him to know her own family hadn't let her live that moment down. Even with it being a private turning point for them, he hated to hear their unconventional turn on had been used against her by others. Nothing could be done about it now. "Let's get out of the heat." He opened the front door, and they moved toward the kitchen. "Jimmie Sue arrived while we were talking. Go and ask if you can help her." He wanted the teenager's mind on other things.

Damien wrinkled his nose. "I don't know how to cook."

"Ask anyway. Jimmie Sue won't let you lift a finger, but she'll be so happy you asked, she'll fix anything you want for breakfast. Maybe later at lunch, one of her apple turnovers will show up on your plate. Don't tell her about Angel's birthday. Or she'll insist on baking a birthday cake and Angel might see it. I'd like to surprise her. We'll pick up one when we buy her presents."

"All right!" Damien wiped imaginary saliva from his mouth and jogged down the hallway to the kitchen.

As soon as Damien was out of sight, Jake took the steps two at a time up to the second floor. He eased open the bedroom door.

Sprawled across the bed, Angel sleepily looked up at him. "Hey," she said in a raspy voice.

"There's my birthday, girl." He leaned down and kissed her temple. Women were so funny about morning breath. "Why didn't you give me a heads up today is your birthday?"

She shrugged. "After Mom died, it became another day. Though Damien usually remembers." Stretching, she looked at him, an unspoken question showing on her face.

"Yeah. He made sure I knew." Jake sat on the edge of the bed and smoothed her hair from her face. "I realized today you were only fourteen when I took you over my knee the first time."

"So. You were only sixteen."

"I thought you were closer to my age at the time. Not

that fifteen or sixteen sounds any better now. I guess it makes more sense why everyone got so incensed by it all." If he had a young teenager daughter and some smart-ass young buck thought to turn her over his knee...maybe he had gotten off lightly. "I'm sorry I treated you like that then."

Angel sat up and hugged his neck.

"You have nothing to be sorry for. That spanking fueled my hormone-driven imagination for years. So you can't stop now." She kissed his neck. "You know you haven't spanked me in days. I'm sure I've been a bad girl. You just haven't caught me," she teased, batting her eyelashes at him.

"You're being a bad little girl now." He grabbed her hand and pressed it to the hardness between his legs. "I have too much to do this morning and afternoon to straighten you out." He pulled down a corner of the sheet and palmed a full breast. "Wait until this evening. You won't be able to sit down for a week."

Her eyes closed, and she moaned. "Promises, promises. I'd love a birthday spanking. Maybe we can try out the toy I bought online."

"That is a thought, too."

She opened her eyes and gave him a sultry look. Fuck, that woman was seeped in depravity as deep as he was.

"I can't wait." Her tongue slipped between his lips and showed him what else she wanted.

When they came up for air, he sucked in a breath, trying to regain his thoughts.

"I want to spend some time with Damien," Jake said. His chin dipped down as he waited for her reaction. "So he's going with me on my rounds." Once a week, he checked in with several of his businesses, answering questions, straightening out arguments among the employees, and other miscellaneous crap that popped up. Considering how she didn't want Damien in the business, she might argue, but he sensed the boy needed some one-on-one time while they searched for her present.

"You're not taking him to the clubs." She dropped her head back and raised her eyebrows.

"What? You're trying to boss me?" His tone threatened in a teasing manner.

"He's my responsibility." Her expression grew serious.

"Your grandfather's will says differently."

She turned her head. The sting of her grandfather's lack of faith in her still stung. "He's relied on me for years to take care of him. It's hard to quit caring."

He smoothed hair from her eyes and cupped the side of her face. "No one expects you to. Anyway, Damien needs guidance from a male perspective." Putting a finger over her mouth, he added, "And Tick isn't exactly the type he needs."

"I'm glad to agree on that," she said after removing his hand. "There are a couple things I can do today."

"Be sure it's something fun." He gathered her up in his arms and gave her a loud smack on the lips. "No work today, birthday girl."

"Anything you say, sir." Her grin looked a little drunk with happiness.

"Now I like the sound of that."

Chapter Twenty-Two

Angel watched all the activity around her. Damien played Skee-Ball against Tick. Their shouts echoed in the large room when the ball dropped into the highest scored circle, causing the lights and bells to go off. Lydia worked a claw in a huge stuffed animal bin while Jimmie Sue looked on, giving advice. A couple of guards eyed a young woman playing a retro arcade game.

In one corner, a group with a seven-year-old girl staring at a large white cake began to sing Happy Birthday. Nearby, kids ran in and out of a jungle gym huge enough to hold twenty kids.

She felt a little lost. She didn't know how to play any of the games. When she was younger, money had been tight, and later, Mac considered it a way to rot the brain, same as watching television. Hopefully, no one realized this was her first birthday party. She didn't want anyone pitying her.

Still, she did enjoy seeing everyone having a good time. Even Jake teased a teenager as they fired matching rifles at deer leaping across a large video screen.

Cutting into the cake slice on her plate, she groaned.

Really, she was full but couldn't resist eating the last bite. Her gaze wandered over the disarray of colorful paper plates, plastic forks, two almost-empty pizza trays, and an ice-cream birthday cake two-thirds gone. Cake made from ice cream became her top favorite dessert from then on.

The bright lights above her glinted off her new diamond bracelet. For the first time in her life, she wore two pieces of expensive jewelry. Her wedding band and the bracelet that Jake had bought her. Pushing wrapping paper to the side, she checked out her new earphones from her brother. She looked forward to using them while she worked out.

Lydia had given her a bottle of the older woman's favorite perfume. Though expensive, no way would Angel ever wear that. Who wanted to smell like their mother-in-law when her husband kissed her? Eww!

Jimmie Sue, always practical, had presented her with a beautiful antique brush and mirror set. It made Angel feel so girly. A rare occurrence.

She'd even felt pretty today. While Jake and Damien had gone off together, she'd visited the local salon and had her roots touched up. For a few moments, she'd seriously thought of cutting off the red and coloring her hair back to a natural color. Then she remembered Jake saying he found her hair sexy, and he loved how her being different turned him on. Well, he didn't say that word-for-word, but she'd been able to read between the lines.

She touched her cheek. It felt funny not wearing the thick makeup that normally whitened her face. She'd decided today to wear a natural color foundation. She wasn't brave enough to go without makeup entirely.

"Why aren't you playing a game?" Jake eased into the chair next to her. "I should've known Damien had an ulterior motive for picking this pizza place."

She laughed as she caressed his arm, enjoying the feel of muscles shifting and tightening beneath her fingers. She never could get enough of touching him and the freedom to do so. "Don't worry. Watching everyone having a good time makes me happy."

"You are a special woman." His thumb glided over her chin. "I like seeing you without your mask."

"Mask?" She shivered, briefly closing her eyes, as his fingers skated down the line of her jaw. On realizing he meant the white makeup, she laughed. "Oh, thanks. I thought I'd try retro." She teased, her face heating up.

"Don't stop wearing the white stuff on my account, though. I like being the only one to see the real you." He edged closer and brushed a kiss across her mouth. He leaned back and his gaze searched her face. "You about ready to go home? Tick said he'd bring Damien home by ten."

Tired to the marrow of her bones, she was happy he asked. She hadn't wanted to hurt anyone's feelings by leaving too early.

"What about your mom and Jimmie Sue?"

"I'm walking them to their cars, but they have their own homes." He raised his eyebrows in a devilish manner.

Having Jake all to herself in the big house for a couple of hours was a wonderful idea.

"Then let's go. I feel an urge to be naughty on the way home."

"I'll keep an eye on you. Don't want to miss a chance to punish you later," he said softly in her ear.

She giggled and covered her mouth. When was the last time she'd giggled like a little girl? Jake made her feel young and carefree.

He pushed back his chair and stood, holding out a hand.

The pleased look on his face brought a different kind of warmth to her face and body. She so wanted this man. Grinning big, she teased internally, *like he has no idea.* She'd been obsessed with sex since Jake first laid hands on her, but once he placed a ring on her finger, she'd become a fiend.

After goodbyes to Damien and Tick, Jake rounded up his mom and Jimmie Sue, and they walked together with Angel trailing behind out into the humid late June weather. Out of habit, she had hesitated inside the doorway, checking her surroundings before following the others. The parking lot's adequate lighting eased her worries a little, but she stayed on alert. Then an odd heavy feeling revved up her senses. Someone was watching. A movement to her right caught her attention. Someone had dashed, hunched down, between two cars on the opposite end of the lot. She glanced over to Jake. The way he laughed and placed an arm around his mom, looking off into the distance, but not directly at their stalker, told her he probably had seen it, too.

Jake turned his head and raised his eyebrows, giving her a quick nod. Yeah, he'd noticed.

She dipped her chin. They understood what needed to be done. The first priority was to make sure the older women were safe in the car and on their way

Slowing down, allowing a couple of yards to separate her from Jake, Angel adjusted the purse's strap on her shoulder. She actually possessed a real one, not a small backpack. When Jake had seen it, his eyes had widen and he teased her about getting girly on him.

Acting nonchalant, she ran her hand down her blouse as if to straighten it. In truth, it was a nervous tic. Every few minutes, she checked her gun, especially when she wore the made-for-women velcro type holster. It wrapped around her ribcage beneath her top. Lightweight and perfect for one of her smaller pistols. The gun rested beneath her arm. If she ever needed her gun, she would have to pull up her shirt, snatch it from under a velcro strip. Simple, right? The only probably was, velcro was a noisy son-of-a-bitch.

Jake stopped next to Lydia's Caddy and opened the door.

A loud pop and the tinkling of glass had everyone ducking. Screams echoed from the car and the building behind Angel. People ran back inside.

In seconds, she had gun in hand, searching for the shooter.

Swallowing her heart, she hoped Jake and the ladies were all right. Not wanting the shooter to know exactly where she was, she kept quiet, not asking if they were okay. Low deep murmurs reached her ears. From the tone, it sounded as if Jake was handling the women.

Running by two crouching, scared teenagers, she motioned for them to stay put. Then she headed to the darker side of the lot where she'd seen the suspicious person earlier. The shooter probably had already moved to a different position, but she hoped to get a visual. Later, she wouldn't be certain why she looked where she did, but she lifted her gun and fired a split second after the muzzle flash gave away the shooter's location.

Jake paced up and down the hospital waiting room.

God, if she didn't survive that bastard's bullet wound, he would never forgive himself for not protecting her better.

Judd Richards charged into the room. His hair stuck up in every direction. As a successful lawyer, he usually was a well-dressed man, but at the moment, he looked a wreck.

"I've got to talk with you, Jake."

"If you don't get the fuck away from me, I'll beat you to a bloody pulp."

The big man's face whitened. "Is he still alive?"

"I don't know what you're talking about. Right now, I don't give a fuck about anyone except the woman who almost bled to death in a filthy parking lot."

"No matter what, please don't kill him." Judd tried to whisper, but failed miserably as the last two words came out in a wail.

Coldness seized Jake's heart. He couldn't feel anything but blind hatred for the man whose son had nearly...he couldn't think about it. He'd deal with Tick later.

Shoulders slumped, Judd's gaze searched Jake's face. No sympathy broke through the wall Jake had built in the last hours. Judd turned and walked out of the room. No one else said a word to him.

The stink of fear filled the room. He wasn't sure if it was because of his continued anger or the news they had begun to expect as the minutes dragged by. She'd been in surgery for two hours now. Though the doctor sounded confident they had gotten her to the hospital in time, Jake knew anything could go wrong.

An arm came around his waist and the familiar scent he loved to immerse in surrounded him, almost cancelling out the stench of hospital and fear.

"Everything will be okay," Angel said.

Jake gathered Angel into his arms and stood in the middle of the room, needing the comfort of a warm body.

"Your mother is a strong woman. Hey, look how long she put up with your dad. A little bullet won't keep her down. You know that," Angel said in a poor attempt at humor.

He pulled away after pressing his lips to her forehead. "I know. Let me chill for a little while."

She grabbed his hand. He shook his head and she released her hold. He went to a small sofa in a partially hidden alcove, giving him a little privacy.

Angel sat at the other end, keeping her distance as he folded his arms. His body closed off from her.

Never had he felt so old. When he'd been told Dick Whitfield had died in a fire, shock had numbed him for a few hours. After they discovered the old man had been shot, sure Jake had felt sad, but more pissed. Never to have the opportunity for the relationship he'd always dreamed of with the old man. Mutual respect, a pat on the back, and a hearty, "Good job, boy." Sounded stupid now. If the old man hadn't changed in all the years Jake had lived around him, he would have never done it.

His mom had been a different story. Of course, she'd given him up when he'd been little, allowing the old man to treat him like shit, but she'd been nearby. Her softness and love had been in the background and on the weekends the old man let her visit. No. She hadn't been the perfect mom, but he knew she loved him.

Jake looked at Angel sitting one cushion over on the sofa. She warily watched him. He guessed he owed her some apologies, but it would have to wait. All he could say was when he lifted his mom and found blood coating his fingers, he went a little nuts. He'd said some ugly things to Angel before the ambulance showed up. His men had backed off, disturbed by his attitude toward his wife. But here she was being patient, waiting for him to come back to his senses.

"Did you put him where I told you to?" He knew the

answer, but hearing her confirm it would loosen the knot in his chest.

"Yes. Dan showed up with the men you mentioned. They took care of him. I didn't follow. Felt it was best I stay and answer the deputies' questions. Sand County's finest is searching the woods near the pizza joint for the shooter. They won't find anything," she said in a soft voice, making sure it didn't carry over to the other occupants in the room.

Nodding, Jake felt the tension in his body release. His men had already scooped up Tick and taken him to the house. He still had to deal with the traitor, but the rat bastard was secured in the basement and would be going nowhere. Once he knew his mom was safe, he would tend to that scum of the earth.

The large door swung open and the doctor, dressed in scrubs, walked in.

Jake met him half way. The seriousness on the man's face caused Jake to pause.

"I'm sorry, Mr. Whitfield..." Blood left Jake's head in a rush. Somehow he kept his knees locked. The buzzing in his ears almost caused him to miss the rest of what the doctor had to say. "For taking so long. Your mother is fine, and you can go back and see her in about twenty minutes. They should have her set up in recovery by then."

At the moment, Jake was unsure if he wanted to hit the man or hug him. He decided to merely nod. Thankfully, Angel came up and asked, "How long will she be in the hospital?"

"The surgery went so well, I believe a few days. The next twenty-four hours will tell us how she's responding. I'll know better then." His confident voice gave Jake some comfort.

"When can I see her?"

"Wait a couple minutes and a nurse will be waiting for you through those doors." He waved to the doors he'd gone through. "She will you let you peek in on her." The doctor absently smiled. "Excuse me, but I'm needed." A nurse stood off to one side, holding out an electronic pad.

Tears prickled Jake's eyes from relief. His mom was okay. When he'd seen the warm blood on his hands and more spreading across her blouse, he'd gone insane. He'd been on autopilot rage for several hours and every bone in his body ached.

"Come and sit back down. Give yourself a moment." Angel sat and patted the cushion next to her.

"No. I rather stand." He twisted his neck. The popping helped ease up the stiffness. "Go on home. I'll be there after I see Mom."

"Your mom...I thought I would go with you—"

"No. You have plenty of things to do. Best for me to see her alone."

He felt her gaze, but the paramount need was to see his mom, to be assured she was alive. Before he walked away, a commotion at the nurses' station caught his attention.

"Oh, there you are, Jake. I filled out all the paperwork. How's your mama?" Jimmie Sue looked pale, her eyes puffy and red from crying.

"She's out of surgery and doing fine. I'm about to go back there and see her."

"May I go with you?"

"Of course, this way." He opened the double doors, waved Jimmie Sue through, and then he looked over at Angel. "I'll see you later."

Her expressionless face told him nothing about how the shooting affected her. Her grandfather taught her well.

Maybe too well. Did none of this bother her? Did she not care about anyone but herself and her brother?

She looked away, stood, holding her purse against her chest. "As you said, I have things to do. I'll go check on Damien."

He watched her walk away. Shoulders straight and eyes forward, she didn't wave goodbye or look back. Something about that interchange felt off to him.

"Are you coming?" Jimmie Sue waited anxiously in the hallway.

"Yeah. Right behind you." He glanced over at the elevators. The doors slid closed. Angel was gone.

Chapter Twenty-Three

"Tell me again why we can't stay in Jake's house?" Damien asked for the tenth time.

Angel leaned closer to the kitchen countertop, pretending to be immersed in cleaning the black laminate. If only she could afford granite ones like those in the Whitfield house.

Shaking her head, she bit her lip, ignoring her brother's nagging and refusing to regret what she'd done. When she had woodenly marched out of the hospital, she'd driven straight to the Whitfield house, threw most of her things into shopping bags, and ordered Damien to do the same. They didn't own any suitcases. When a person never went on vacation, the extra expense was unnecessary.

"Why?" The confusion in his voice matched her own twisted thoughts.

"Because the danger is over. We got the shooter, and we'll be safe here now." She tried her best to keep it simple and filled with the truth. Only she had yet to tell him his good friend Tick had been involved.

Scrubbing at the stubborn stain, she used the easy,

repetitive activity to keep her mind off Jake. So far, it had worked to hold back the tears. Her plan was to wait until bedtime and then she could press a pillow over her mouth and let go. Maybe then Damien wouldn't hear her act like a fool.

"You're acting strange."

"How's that?" She was, but she wanted her brother to say how and then she would correct it.

"First of all, you've rubbed that one spot so long, I think you made a hole in the laminate."

She looked down. He was right. She'd ruined it. Trying to act like she didn't care, she tossed the cloth into the sink.

"How about I order us some pizza?"

He pulled his head back as if she struck him. "At eleven o'clock at night, and after we had pizza last night? You never let me eat anything after nine and never pizza two nights in a row. That proves it. Something is wrong. Did you and Jake have a fight? Where's Tick? He disappeared last night and usually he checks on me by now. At the least, he texts me goodnight."

"Listen, Jake and I are having a few problems." On seeing his worried look, she added, "We probably won't divorce, but I think it will be best if we live apart."

"Is he going to prison?"

"What? No. Nothing like that." She gave him a hug. Poor kid thought when an adult dropped out of his life, it was because they'd been incarcerated. *Thanks, Dad.* "We just don't see eye to eye. We may work things out or we might not. Whatever happens, you and I will be together until you go to college. Then who knows, I might follow you there and rent an apartment off campus."

"Yeah, like that's what I want. My big sister looking after me while I'm at college." He shook his head.

Squeezing her back for a second, letting her know he was teasing, he released her. "I'm going to bed. I'm tired, and you're not making any sense." He rubbed his eyes with his fists. The same way he did when he was five. He stretched his back, raising his arms above his head, touching the top of the doorway with the tips of his fingers—he so could not do that at five—and then walked down the hall toward the bedrooms. He'd grown so much.

She had to admit he was right. She wasn't making sense.

Her mobile phone buzzed. She looked toward the kitchen table as the phone rattled precariously close to the edge. Probably Jake. She'd been ignoring his and everyone else's calls and texts since she'd left the hospital in the early morning hours. She was probably acting immature, but she wanted a little time to think over everything.

She stretched out on the couch, refusing to go to her lonely bed. Already she missed Jake so much she ached. Having his attention and being able to caress his body whenever she wanted had become like a drug. The way he held her at night, his touch, voice, taste. Oh, God, she wanted him. But he didn't truly see her as a partner or equal in any way, no matter how many times they talked about it. She was nothing but a soldier to him. Someone to follow his orders. For that matter, except for giving her some of the best orgasms of her life, he acted as if she didn't have feelings.

After the shooting, it had been bad enough when he called her stupid and spoke so condescendingly to her in front of his men. Many people said things in the heat of the moment they regretted later. She'd been willing to forgive. But the final nail in the coffin had been the way he'd dismissed her at the hospital. She'd wanted to be with him, to support him when someone he cared about was hurt. She didn't deserve to be treated like a stranger.

How would he have acted if she'd been the one in the hospital bed? Would he view it as an inconvenience?

Looking at the ceiling, she shook her head, covering her eyes before digging fingers into the tresses and pulling in frustration.

Best to stop thinking about it. No reason to borrow trouble. She had enough without trying. Time for her to move on and quit feeling sorry for herself. His mother was fine. The bullet had gone through her right side, not hitting any bone or major arteries. Of course, Jake was upset and not thinking straight. He hadn't meant it the way it came out. As if he didn't want her near him, not being family or a friend, she didn't belong, or she was nothing to him.

Despite telling herself over and over again he'd been upset and not thinking straight, she couldn't stop the darkness warping everything he said and how she felt. What did she know about having a close-knit family? Or being a wife? She had Damien and no one else.

She turned over and clutched the throw pillow to her mouth and cried.

Jake glared at the phone in his hand. Where the hell did she go?

From what one of the guards reported, she'd stayed for about an hour and then hustled out her brother with several plastic bags. The trackers he had inserted no longer worked. She obviously pulled her and Damien's chips. As soon as they relayed what they knew—a hell a lot that was—he'd sprinted up the stairs. Several bare hangers and a couple of empty drawers told the story. She had run away again.

He hit her number on his phone again, waiting for an answer by her or her voicemail. As soon as he heard the recorded message he ended the call. Fuck.

Closing his eyes for a few seconds to regain his composure, he stared across the bare space at the man sitting in a chair. Through a secret doorway in the basement near the media room was an area with no windows and only concrete blocks painted white and a large drain in the middle. A couple of steel poles held up the house, breaking up the bareness, and between the posts sat Tick Richards, tied by his arms and legs to an ugly, green plastic chair.

Dan had worked on him for the last two hours until Jake arrived from the hospital. As a rule, Jake normally handled the softening up, beating the shit out of whoever sat in that chair, before the interrogation, but with his mother being involved, he wanted Tick to live long enough to give details.

Walking around to face the man he'd considered a loyal employee, Jake stopped a few feet away and stared. Blood, shiny and thick, soaked one thigh. His torn shirt revealed thin slashes across his hairy chest. The man's right hand had three broken fingers. One eye and cheek bone were swollen and plum colored. Several large bruises dotted the top of his bald head. Tears streamed down his face.

Later, the sight would bother Jake and sadden him, but for now he needed to remain strong and find out who all were involved.

"Tick, you've been part of my family for most of my life. You've eaten my food, drank my liquor, and slept under my roof. I don't understand why you'd betray us like this. For that matter, what in the hell has my mom done to you but treat you with kindness?"

"I know, I know," Tick sobbed out each word. "I didn't mean to shoot her."

"Then who in hell were you aiming at?"

"You."

Jake tried to hold back his surprise, but he knew his eyebrows had shot up. He really hadn't expected that.

"Why? What are you hoping to gain?"

"Why? Why?" Tick's hysteria increased with each word. "You and your brothers are no different from your dad." Spittle gathered at the corners of his mouth. "You use people. Treat them like shit. You all deserve to die. Just because your dad helped me get rid of that girl, he thought he owned me. Could talk and treat me any way he wanted."

"That girl was the Sand County Sheriff's daughter, you ass-wipe. If they had a clue you or anyone connected with the Whitfields had been involved, we all would've gone down. Bad." He inhaled deeply, trying to calm the anger growing by the second. To think he'd believed Tick loyal and his father couldn't be trusted. The jury was still out on Judd. "Did you really think you could get away with it? That we wouldn't catch up with you?"

Tick's crazed laughter echoed in the room.

After a minute went by without Tick letting up, Jake nodded to Dan. The man lifted a hammer and brought it down on an already broken finger.

The scream nearly pierced Jake's ears. The room was sound proof, but didn't muffle the sound inside.

As Tick didn't have hair to hold his head up, Jake grabbed his ears. The big man closed his eyes.

"Listen to me, your dad begged for me not to kill you. You and I know there isn't any hope of you living another day. But I can make it quick and give your ashes to your dad." Jake knew Tick understood he meant no pain in the method of ending his life. "Did you have anything to do with killing the old men?"

At first, he thought Tick wasn't about to answer. Then the man opened his good eye. Such hatred stared back.

"It was Matt and I. We'd been practicing for years. He took out Mac and I shot the old bastard. It felt real good. You should've seen your old man's face. I wish I had a picture. He couldn't believe I had killed him."

The hostility flowed from every pore in the man.

"Did your dad know?" Jake had to be sure the betrayal didn't go too far.

"He's too much of a coward. He thought asshole was his friend. I tried telling him Dick treated him like dirt."

"Did you play a part in the shooting at the funeral?" He needed to know how much Tick and Matt had done.

"I'm not that stupid. Matt arranged it without talking to me. An old buddy of his. He also was the one who tried to take you out at your wedding. He deserved to be killed for being such a lousy shot."

The old buddy had been the guy in the tree Angel had killed.

"Why did you kill Matt?" Something deep inside said Tick had done it.

"He got scared after the wedding and wanted to tell you the truth." Tick's forehead wrinkled and his eyes closed for a moment, either from the pain of the wounds or from the memory of his friend's death. "For some idiotic reason he thought you'd be happy we'd taken out the old men. That you'd reward us. I had to stop him. He'd always been an imbecile."

Jake let him go and stepped away.

"Did the old man's cousins have anything to do with any of this?" He had to know if it truly stopped with Tick. He'd believed Tick about Judd.

"I want to tell you so bad that they did. They're as big

assholes as Dick Whitfield. And just thinking of you spilling blood all through Marystown makes me happy. But I can't. They didn't, but I will say you need to keep an eye out. They've been telling people they are taking over. They have help from someone, but I don't know who. They're saying you're bringing in the Atlanta mob, and if not stopped, you'll throw the whole town to the wolves."

No surprise there. Jake had suspected they were behind the rumors Ethan had heard.

"Tick, I still don't get it. I can almost understand taking out the old men. There has been many times I contemplated it. But why me and my brothers? Hell, what about Damien? Was that Matt?"

"Damien. The kid had left his key and decided to break a window to get inside. He'd gotten me to lie about it. Sometimes he surprised me with his deviousness, and that's because he's a good kid." The last few words came out sluggishly. His loss of blood was finally catching up with him. A steady stream had trickled down his leg and pooled around one foot. Others dripped beneath his chair.

"What about the shooter at the cabin?" They had thrown the body into the swamp, but so far all they knew was he'd been from Tennessee, not Georgia. And that had been from the license plate on the car they had found near the cabin. It had been registered to a nonexistent business.

"Have no idea. You do have a lot of people wanting you dead." The macabre grin warned Tick liked the thought.

Jake began to pace. That tied up most of the mysteries, but could he trust what Tick said? Was he telling the truth? Was it all a big setup and Tick was willing to die for it? Fuck. He didn't know what to think. The part about the cousins not being involved in any of the deaths or shootings, did hold a ring of truth to it. So far, he hadn't mentioned a certain ex-FBI special agent.

"Boss."

Jake looked at Dan standing over Tick.

"Yeah?"

"He's dead. When he sagged in the chair, I checked his pulse. No heartbeat." Dan pressed two fingers to the side of Tick's neck.

A combination of the gunshot, loss of blood, and work over were too much for his heart.

"You know what to do with the body. Be sure to pick out a nice urn for Judd." Rubbing the back of his neck, he ached all over. It had been a long day. Tomorrow, he would find out where Angel had landed. Then he'd figure out how he could get the news to his brothers. They would want to know their old man had been revenged, and they could come home.

Only, he wasn't sure how Angel would take the news. She'd wanted her pound of flesh, and by not letting her talk with Tick, he'd kept her from having closure. On top of that, he still had to apologize for all of the things he'd said the night of the shooting,

Shit. He had really fucked up.

Chapter Twenty-Four

Jake eased the car to a stop in front of the mobile home. No cars out front, but the detached garage stood in the back. Lights shone through the thin curtains. What the hell was she thinking? How many times had they talked about how dangerous back lighting could be in their business? She needed thicker curtains. Otherwise people would track her movements through the place and shoot. For that matter, the same with the prefab thin walls. She needed to be in the Whitfield's brick house.

His phone vibrated in his pocket. Shifting in his seat, he pulled it out and read the text message.

Are you coming inside or staying outside like a coward?

Damien. The teenager had guts.

He looked up and caught a curtain flutter. The teenager was right. With a deep breath, Jake exited the car and strolled up to the front door. Raising his hand to knock, the door opened.

Instead of Angel, Damien pushed his way out, partially closing the door behind him.

"Man, I don't know what you did, but you got to fix it. She won't listen to me. I want to go back. After living in a real house, I can't take this piddling ass place. She can hear everything! You know? Ev-ery-th-ing. A dude can't have any privacy. You know?" The teenager widened his eyes as his head bobbed up and down, emphasizing his distress. "And food. I really miss Jimmie Sue's cooking. Have you eaten anything my sister has cooked? No? I swear you don't want to."

Locking his jaw to hold back the laughter, Jake, unable to look Damien in the eye for fear of letting go, carefully looked over the teenager's head into the living room as he pushed the door back open.

"Where's your sister?"

"That away." He nodded to the right. "She's in the kitchen. I have no idea what type of concoction she's mixing up. She swears she follows the recipes in the cookbook, but I don't know, man. You got to stop her. Please take her back. Whatever the hell she's done, she didn't know better."

"So now, it's something she did?" Jake shook his head. The teenager was a riot. Actually, a good kid. A lot of it had to do with having a sister like Angel.

"You're killing me. You two are nuts for each other. Nuts being the key word here. I know none of us are right in the head. So yeah, you need to forgive each other, and let's get back to the big house. I've promised a couple of my friends we could play the newest For Honor. Tick said he'd show us a few Easter eggs he'd found in the game."

Jake ignored the last sentence, though his throat closed up for a second. Hell, he hadn't thought of how Tick's death would affect Damien. Later. He would deal with telling Damien after settling things with Angel.

Slipping around the teenager, Jake walked into the

living room. He'd never been in her home. Big red athletic shoes were strewn at the end of the couch. Definitely Damien's. Keys and a purse on the coffee table with a newspaper opened over a chair's arm. Messy, but the way a real home should be, nothing like his big empty one. That was, except when Angel lived with him. It had felt like home then.

He looked to the left. A small hallway led to what he guessed were bedrooms. What did Angel's look like? Frilly, showing her girly side. Or simple and plain, revealing her no-nonsense attitude. That question could be answered later.

Forcing his attention back to finding the kitchen, he moved around a table and chairs on the right and through a swinging door. Her back to him, she stirred something on the stove. She wore her black hair twisted into a knot on top with red tips pointing everywhere. The dish cloth hanging over a shoulder wrapped up the look of Susie Homemaker. She wore a green top and faded blue jeans, nothing of her usual black. The soft cotton hugged her womanly hips and cupped the full ass he loved.

He stood and stared, unsure what to say to her.

When he'd seen the blood spilling from his mom, he'd gone a little crazy. Cursing and hollering at everyone around him. He tried over and over again to shut his mouth, but the blood coming from his mom's body blinded him to the destruction he left behind. Lydia had never harmed a soul. Though she hadn't been the most normal and protective mom—he'd done more of the protecting even as a kid— she'd shown him the importance of being tender with the gentler sex. She'd taught him women were not the evil, deceitful creatures his old man had ranted and roared about.

"How long are you going to stand there and stare at my butt?" Angel turned, one dark eyebrow lifted. "So you're here to apologize. Personally, I think it is only fair you get on your knees." Eyebrows raised, she didn't believe he would do it.

Well, hell. Whatever he needed to do, he would. That was as much as his pride allowed. He went to a knee, resting his arms on the raised one. He lifted his head to look at her. "I'm not good at doing humble, but you deserve a knee. That much is for sure. I understand why you're pissed at me."

Her eyes narrowed. Her doubtful expression confirmed she believed there was a trick to his admission.

She fingered the handle of a knife sticking out of her pocket. "I did everything you wanted and you embarrassed me in front of your men," she flatly stated.

"What can I say? I was out of my mind. Nothing had ever happened to Mom like that. I went crazy and said things I didn't mean." He released a long sigh, nodding. "It was inexcusable. I'm sorry." Fuck, that was hard. Yes, he was in the wrong, but he couldn't remember the last time he willingly apologized without the shit being beaten out of him by his old man. "And they're *our* men. And I regret doing that."

She blinked and looked away. Her face stiff from holding back her emotions. Damn, he'd hated she felt a need to hide anything from him, especially her feelings. After the time he tracked her down to the motel, it had been with other people. Never him.

Damn it. She stared at the floor and then ceiling, still refusing to look him in the eye.

"I swear, Angel, I'm sorry. You have no idea how much I hate myself right now."

Fuck, he was glad he hadn't completely lost his mind and hit her. Even at the peak of his anger the thought had never crossed his mind, but he'd worried about it most of his life. He was his father's son. Yet, he respected women too much for that. Fuck to all hell, he loved her too much. Yes, for days now, he admitted he loved her. Maybe in some ways, the way he felt had come about too quickly. Deep inside, who knew, he may have started to fall for her all of those years ago. And since then every woman he met never measured up. Only Angel. She was everything he'd ever wanted in a woman: strong, courageous, loyal, daring, straightforward, and sexy as hell.

"Sugar, you've got to tell me why you're so mad. I'm sure it's something I've done, but you have to remember, I haven't been in my right mind."

Her eyelashes fluttered as if clearing her mind, possibly coming to a decision.

"I'm not good at playing games," she said. "I've had enough drama in my life. So here it is. You were forced to marry me. I understand that. Now, after everything we've gone through, done, and planned, do you want to stay married? If you don't, I won't fight you. Whatever the old men put into their wills is bullshit. We don't have to abide them. Richards will do as we say. I know it and you know it. So tell me the truth." Tears welled up in her beautiful green eyes. It killed him to see her so unhappy. "Am I good enough to be your bed partner, but not good enough to be the woman who stands at your side in sickness and health?"

Then it struck him. He'd sent her home from the hospital. At the time, he'd been worried about his mom, and when Angel offered to go back to his mom's room, in the back of his mind he'd seen her slumping shoulders and dragging feet. She'd been bone tired. He hadn't wanted her to become ill and two of the most important women in his life in the hospital.

In less than two weeks, she'd been through so much. Her grandfather died. She'd killed two men and shot another. She needed her rest, uninterrupted rest, but she'd been worried about his mom.

He'd never considered how his family was hers now. They were each other's family.

No matter how strong-willed she'd proven to be around him, he had refused to accept the truth: he needed her as much as she needed him. His determination to be a strong fortress for those he cared about in the midst of the chaos wasn't working. Her touch, her support, and care mattered more than he had ever expected. By remaining alone, holding the fort without help, he'd given her no option but to leave.

He lowered his other knee and rested on his heels, hands on his thighs. His head down. She deserved more than he could ever give her.

Lifting his head, he decided to lay it out like a man.

"Angel, how any man as cursed as I am could luck up with you as his wife, I'll never know. My mom and I would be dead now, if not for you. That evening in the hospital, all I thought about was how exhausted I was and how you had to be twice as weary. That you needed to go home and not worry about anything. I swear that was it. I'm sorry if you thought anything else. Why didn't you call me out on it?" He lowered his voice. She needed to understand he wasn't angry.

Her voice cracked, sorrow making each word husky. "I thought you were ashamed of me. That you were tolerating me being by your side, using me." Using her thumb and forefinger, she wiped her eyes, blinked, and then knelt in front of him. "I love you. I guess I've loved you all my life. I don't understand why. Really, why should it make any sense? A person just knows."

He reached for her arms and pulled her on top of him as he straightened his legs and leaned back against a cabinet. "No, baby, it shouldn't make sense. Fuck. I love you more than I thought I was capable of. You're part of me. Without you, I'll never be whole."

Unable to resist, he kissed her. Her lips were soft and giving. Just like she always was in bed. A tough cookie out in the world, but in their private world, all marshmallow insides.

He squeezed her tight, and she returned the gesture. Their lips parted, and she rested her cheek on his shoulder. A few seconds passed before he felt her body shake.

"Oh, don't cry. I thought we patched everything up."

Her head moved up and down. "Yeah, I just never believed you could love me back."

"Oh, damn, Angel. You're so lovable and sexy, it's amazing all of the assholes in Marysville didn't know it."

She laughed. A good solid laugh he realized he loved to hear.

"Thanks." Her gaze darted to the side.

"What? What's wrong?"

"I really want to go to the hospital and visit your mom."

Chuckling quietly, he squeezed again. "You bet, but why is it so important for you to see her? She's going home tomorrow afternoon."

"I think your mom and I got off on the wrong foot, and I want her to see I care."

"Sure. We'll do that right after we move you and Damien back into the big house."

"Big house?"

"That's what your brother calls it."

"Did you tell him that's a term for a prison?"

"Nah. He can call it anything he wants as long as you call it home." He grinned down into her sweet face. That was when he noticed she wasn't wearing her white makeup. Maybe she was deciding to quit hiding behind it.

He caressed her cheek.

"I like that. Home. Wherever you live," she said in a soft voice.

Another deep kiss had him stretched over her on the floor, his arm beneath her head, protecting her from the hard surface.

"How about you show me your bedroom? It'll be more comfortable. And if I remember correctly, you're due for another spanking."

"You think so?" Her eyes sparkled with excitement beneath heavy lids.

"Yeah."

"Good. I was beginning to worry you'd turned in your man card."

He laughed and helped her to her feet. After a slap to her ass, he threw an arm over her shoulder and strode through the living area and down the short hallway. Damien was nowhere in sight.

"Where's your brother?"

"He's visiting with his friend a couple doors down."

Recalling what Damien said about the thin walls, Jake was happy the teenager had deserted the place. Wouldn't want him charging in to save his sister at the wrong time.

She opened the bedroom door. He started to follow, but stopped and pulled his head back in disbelief.

"I knew you liked to read, but I had no idea." He nodded toward the other side of the room. One whole wall had shelves upon shelves of books. From what he could tell most were hot romances. He chuckled and turned to her. "How about you reading a couple hot scenes of your favorite ones?"

"How about a spanking scene? I have just the one," she said with a sultry smirk.

His heart jumped and heat flooded his body. He never thought it possible to feel so out of control and in love with a despised Tally. Guess he just needed to marry her and change her name. Hell, he didn't care about her name. All that mattered was she belonged to him.

Chapter Twenty-Five

The light heating her face came at a strange angle. Angel cracked opened her eyes and quickly pulled a pillow over to block out the rays. A delicious twinge shot across her buttocks and down her legs. He'd shown her how much he cared for her, and she'd orgasmed so many times, her whole body ached.

Stretching, easing the twitches and pains, she rolled over and reached out for Jake. Warm skin met her fingers. Jake. He'd stayed. He'd slept at her place in her small double bed.

For years, she'd imagined him being in her room. But the dream had a fancy bed with wispy curtains blowing in the breeze as they kissed in slow motion, their hair tangling in the wind. Biting her lip to stop her laughter, she leaned over, pressed her lips to his chest, and inhaled with satisfaction. She savored his scent. The man did smell good. Soap with a faint hint of smoke and hot male.

Unable to resist, she licked his skin from one tight little nipple to the other. The hair at the center of his chest tickled her tongue. Resting her ear over his heart, she enjoyed the strong thumping. The speed picked up as her hand followed the dark trail to his hard, thick cock. What a great feeling knowing she could make the big guy react like that. Baring her teeth, she nipped a path down until she flicked her tongue at the tip of his cock and scraped her teeth gently across the ridge.

He jumped. "Fuck, Angel, you're killing me." His voice deep.

"Did I hurt you?" She knew he liked a little pain, too.

"Kiss it and make it better." His hand smoothed the back of her head. "Please."

Her eyes closed for a second with a sigh. The sweet, softly spoken request from the hard man brought such tender feelings, cementing her love with a simple word.

She swirled her tongue around his slit and then over the cap. When he hissed, she smiled but continued to bathe the sensitive head. By the time she sucked his cock to the back of her throat, he released a groan with each draw.

"Hell, yes. That's it. Take it all the way. Oh, yes. I fucking love your mouth."

Stretching her neck, she swallowed his length past her gag reflex. She breathed hard through her nose, ruffling the hair at the base of his shaft. All the times she'd practiced with a dildo and watched the lessons online paid off. As she backed off, he began to orgasm, and she sucked hard.

"Fuck, yes!" His scream echoed in the room.

Did Damien hear Jake's scream down the street? Who cared?

She fought the giggle working its way up from her heart.

After a resounding pop, she rested her cheek on his flat stomach. Smiling from the happiness filling her, she stared at his beautiful cock, soft and partially extended against his thigh. Unable to hold back, she carefully traced a vein down the length. It twitched, and Jake grabbed her wrist.

She lifted her head to look at him. His gaze was serious as he dragged her hand to his mouth and kissed the palm. Pulling from his hold, she scooted up his body and stared into his eyes with a tilt of her head.

"Enough, sweetheart. Give me a few minutes. Maybe an hour. Maybe tonight? Shit. You are something. How did I get so lucky? I never thought I'd be grateful to the old man." He looked at her with such tenderness, she felt tears build up.

"I'm the one who's lucky."

Kissing him was something she would never get tired of. His tongue thrusting and licking her mouth had her throbbing with want. Knowing that he could probably taste himself, her pussy clenched. That was such a sexy thought.

Breaking off the kiss, he leaned back, breathing hard.

"Sugar," he said. "Sugar. I have to go and tend to a few things this morning."

"Tick?"

His face shut down. She hated when he did that.

"Forget about Tick," he said. "He's the least of our problems. We're still in danger from the Atlanta mob and that bitch of an ex-FBI agent." He pulled her into his arms and kissed her temple. "I have to get with my brothers and talk about what's happened and who's involved."

"Have you heard from Sen or Quinn's daughter?"

"Nothing. I would be really worried but Sen has always been good at taking care of himself. He'll protect Tessa."

"He cares about her?" Something in his tone had indicated that.

A crooked grin brightened his face. "Yeah. He's had a

thing for her for years, but Quinn hates his guts. Quinn's old man died fighting in Vietnam."

"That's sad on so many levels. Mostly, I'll never understand how people can condemn a total culture, race, or religion for the actions of a few." She hurt for Sen. She better than most understood how it was to love someone with no hope.

Clasping Jake's big hand, she brushed her lips over the back of his hand and pressed it to her cheek. But look what time took care of. She still couldn't believe he loved her. From the way he looked into her eyes, she knew he'd been telling the truth.

"If anyone can win over Quinn, it'll be Sen. He has more tenaciousness than anyone I've ever met," Jake said, smiling sweetly at her. Her heart warmed.

"What about Ethan? Is he still in Marystown? You don't think your cousins will try something?" Knowing his brothers were as important to Jake as Damien was to her, she wanted everyone to be okay.

"I heard from him yesterday. He's back in Nashville. He's certain by the end of the day he'll know who Carleton is working with."

"The cousins still up there?"

"Nope. They're back at home. Probably still planning a way to take over Whitfield Industries. They're that stupid." He slapped her butt. "Time to get packing and moving yours and Damien's stuff to the big house."

She laughed, shaking her head, and murmured, "Big house. Too funny."

At lunchtime, Damien showed up and helped, excited about the permanent move.

"Wait until Tick finds out I beat Chris at Halo 5. He

won't believe it." Damien threw his bag into the back of the truck Jake had one of his guards bring.

Anyone else, Angel could hide her feelings from, but not her brother and not Jake. When he turned to say more to her, he stopped.

"What's wrong?" Damien asked.

She looked over to Jake, trying to decide how to give the bad news to her brother.

"Tick's dead," Jake said. Only a man would think something so blunt was okay.

"What?" Tears filled her brother's eyes. Angel started to move toward him. He held up his hand. "No, Sis. Don't. I want the truth. I knew something happened, and it wasn't good, but I trusted you to tell me. You haven't. I want to know now. I want to hear it from Jake."

Oh, God, when had he grown up?

"Tick and his cousin killed the old men and had been involved in the other shootings. He killed his own cousin and burned his body above the garage, trying to hide his guilt. He tried to shoot me and missed, hitting Lydia."

Looking a little lost, Damien nodded. The movement released the tears. Streams flowed down his cheeks though he didn't make a sound.

Angel fisted her hands. Oh, God, she hurt for him. She wanted to punish someone for hurting her brother. Tick. His jealousy caused so much pain for so many people. How could he be so blind? The brothers had wealth, but Angel knew Tick's dad wasn't poor. The man had a father who loved and cared for him. That was much more than the Whitfield boys ever had.

Using his T-shirt to clean his face, Damien sniffed and then cleared his throat. "When's his funeral?"

Jake shook his head. "No funeral."

"I see. The bog."

One of Jake's eyebrows lifted.

Damien rolled his eyes. "I'm not stupid." He rubbed the back of his neck. "What about Mr. Richards? He deserves to bury his son. He was Mr. Whitfield's best friend."

"Traitors don't get treated that way."

"Sounds like you're punishing Mr. Richards, too." Damien looked up to Jake, squinting one eye in the late afternoon sun. "It would be a favor to me. I liked Tick. He never did anything to me. If there is anything about the body to give away what happened, Quinn can fix it. I heard about a few things that can be done to hide gunshots."

"Damien, where are you hearing this crap?" She felt uneasy by his knowledge.

"Sis, you're kidding yourself if you think I'm not a Tally. Granddaddy didn't ignore me all the time. He told me stuff."

She covered her mouth. Everything she'd done to protect him had not been enough.

"Hey, don't worry." He walked over and hugged her. When had he grown another inch? He could look at her eye to eye. "I'm still planning to go to college. I figured Whitfield Industries will need a good acccuntant. I like numbers." Releasing her, he turned back to Jake. "What do you say?"

"He wasn't shot. He actually had a heart attack."

"Torture can do that," Damien stated.

Jake nodded. "Okay. I'll make a couple calls. Richards can have his son's body for burial."

"Good. I'm glad." Damien gave a half smile and climbed into the back of the extended cab truck.

"Oh, no," she softly said.

"What?" Jake asked.

"He's grown up, and he's got you wrapped around his little finger."

"Fuck, no. You have me wrapped around yours. He just never asks for anything, and I had been rethinking it, anyway."

He walked her to the passenger side of the cab. Before they reached the door she leaned up. "Have you recovered, old man?"

Jake gave her a puzzled look and then his face cleared up. "You bet. And thank you, God, for king-sized beds."

Laughing they headed back to the big house on Whitfield land. Not a prison, but a home that would be filled with laughter. She couldn't wait until all the brothers were back. At least, no one would be shooting at them.

Chapter Twenty-Six

Jake inhaled on his cigarette as he placed his heel on the porch rail. The occasional breeze cooled the sweat on his forehead. He needed to break the smoking habit, but it helped him think. For the last two weeks, he'd settled in Angel and Damien and kept in touch with his brothers. It had been a big relief to hear Sen's voice. Though he never admitted it, he had been concerned about Sen. If he could've pulled the man through the phone and hugged him, he would have.

"They're late."

Bringing the chair's front legs down and placing both feet on the porch, he patted his lap. Angel walked over and sat, circling an arm around his neck.

"Yeah. Could be the traffic." At that moment, a roar sounded down the long drive. Ethan sat on a mean-looking Harley, gunning the motor, probably to hear the roar of the engine and to scare the woman on the back. Her long brown hair flowed behind her. Jake barely recognized the manager of Scene 69. Karma. She was several years older than any of them. Seconds behind the motorcycle, a black Camaro sped down the drive, rumbling and slick-looking. Jake didn't have to guess. Sen had talked about buying one for years. The window slid down. Yep. It was Sen with Tessa up front.

"I can't wait to hear their stories," Angel said with anticipation in her voice.

"Me, too. Then we'll party. We all deserve it," Jake said as he nodded. "The roof on the old place might fall in." There had never been so much to celebrate. Hell, there had never been happiness in its walls.

Everyone seemed to be enjoying life again. Even his mom had stopped by and talked about planning a trip to the beach.

He kissed his wife. The woman of his heart.

Love was blossoming and filling the Whitfield place. Their home.

Excerpt of Sen's Book

Next Southern Crime Family novel (*Unedited*)

Sen ducked into the well-lit doorway beneath a brown cloth overhang with Quinn Funeral Home printed in white. He looked around and then punched in the code as he turned the knob with his right hand. His left remained in his hoodie pocket to keep blood from dripping on the cement. Good thing he'd changed after the funeral. He would hate to ruin his suit jacket.

"Dammit, Quinn," he murmured as he tried to twist the door knob. "What's with bolting the backdoor?"

The owner had never done that before, knowing how the Whitfields often had injuries needing stitches or minor surgery without it being on public record.

Jogging around to the front, Sen slowed and checked the empty parking lot before strolling through the front doorway. Thankfully the viewing rooms were empty of the living this late in the evening. He edged around a corner into a long hallway and passed the office where he heard the security guard talking on the phone. A few more steps and

Sen reached the door marked "Employees Only" that lead to a small anteroom filled with extra folding chairs. On the other wall was another door marked "Keep Out." He typed in the code—hopefully they hadn't changed it—and it quietly opened onto a landing with steep stairs.

He released a sigh and then softly padded down the steps until he almost reached the prep room.

His skin crawled as the smell eased into his nostrils. Not the smell of decay, but the sickening pickle odor of formaldehyde. The scent turned his stomach, and each time he entered the room, he'd hoped to never inhale it again.

He peeked around a partial stairwell wall and cringed as he spotted a body of an elderly man laid out on a metal table. A cloth covered the male from the waist down. That stopped Sen.

Quinn never covered the bodies. Not that the old fart was a pervert or anything, as far has Sen knew, he just treated each body as if it was sexless. Nevertheless, his attitude didn't make a visitor comfortable around the naked corpses.

After taking a couple more steps, he peeked over the banister to check the rest of the room. He spotted a slight-built woman standing near a sink, taking off a mask and gloves.

Fuck, fuck, fuck.

Sen leaned back against the wall, face toward the ceiling, and thumped his head on the cement blocks a couple times in frustration. Closing his eyes, he waited a few seconds as he tried to pull himself together. If he could go somewhere else to get stitched up, he would. But the way his pocket felt beyond soggy, he better make it sooner than later.

Not that he didn't want to see her, but not now, not like

this. Maybe in another month or so when all the shit that was going on in his life was over. The dumbass at the pawn shop had fired his fucking gun when Sen had questioned him about the scumbags who killed his father. It would be the second time she'd patched him up. She'd begin to think he was a hotheaded asshole.

Exhaling without a sound, he was wasting time and nothing was being solved. Time to get his arm seen to and the hell back on the road to find out where the dickhead slinked into the shadows.

What a hell of a week it had been. Between being fired on at his father's funeral and then in one of his own shops, he felt like a bull's eye was painted on his back.

Time to grow a pair and talk with the girl and get his arm stitched.

With a deep breath, he straightened and opened his eyes, staring directly into the most beautiful pair of expressive green eyes he'd ever known.

How had he not heard the steps creak? The woman was sneaky quiet.

Tessa wiggled her fingers in a wave at Sen. Her eyes twinkled. She appeared happy to see him. His heart thudded. That felt good and bad at the same time.

Without a word, he pointed to his left arm.

Her forehead wrinkled in concern as her face paled.

Damn, he hated for her to be upset. He didn't have time to explain. All he needed was for her father to show up. Maybe one day, he'd find a way to see her without the threat of her dad trying to kill him. Yeah. Like he needed another person trying to blow him away.

She waved him over to a beat up black leather chair positioned before a desk in the far corner. He knew the drill. Taking a seat, he dropped the hoodie easily enough.

His next movements tested his pain tolerance. With one hand, he grabbed the end of his tee shirt and pulled it out as he tucked in his elbow. He jumped when he felt cool fingers slide over his heated back. Tessa lifted the shirt over his head before carefully pulling it over his wounded arm and off. Her help worked. No groans escaped his lips. Though really it didn't matter. Tessa was deaf. From what he'd learned, she'd been that way since the age of five from a bad bout of the mumps.

This wasn't the first time she'd sewn him up. Over a year earlier, he'd been sliced by a knife in the ribs during a bar room fight. He broke it up, but not without a memento of his interference. Shows how intelligent he could be at times. When he'd shown up, she'd been alone then too. The scoop around Marystown was she'd moved her apprenticeship to her dad's place. Her presence proved the gossip right. That time, when she finished the last stitch, her dad had arrived. Considering how Quinn felt about him and how he'd carried on, a person would think he'd walked in to see them naked and getting it on.

If not for Sen's father, Tessa's dad probably would have shot him where he stood. It was one of the few moments he'd been thankful to his old man. So for some time, he'd avoided the funeral home and only running into Tessa a couple times in the grocery store. They'd nodded at each other, but that was all. Then a couple months ago, a bullet had gone low and taken a chunk of meat off his thigh. At this rate, he would look like Frankenstein's monster.

At the time, chances were Quinn would be working with his daughter. So Sen had taken care of the stitches himself. He hated it when Quinn patched him up anyway. The man always claimed to be out of pain killers. Strange enough, he had plenty whenever Jake came in, while Ethan preferred the pain and wouldn't let Quinn do it. Crazy son of a bitch.

Tonight, when he decided to come there, he'd been desperate. If the slug wasn't still in his shoulder and he could reach the spot, he would of taken care of the wound himself. No matter what the asshole, Quinn, thought about him, Sen needed someone to do it who wouldn't report to the police.

He jerked away when fire shot down his arm. She grabbed his wrist, holding on with a strong grip, to probe and squeeze the wound again.

"Watch it," he said between gritted teeth, his eyes meeting hers.

With a questioning look on her face, she waited for him to explain.

Tessa read lips fairly well, if people talked slowly and distinctly while facing her. Still she couldn't catch every word as many were formed the same way by a person's lips, especially if the person gritted his teeth. Just as he was doing.

He tensed. Though he'd wanted to wait until he'd improved, he decided now was better than never. He carefully raised his bloody left hand to his right, pointing each index finger at the other, twisting his wrists as the fingers met as close to his left shoulder without screaming in agony. It was one of the first signs he'd learned. He'd known he would be in pain the next time he saw her.

Her face lit up and her hands began to fly. The two years of classes he'd taken helped a little beyond the basics, but he missed a lot of what her hands told him. It wasn't like he had anyone to practice with at home and he missed a few lessons.

"Whoa, whoa. You're going too fast." He signed as he

spoke. The teachers had tried to break him of the habit of speaking while signing, but he lapsed whenever he became annoyed with his ability to keep up. He wanted her to understand everything he said, hell, signed. So maybe she could understand the gist between reading his lips and hands.

With a big grin still on her face, Tessa's hands moved a little slower.

You learned ASL, when?

Been going to classes, he signed and refrained from saying the words. *I'm not good at it. Slow.*

I think you are doing great.

He felt like a million bucks and made sure she could see it on his face. Most of his life, he hid his thoughts and feelings, but for Tessa he'd put them on full display to communicate with her. Otherwise, learning ASL, American Sign Language, would be for nothing. It was more than just hands.

They stared at each other for a long minute until the ache in his arm reminded him of why he was there. Unsure of how soon her father would be back, he needed her to do her magic before Quinn showed up or Sen bled to death.

Sen pointed at his wound.

Looking abashed, Tessa held up a finger, asking him to wait, and she began arranging an assortment of sutures on a tray, alcohol wipes, tweezers, and other items he didn't want to think about. She directed him to sit further back in the leather chair. Once his head settled on the padded headrest, she stuck an hypodermic needle near the wound. The intense pain steadily faded away. In no time she pulled out the bullet, sewed, and cleaned him up. She was efficient and had a light touch.

She pointed to a container on the desk next to him.

He leaned over and picked up the small glass of orange juice and downed it. It reminded him of when he'd donated blood. With careful movements, he slid the glass back onto the desk as he watched her toss the stainless steel instruments into a sterilizer and throw bloody gauze and other used pads into a bio hazard bin. Why would a funeral home need to sterilize anything? He really didn't want to know the answer.

Most men wouldn't call Tessa beautiful. Then again, most of the males he knew were dumbasses. With her long curly red hair tied in a ponytail and pale skin with freckles across a pert nose, she looked like a fire goddess. Those big green eyes had been the first feature to grab his attention, though he admitted her long legs and nicely rounded breasts and ass received equal shares of his scrutiny.

Unable to take his gaze from her, he soaked in the sight of her walking toward him. He moved his legs apart to allow his junk some room. His bare nipples pebbled. Maybe she wouldn't notice his reaction. It could easily be from the chilly room though he couldn't say the same about his dick. Being a good girl that she was, she kept her attention above his waist, not noticing his hard-on.

She handed him his black hoodie and a clean blue scrub shirt. Most likely one of her father's.

Put this on or you will get cold and sick. Her delicate hands signed as she shifted her body.

With his right hand, he pressed his closed fingers to his lips and lowered them slightly toward her.

Thank you.

You are welcome. She dropped her hands to her waist. Biting her bottom lip as if holding back her laughter, she dipped her head and stared up at him from beneath her eyelashes.

Funny, what? He signed.

I'm happy you are signing. Nice to have a new person. No boring same-old, same-old.

He understood. Not many people in Marystown knew ALS. So he imagined just signing with her dad had become confining. For over a year, two times a week, and sometimes as much as three times, he'd drove out to Sand City to learn and still hadn't mastered it.

As soon as he pulled on the loose shirt—her dad was a wide man—with her help, so not to pull the stitches, his cell phone vibrated. He dug into his pants' pocket and pulled it out. He had a voicemail.

Jake's concerned tone came across easily enough in the voicemail. "You, bastard. Give me a call. I need some answers and I want to know you're okay."

His brother would have to wait for the return call.

Being the eldest of the three, Jake was often the worrier. Actually, he was Sen's half brother, just as Ethan, the youngest, was half too. They each had different mothers. Their father never married their moms. A true asshole as the brothers were only months apart in age. Their asshole of a father was dead. How many times must he tell himself that? Shot and body burnt in his nightclub, his old man hadn't been alone. The Tally patriarch had died too in the same place and same method. Sen still had a hard time believing all of it. His old man had treated him like a dog to be trained and set on the world with a long leash. So he wasn't necessarily broken up by his death, but he'd been surprised by the grief that tightened his gut by the news. He had been his father after all. Then he'd learned the old men had left wills tying the two families together through marriage. Jake being the sacrificial lamb. Thank God, he was the second son. The bride-to-be with her hair dyed black and red tips, goth makeup, and leather get-up was a bit more than he could handle. He wanted to wake up in the mornings with his nuts and cock still attached.

Just then, a cool hand took his left one and began wiping at it with a wet cloth.

Tessa kept her attention on cleaning the blood from his fingers. She carefully removed the dried and congealed mess between his fingers, even soaking the cloth a little more and seeing to his fingernails. Not since he was a child had a woman ever tended to him so well. The room blurred a little. He inhaled long and deep. Well, hell. He'd forgotten to breathe while watching her. She was just so damn fascinating.

She stepped away and quickly returned with a paper towel to dry his hands.

Once again, he signed *thank you.*

With a big grin on her face, she moved to the large red bin and tossed the bloody wadded paper inside.

Taking another deep breath, he forced his gaze away and stared at his cell phone, using it as an excuse to appear unfazed by her care.

The afternoon had been crazy. How insane had the old man been to be in negotiations with the Tallys? The two families had hated each other for over fifty years. All due to Mac Tally stealing a woman from Dick Whitfield. Most of his life, Sen considered it to be the most idiotic thing he'd ever heard.

Then he met Tessa. He finally understood. Despite her dad's feelings about him, he wanted her. Sen had been working toward this moment for a long time. Though they met up tonight by happenstance, he didn't care. It was fate.

The longer he watched her moved around in the mortuary, the more he became torn between taking her with him and keeping his distance. The way bullets flew around the cemetery and pawn shop, the people after him and his brothers cared little of who was caught in the crossfire. So the best place for her to be was away from. Only he was uncertain he could manage that.

Besides, the dumbnut in the pawn shop had shouted something Sen had found of interest.

"Just as I hoped," the stringy haired psycho had said as he snatched up the gun and shot at Sen. The man had terrible aim.

Fuck. Why had it been loaded? All guns were to be checked for ammo and the cartridges locked away by his manager on entrance into the store. The man would be looking for a new job tomorrow. Until then, he had enough sense to duck behind the counter on the other side of the bullet-resistant glass.

Sen hunched behind a display of musical instruments. He'd already pulled his gun from the shoulder rig beneath his hoodie.

"Put the gun down or I'll be dumping your dead ass in the trash," he shouted, aiming his weapon in the general direction of where the bastard had disappeared. Despite his threat, he only wanted to wound him. The asshole needed to be alive to answer questions.

"I'm not giving up that easy. I need the money. The contract on your head is massive. You and your brothers are no more than the walking dead." The man slammed into a stand of bicycles and scrambled to his feet behind another group of shelves..

Sen shot several times in the general area—good thing the building's walls were made of cinderblock—hoping to frighten the man into giving up.

"Put the fucking gun down," Sen repeated.

"I'll be back. When you least expect it and before someone else gets to you first." Another bang filled the air as the man fired over his shoulder and crashed into the door, shattering the glass, as he exited at a run.

Sen felt the sharp pressure to his arm as he headed toward the door. He'd been shot. When his brain caught up, the stinging heat and wetness flowing down to his elbow would soon be topped by blessed numbness until the wound was cleaned. Then it would feel like burning hell.

He'd ignored the wound as he chased the man a block or more. When his visual became blurry, he realized the bleeding hadn't slowed and he gave up catching the bastard.

That was when he decided to stopped by Quinn's and have it stitched up.

If what the psycho said was true, anyone who hung around him would be vulnerable.

Sen looked at Tessa. She glanced over her shoulder at him and smiled.

His gut clenched. He'd kill anyone who would harmed a hair on her sweet head.

About the Author

CARLA SWAFFORD loves romance novels, action/adventure movies, and men, and her books reflect that. And on top of all that, she's crazy about hockey, and thankfully, no one has made her turn in her Southern Belle card.

So, it's no surprise she writes spicy romantic suspense filled with mercenaries, motorcycle one-percenters, and southern criminals. And in the last few years, she's included sexy hockey players in books without suspense, except for the kind that asks, how will they ever find their happily ever after?

Married to her high school sweetheart, she lives in the Southeast U.S.

To find out more about Carla, be sure to visit her Facebook and TikTok pages or join her newsletter on her website. www.carlaswafford.com.

Also by Carla Swafford

Series: Brothers of Mayhem

Hidden Heat

Full Heat

Above currently published by Loveswept, an imprint of Random House in ebook only

Naked Heat

Series: The Circle Mercenaries

Circle of Desire

Circle of Danger

Circle of Deception

Above previously published by Avon, an imprint of HarperCollins.

Circle of Dishonor (novella)

Circle of Defiance (novella

Kidnapped For A Day (short story)

Above novellas and short story available together in one paperback

Series: An Atlanta Edge Hockey Romance

Crossing The Line

Fake Play

Series: Southern Crime Family

Jake

Sen (coming soon!)

Ethan (coming soon!)

Small-Town Romance

Loving The Small-Town Preacher's Son

Loving The Small-Town Hero

* 9 7 8 1 9 5 6 5 1 8 0 5 4 *